# Operation Sex Kitten

San Diego Social Scene, Book #1

Tess Summers

I0586728

Published: 2017

ISBN: 978-0-9994319-2-4

Published by Seasons Press LLC.

Copyright © 2016, Tess Summers.

Edited by Rebecca Gilbert and Kasi Alexander.

Cover by OliviaProDesign.

# Dedication

For everyone who supported me when I dared to dream of a life outside the box.

# Acknowledgements

Mr. Summers—you're my real-life hero. I love you.

Summers' children—I appreciate you putting up with my wacky hours and distracted staring into space. Thank you for loving me through it all. You are my reason for being.

JM—thanks for being my sounding board as I brought the characters to life. Your advice and wisdom helped me make this book possible and your "of course it's going to be published" attitude gave me the courage to make it happen.

My Bad Girls Club: Janece Ellers, Elle Pawley, and Marty Wenzel. Your encouragement kept me going. As did your demands for more chapters! I couldn't ask for more supportive friends. I love you bitches.

Laura Paul Giovanini—Thank you for your graphic design brilliance, but more importantly, thanks for being my friend for almost my entire life.

Doug Hall—thank you for being brutally honest. There isn't a doubt in my mind your observations made this book better.

Shasta Crabb—comma splices... I know, I know! You have a gift.

Andrew Hall—I don't know what I would have done without your sage advice. You are quite simply, brilliant.

Rebecca Gilbert—thank you for being an amazing editor. I thank you from the bottom of my heart for all your help and care with my first book.

Kasi Alexander—your editing abilities are almost superhuman. Thank you for doing such an incredible job.

The Writing Community—I can't believe I've learned so much in only one year. It's all thanks to you. You are an amazing, supportive, fantastic group of people. Thank you from the bottom of my heart.

My readers—I am humbled that you have read my work. I sometimes pinch myself that I am able to share my imagination with others. Thank you for supporting me.

# Table of Contents

Dedication ......................................................................... iii

Acknowledgements ............................................................iv

Prologue .............................................................................. 1

Chapter 1 ............................................................................3

Chapter 2.........................................................................23

Chapter 3..........................................................................33

Chapter 4..........................................................................42

Chapter 5.......................................................................... 46

Chapter 6..........................................................................63

Chapter 7..........................................................................73

Chapter 8..........................................................................87

Chapter 9........................................................................103

Chapter 10 ...................................................................... 121

Chapter 11...................................................................... 132

Chapter 12 ...................................................................... 145

Chapter 13 ...................................................................... 152

Chapter 14 ...................................................................... 166

Chapter 15....................................................................... 173

Chapter 16 ......................................................................180

Chapter 17.......................................................................190

Chapter 18 ..................................................................... 201

Chapter 19 ...................................................................... 217

Chapter 20...................................................................... 238

Chapter 21 ...................................................................... 244

Chapter 22...................................................................... 264

Chapter 23 ...................................................................... 284

Chapter 24 ...................................................................... 313

Epilogue ......................................................................... 330

A Note From Tess.............................................................333

*The General's Desire* ......................................................334

*Playing Dirty* .................................................................335

*Cinderella and the Marine* .............................................336

San Diego Social Scene......................................................337

Agents of Ensenada..........................................................338

Boston's Elite series ..........................................................339

Wounded Heroes...............................................................340

San Diego After Dark ........................................................340

The Mister Series ..............................................................340

About the Author...............................................................341

Contact Me!......................................................................341

# *Operation Sex Kitten*
## San Diego Social Scene Book One

# Prologue

*Ava*

"Maybe sex like that only exists in the movies." Ava sighed as she flung her arms to her sides for dramatic effect after watching a steamy sex scene in a movie she and her best friend had rented.

Anne looked at her like she was crazy. "Didn't you and Brad have sex like that, ever? Even in the beginning?"

Ava frowned. Obviously they hadn't, or she wouldn't have said that.

"Oh, honey, then he was doing it wrong. Did he ever, you know, satisfy you?"

"I think so?" Ava wasn't quite sure.

"You think so? You *think* so? Then he really was doing it wrong." Despite Ava's obvious discomfort with the conversation's topic, her friend pressed on. "Well, have you, uh, been taking care of things yourself now that you're single?"

Ava gave an inquisitive look; she wasn't exactly following.

"You know, are you being the *master* of your domain?"

It finally dawned on Ava that her friend was referring to masturbation. Embarrassed, she quickly replied, "Of course not!"

"My beautiful friend, if *you* can't get yourself off, how do you expect your partner to?"

Two days later, a gift basket with a vibrator, XXX-rated videos, condoms, lingerie, a bottle of wine, and other 'goodies' was waiting on the pool house counter when Ava walked in the door with a card that read, *To discovering new things*. She was mortified at the idea her parents would walk in and find it on the counter, so she stashed it in her closet.

It took a week before Ava opened the contents of the basket and only did so to stop Annie from pestering her. She watched a video, embarrassed at first, but then became intrigued, amazed that women were that bold. With the help of her new device, she soon discovered that the idea of being more daring turned her on. She went online and started reading erotica and was left wanting to experience what the characters she read about experienced. *No wonder Brad left me*. Ava decided she would use her newfound sexuality to win him back and show him she was sophisticated and sexual. Set to close on her new condo that following week, she now had a new mission. Operation Sex Kitten was about to commence.

# Chapter 1

*Ava*

"Ava, Ava Ericson, that's you, isn't it?" Even half awake, Ava recognized the thin voice of her parents' elderly neighbor, Mrs. Marten.

"Yes, Mrs. Marten, it's me. What time is it?" She sounded more snappish than she intended.

After hanging up the phone with the widow, Ava ran a brush through her hair and was out the door without thinking, but by the time she drove through the guard gates of her parents' upscale neighborhood, she was fuming. Mrs. Marten had called to inform her of quite the party happening at the Ericson place. Normally, she would have congratulated her parents on throwing a bash wild enough to upset the neighbors. With the exception of their annual Halloween shindig--which was a far cry from normal--their stuffy dinner parties usually ended by nine-thirty p.m. But unfortunately, her parents were away on a two-week cruise, leaving her youngest sister, Grace, home alone to prepare for her freshman year in college that was still two months away.

As Ava turned onto the familiar cul-de-sac, she was a little taken aback by the cliché of the scene at the end of the street. It looked like something straight out of a bad teenage movie, where the characters attend a party that gets out of control. Cars lined the long driveway to the house, parked haphazardly in the manicured hedges and on her mother's well cared-for flowerbeds. Underwear now adorned the garden statues. With no more room in the driveway, a yellow sports car parked in the curve of the street, blocking a fire hydrant, and an old car with a faded blue paint job had jumped the curb and was sitting with two wheels next to one of the brick pillars at the entrance and two wheels still on the street. Amazingly, the for-sale sign still stood intact. However, when she stopped in front of it, she saw that someone had drawn a mustache on the agent's face on the sign--her face.

Ava shook her head when a roll of toilet paper was fired through the air from the window above the front entrance of her family's traditional brick Tudor. *I'm going to kill her*, she thought as she pulled her Prius into Mrs. Marten's circular drive and parked right outside her front door. The tiny woman was waiting for her as she got out of the car.

"I didn't know what else to do, Ava! I didn't want to call the police but this has to end! Oh, it's a good thing the Clarks are out of town!" The Clarks were the neighbors that lived on the other side of her parents. Mr. Clark was known for his pristine lawn, immaculate home, beautiful and much younger third wife, and horrible temper.

"Thank you for calling me, ma'am. I'll take care of it." She reassuringly patted the elderly woman on the shoulder. "You go back inside now."

She waited until the neighbor had made it safely back inside before turning to the task at hand--beating the shit out of her sister.

Ava shook her head the whole time she marched up the driveway to her prestigious real estate listing and parents' Tudor, keys in one hand, cell phone in the other.

Walking into the large foyer of the house, Ava was given a warm, drunken greeting by her little sister's best friend, Jill, who was weaving at the landing of the large, cherry staircase that stood at the front entrance. The longhaired girl gripped the banister while she stumbled down the stairs to where Ava was standing.

Ava steadied her once she reached the bottom before gently asking, "Honey, what is going on here?"

"We're having one last hoorah with our class!" the intoxicated friend shouted, and raised her red plastic glass, as if giving a toast.

"Jill, listen to me. Where is Gracie?"

"Oh, she's around here somewhere," Jill slurred as she motioned with her glass, spilling beer everywhere, then abruptly sat down on the steps.

"You stay there. I'll be right back."

Ava surveyed the house. Beyond the staircase, every seat in the living room was occupied and she could hear loud music and noisy, indistinct chatter coming from the kitchen. At that moment, she was very glad her parents had heeded her advice and removed the valuables while the house was being shown to potential buyers. It wasn't going to help the destroyed furnishings that were still there, but at least the blow to Grace's bank account would be lessened. She couldn't believe she was worried about Grace's bank account at a time like this! She was too much like her mother. Grabbing the arm of the next young man who walked by, she asked, "Do you know where Grace is?"

He grabbed her hand and started stroking it. "Hey, beautiful. It doesn't matter where she is. Come have a drink with me."

She couldn't believe it. Was the boy, who was obviously not even of legal drinking age, actually hitting on her?

She pulled her hand back like it was on fire, flashed a look of disdain that conveyed, *You've got to be freaking kidding me*, and then with eyebrows raised, said sternly and slowly, "Where. Is. Grace?"

He threw his hands up chest high. "Whoa, babe, sorry. Chill. Last I saw her, she was out by the pool."

Ava suddenly became self-conscious of her appearance. She was pretty much in her pajamas--a pair of sports shorts and a tank top--and had only taken the time to put a bra on and brush her hair while putting it in a ponytail before heading out the door after receiving the neighbor's call.

Ava entered the kitchen and wove her way through the sea of scantily clad teenagers, many under the influence of alcohol, and even more acting like idiots, until she reached the doors leading to the pool area. She stepped down through the French doors onto the patio and spotted Grace. The tall, beautiful blonde was holding court with three shirtless, muscular young men in board shorts and flip-flops.

At this point, Ava was livid. How could Grace be so damn irresponsible? She already knew the answer. Ava was the second oldest child in the family and the eldest girl. Steven, her older brother by a year and a half, was a second-year medical resident on the other side of the country. They were thick as thieves growing up and she still considered him to be one of the few people she confided in. Her parents had difficulty conceiving again and it was almost six years before her middle sister, Hope, came along. Two years later, her mother was pregnant with Grace. Gracie was the quintessential baby of the family. She got away with pretty much everything and didn't have a care in the world. Conversely, Ava took on the eldest child traits: bossy, responsible for everyone, overachiever. Steven shared only one oldest child trait with her--overachiever.

As she approached, her little sister caught sight of her and the previous huge grin on the younger girl's face fell into a look of fear.

"What the hell, Grace? Get everyone out. Now."

As soon as she said it, the realization that many had been drinking so therefore could not drive, hit Ava. "Wait, hold on, they can't drive if they've been drinking." A picture of Mrs. Marten's worried face popped into her head, so she continued, "But they still need to go!"

"Luckily, I have everyone's keys," Grace proudly exclaimed while holding up a sack filled with what Ava assumed were the attendees' car keys.

"Okay, well they either need to be able to drive home or I am calling their parents to come get them." She hoped that even though most of these kids were technically considered an adult, as they were over eighteen, it was still an effective threat.

Ava used her sister's shoulder to steady herself and climbed onto a stool, cupped her hands around her mouth and yelled, "Party's over! You need to go home!" Not one person even acknowledged her. She took a deep breath and tried again, louder this time. Still nothing. She looked down at Grace, who simply shrugged her shoulders. Mustering up her deepest cheerleading voice, she tried one last time and felt like a substitute teacher in a gym class, attempting to get anyone's attention and being ignored by everyone.

*Kids these days have no respect for authority. Now what?* Ava slid back onto the seat of the stool. She needed to think, away from the yelling and the loud music. Feeling something pinch her thigh as she moved her feet to the footrest of the stool, she reached into her pocket and pulled out her keys and cell phone, then walked over to the pool house. Unlocking the door to her old place, she slid inside, hoping unnoticed, and locked the door behind her. Luckily, Grace was never given the new keys when her parents changed the locks before she moved in, so it had remained untouched by the partygoers. Sitting down at the kitchenette and putting her hand on her forehead, she truly was at a loss. She looked at the clock and realized it was too late to call any of her colleagues for assistance. She hated to do it, but she decided to call her dad's brother, Richard. He was godfather to all of Robert and Francine's children and, although he'd probably be more pissed than Ava, he definitely was authoritative.

She was surprised when her Aunt Mary answered after only the first ring.

"I'm so sorry to wake you. It's Ava, may I speak to Uncle Richard?"

Aunt Mary informed her that she was wide-awake and that her husband was out of town on business. "Is there something I can help you with, dear?" her aunt asked.

"I've just got a problem that I might need some muscle to help me with," she replied.

"Can't Brad help you?" Her aunt didn't know they had broken up? How did she not know? Ava realized she hardly ever saw her aunt anymore and supposed that when she did, it hadn't come up.

"Good idea. I'll give him a call." Now was not the time to go into the fact the two hadn't been a couple for almost a year. She thanked her aunt and hung up.

Ava sat still for a long time. Should she call Brad? This might fit nicely into Operation Sex Kitten, her mission of getting him back. She could be the damsel in distress, he could come save her, and she could thank him by blowing his socks off with her newfound sexual prowess. Prove to him that he was wrong about her 'lack of sophistication.'

She hadn't seen him since that day at their almost-apartment and hadn't actually talked to him in over two months, not really having a reason to do so. Since deciding she was going to get him back in her bed, she had started looking for one. In addition to wanting to show him her brand-new sexuality, she missed having him in her life, and, truth be told, her pride was hurt at how easily he let her go. Now she had a legitimate reason to call him--she truly needed his help and he could be her knight in shining armor. She dialed Brad's number and was pleasantly surprised when he answered on the third ring. "Well, hello there!"

"Hi Brad, it's Ava. Hey, I'm sorry to bother you but I have a problem and I think you might be the only one who can help me." *Ooooh, good job, play on his ego.* "My parents are out of town and I didn't have anyone else I can call." *Let him know I'm not dating anyone.*

"Well, I'm out with..." he hesitated then finished, "friends. But what do you need?"

She then explained about Grace's party and how no one would leave. She ended her story with, "I don't know what to do. I need you, Brad."

"Jesus, Ava. Seriously? What do you expect me to do?"

"I don't know, I--"

He cut her off. "You need to call the police. I can't help you. Sorry."

Embarrassed now for calling him, she mumbled, "It's okay. I appreciate--"

He cut her off again. "Listen, I gotta go. Good luck." He hung up.

She laid the phone on the table as a few tears streamed down her face. That did not go at all how she wanted.

*You didn't even try to flirt with him, you idiot!*

It was obvious he was not interested in her anymore. Who could blame him? She thought their time together and giving him her virginity might have meant at least something, but try as she might, she could no longer deny he didn't give a damn about her. She had almost convinced herself over the last year that he actually did, he had just gotten scared. Cold feet. But when her brain, the rational side of her, would ask why he hadn't tried to see her once since they'd broken up, her irrational heart never could come up with a good answer. Not for lack of trying though. The reality of it was like a slap waking her up from a dream.

"Thanks for nothing, Brad," she whispered while hopping off the barstool and walking over to the refrigerator. She was now more determined than ever to get him into bed, if for no other reason than to show him what he was going to be missing. She loved it when she got pissed, it made her spunky--at least temporarily. She let herself relish the thought of him being full of regret, then realized she needed to learn a thing or two about sex first and had to find someone experienced who could teach her.

She grabbed a water bottle and took a sip. With a deep breath, she walked out the pool house door just in time to see the patio furniture get thrown into the pool.

*Oh, hell no.*

Watching the table and two chairs sink to the bottom, she stormed past Grace and grabbed the bag of keys off the side table next to her lounger. Her sister, who, judging by the look of surprise on her face, seemed to have forgotten her oldest sister was even there, yelled after Ava as she marched into the house. The elder sister put her hand up in the air and kept walking. Pushing her way into the main house, she hesitated only briefly before following where the very loud music was coming from, and was strangely happy it was from her parents' stereo. At least she knew how to operate that. When she shut it off mid-song, it created the dramatic effect she was looking for. Having everyone's attention now, she was in full-on bitch mode.

With a loud, stern voice she yelled, "Listen up. This party is over." Everyone groaned. She held the bag of keys up. "Unfortunately, you aren't going anywhere until I'm convinced you can drive. If you'd like to fight with me about this, I'm happy to have an officer of the law explain your options as he drives you to jail." More groaning from the crowd. "Don't push it, the chief is one of my closest friends and I have his personal number on my speed dial." Okay, that was a lie. She knew the chief, but certainly wasn't his close friend and she definitely didn't have his personal number. "If you have a cup with alcohol in it, dump it." When she saw people start chugging, she raised her phone, intimating she was going to dial the police. "Do you think I'm joking? I said *dump it. Now.*"

To her surprise, they obliged, lining up at the sink to dump their drinks, some still sneaking sips as they waited their turn.

She continued, "Now, the music will stay off and once you've sobered up, come see me for your keys."

People started milling out to the pool area and before she knew it, the pool was full of teenagers. She had a few people approach her for their keys; three were still intoxicated and three were not. After giving the clearheaded kids their keys, she told the other three they needed to sober up first. Only one argued, citing he had a curfew. "I guess you should have thought about that," was her only response before turning to check on the rest of the house.

She went upstairs to find her parents' bedroom suite still locked and untouched. Her parents always locked their suite when they went out of town. Her father had heard too many horror stories of fellow attorneys' children letting their friends in the house and important client information disappearing. The lock wasn't an interior door lock either. It was a deadbolt with a keypad. Her parents had finally given her the combination code when she listed the house for sale in order for her to be able to properly show the entire home to prospective buyers.

After inspecting all of the upstairs, she made her way through the rest of the house, still clutching the bag of keys. She had made the rounds through the kitchen and living room when she realized there was still the keg out by the pool.

*Shit.*

Running out to the bar by the pool, she started rolling the keg out the gate to the driveway, where she was planning on opening the tap and letting it drain onto the grass. It was pretty heavy and she was struggling to roll it straight. Her sister's friend, Jill, stood in the front doorway, calling her name.

After almost getting the barrel of beer to the other side of the driveway, she called out to the girl, "Honey, I'll be there in a sec."

She made one more rotation with the keg and looked up, startled to find a grown man frowning at her, but even more startled at how amazingly good-looking he was. The dark hair by his forehead was lightly tousled, like he'd run his fingers through it out of frustration. She knew the feeling. He was dressed as though he'd been out for the evening--shiny black shoes, black slacks and a cobalt-blue button-down shirt that matched the color of his eyes almost exactly. His shirt was unbuttoned at the neck and his rolled-up sleeves allowed her to see his very expensive TAG watch. She imagined he'd probably been wearing a tie and jacket earlier in the evening.

"Who the hell is in charge around here?" he growled.

*Seriously, dude? Save it.*

"I guess that would be me, at the moment," Ava responded coolly. She wasn't in the mood, and gorgeous or not, she wasn't about to put up with his shit.

His eyes flashed a little. "So you're the one who is holding my nephew against his will."

She burst out laughing, expecting him to as well. He had to be teasing. Didn't they have some comradery being sober grown-ups in the midst of the intoxicated teenage drama? However, he was still not smiling. *Was he actually serious?*

"Well, if by 'holding against his will,' you mean not letting him drive drunk and plow into an innocent family of five, then yeah, I guess I'm the guilty one."

He continued snarling. "I guess you should have thought about that before providing alcohol to underage kids. I don't appreciate being called away from a date to fix someone else's bad decision making."

She opened her mouth to let him have it, but couldn't find the words and stammered a little more. *Who the hell does this guy think he is?* Just then, Jill was standing next to her and tapped her on the arm. "Ava, I got sick in the den bathroom."

Stroking the girl's arms up and down, Ava asked, "Did you make it to the toilet?" Jill nodded and Ava brushed the upset teen's hair out of her face. "So, sweetie, are you okay? What's wrong?"

"The toilet in the hall is overflowing."

Ava closed her eyes. This night kept getting worse. She sighed, then looked back at Mr. Gorgeous Asshole.

"Since we're sharing our evenings, Mr.--"

"Travis."

"Since we're sharing our evenings, Mr. Travis. Let me tell you about mine. I was at home, nestled in my bed and getting ready to watch Justin Timberlake on the *Tonight Show*. I had just gotten cozy and comfortable when my phone rang. The dear, sweet, elderly lady from next door," she motioned toward Mrs. Marten's home, "was on the other end, scared out of her wits because of the raucous party taking place at the Ericsons'. Now, since I am the responsible daughter and my parents are out of town, I felt compelled to come over and deal with the situation. So here I stand, in my pajamas no less, getting ready to dump a keg full of beer, while patio furniture sits at the bottom of the pool and the inside of my parents' home is trashed—the house which, by the way, I have an appointment to show tomorrow afternoon to potential buyers. In the meantime, I'm trying to keep track of fifty teenagers to make sure they don't cause any more damage or worse, get on the road and kill themselves or someone else and scar me for life with guilt. Oh, and to top it all off, apparently I now have an overflowing toilet I get to deal with. So please, give my condolences to your wife, girlfriend, business partner, priest, or whomever for interrupting their evening out. But as far as you're concerned, to quote an old country song, my give a damn is busted."

Jill looked at Ava wide-eyed. Ava knew Jill had never seen her mad. It probably didn't help the girl was still intoxicated. Mr. Travis, on the other hand, wasn't fazed a bit by her tirade.

With a smug grin, he asked, "Where might you be keeping my nephew, in order to keep him off the road and, as you put it, not kill someone and scar you for life?"

The look she shot him was filled with daggers. "Look around," she said while gesturing at their surroundings as if to imply he was helpless and she wasn't about to enable that. "I'm a little busy at the moment." With that, she headed into the house.

Sure enough, there was water flowing from the hall toilet onto the bathroom floor. The river hadn't made it out the door but there was enough water to make a nice sloshing sound as she made her way to turn off the valve. Unable to get it all the way shut off but close enough that it was now a slow trickle, she looked down. Thank God there wasn't anything too disgusting that appeared to be causing the problem. She'd just need to plunge it and since it was no longer flowing steadily, that could wait for a few minutes.

She made her way back to the kitchen where Mr. Gorgeous but Grouchy was now standing and Jill was sitting at the island.

Approaching her sister's friend, Ava inquired, "Can you do me a favor?" Jill nodded. "Will you make a sign that says, *out of order* and tape it to the hall bathroom door?" Jill said she would, but Ava knew the chances of that actually happening were slim.

On to the next problem. "Did you find him?" she asked the still frowning, handsome man.

"He's looking for his shoes," he responded, exasperated, and she began fishing through the bag of keys.

"What kind of car?"

"I have no idea what kind of car he drives."

She handed him the bag of keys. "Be sure to get them back to me before you go." She turned to head back outside to empty the keg. When she got there, she found two boys refilling their red cups.

"You have got to be kidding me!" She grabbed them both by the ears and marched them inside to the kitchen sink. She had no idea what had come over her but she had had enough of being disrespected tonight by men of any age. "Dump them!" She motioned to the beers they were still holding. They obliged and she released their ears, then held out her hands. "Give me your phones!"

They both begrudgingly handed over their phones.

"You!" She pointed to the taller of the two boys. "Who am I calling to come get you?" She started scrolling through his phone.

He replied sheepishly. "My mom, I guess."

"Your mom? Oh, really nice. Your poor mom is going to have to get out of bed and come pick up her dumb ass son at midnight, because he's too drunk to drive home."

He slunk down and said, "I actually rode with him," gesturing to his companion.

"You!" Ava now focused her attention on the shorter boy. "Who am I calling to come get you?"

Mr. Travis stepped forward, looking amused at what he had just witnessed. "That would be me." He growled at the two boys, "Wait for me by the front door."

She shot him another look. "Why did he call you and not his parents?"

"My older brother, his dad, is a former Navy Seal and would kill him if he knew he was drinking. He thought I would be more sympathetic to his plight and the less scary option." He leaned forward and said softly, yet, matter-of-factly, "He was wrong."

She suddenly felt a bit of sympathy for his drunken nephew and what he was likely to endure tomorrow, hungover and at his uncle's house. Probably up at dawn for some intense chores or calisthenics, or both.

"I almost told him to call his dad but then I was curious how my nephew could be trashed after simply spending time at his friend's house and wanted to know who the idiot was that provided him with the alcohol."

She hoped he wasn't implying she had been the hostess of this shindig. "Yeah, I'd kinda like to know that too," she snapped back.

He looked around at the disaster of what was normally a beautiful home and said almost civilly, "Well if you figure it out, you should make them in charge of clean up. Isn't this place for sale?"

Ava sighed. "Yes, and I have a couple that specifically called to see it tomorrow. Guess I'm going to have to find some alternatives for them to take a look at." Why was she telling him that? It wasn't like he was going to care.

He handed her back the bag of keys and she asked, "Did you figure out what key you were looking for?" *Too bad if you didn't. Oh, who am I kidding?* She had to get better at staying mad at people and being bitchier, even when they decided to play nice.

Before he answered, it dawned on her. "Is there someone to drive your car back for you?" She was annoyed with herself for insinuating she would help. He could kick rocks and figure out something on his own. "Can your wife help you?" *Dammit. That came out like I'm trying to find out if he's married.* Although, he was really good looking...

He turned towards the entrance. "I'm not married, and I walked here. I live around the corner. Probably another reason he called me." With an air of superiority, he called over his shoulder as he strode down the hall, "He'll come get his car in the morning."

The water from the bathroom had seeped under the door and made its way to the entrance, where Mr. Travis' very contrite nephew was waiting with his friend at the bottom of the stairs. Even intoxicated, the kid knew to be humble around this man. He motioned for the teens to follow him and walked out the front door, leaving the boys to follow, staggering and slipping in the water as they tried to keep up.

"Bye! Nice meeting you too! You're welcome for making sure your nephew didn't kill himself!" She waved as the door closed. He had been dismissive of her and that had done the trick of getting her annoyed with him again.

She surveyed the house. Red cups, bottles, and trash were everywhere, but that would have to wait until tomorrow. Besides, Gracie wasn't getting out of cleaning this up. Heading back outside to try to empty the keg again, she saw a stack of unused cups on the counter and grabbed one. At this point, she might as well have a drink too.

Holding the tap in one hand, letting beer flow all over the front lawn, and her cup of beer in the other, Ava realized it tasted gross and reminded her of the bad parties she had attended in college. Dumping it out, she suddenly remembered the overflowing toilet.

She sighed and let out a few expletives before running to the front door. "Please have put the sign up, Jill!" she pleaded silently as she made her way to the downstairs guest bath. There was no sign on the door, but there was Jill, sleeping in a chair in the sitting area just outside the restroom door, with the sign she'd made still in her hands. Ava smiled at the sight of the girl, then grimaced when she opened the door. "Where the hell do they keep the plungers around here?" she asked out loud as she looked around. Probably the garage.

Her wet shoes made a squeaking sound on the wooden floor as she carefully started to make her way to the garage. The last thing she needed was to fall and break something. As she passed by the front door, it opened. There stood Mr. Travis. He had not gotten any less grumpy in the ten minutes since she saw him last. If anything, he'd gotten grumpier.

"Genius forgot to get his phone back."

She jerked her head toward the kitchen. "It's probably on the counter."

He eyed the floor. "Why haven't you gotten that mopped up yet? You need to get it cleaned up before someone falls."

*Gee, ya think?*

"I'll get to it in a second." She didn't like him telling her what to do. "I'm on my way to the garage to look for a plunger."

"No, you need to deal with the water first. Someone's going to get hurt." It wasn't a suggestion, it was a command. Ava got the feeling that was how he usually dealt with people: demanding, not asking.

"There's towels in the hall closet. Knock yourself out." She continued on to the garage.

She was annoyed at his tone and the implication that she didn't know how to prioritize. But shit, he was right. That irritated her. *Here it was, twelve-thirty a.m. on a Friday night and I'm dealing with a clogged toilet. I shouldn't be dealing with this, I should be home in bed; I have clients in the morning. No, actually, you know what? I should be out on a date, dammit.* Then again, that would require her to actually have someone to go with. Unlike her ex, who apparently had plenty of women to go on dates with, there was not one prospect on her radar. Oh, not to mention that awesome reality check Brad gave her tonight. He couldn't care less about her, in spite of having dated her for two years. So, the last thing she needed on top of everything else was this guy being right.

She heard the front door open and close again before she reached the garage. *Thanks for your help, jerk.* Then her reasonable voice chimed in. *You can't be mad at him; this isn't his problem.* But she wanted to be mad, at least at someone sober who would comprehend that she was actually pissed off. Not to mention, he was a jerk. Besides, he had been the only one she'd been in contact with tonight that she could be snotty with that would appreciate it.

Except Brad. She should have been snotty with him. She should have been rude a year ago, standing in that apartment kitchen. She should have yelled, thrown things, swore, *something*. Instead she had just stood there, tears streaming down her face, asking why. He never did give her a sufficient answer, only that they were too different. He couldn't see himself married to her. For the last year she had beaten herself up. Was she not pretty enough? Sexy enough? Sophisticated enough to be an attorney's wife? She decided she might be on to something. Her father was a federal judge but had been a partner in a prestigious law firm before accepting his judicial appointment. Growing up, she had watched her mother get ready for charity balls, dinner parties, and the like. Her mother was drop-dead gorgeous and oh-so-sophisticated. Ava took after her mother in looks- -blonde, green eyes, and petite, but definitely not in her sophistication. Ava was awkward and had absolutely no finesse when she talked. Her siblings were all blonde and green eyed like her, but they were tall, like any good Swede should be. Ava was at least seven inches shorter than the rest of her family. Her dad used to tease her that she must be the mailman's child. She was going to keep working on the sexy and sophisticated part; it was the only way she even stood a chance to get Brad back.

She scoured the garage's neatly lined shelves, opened all the built-in cabinets, and even went through the gardening closet. No plunger. Then she remembered telling her parents to get rid of it when they cleaned out the house as they got ready to list it for sale. "It gives off a bad impression to potential buyers," she told them. She'd heard that at a seminar she'd just gotten home from.

"I'm such an idiot," she groaned and slumped her shoulder into the door leading back into the house. Just then, someone on the other side opened the door and she clumsily fell through, right into Mr. Gorgeous Grouchy's chest.

# Chapter 2

*Ava*

The gorgeous uncle had changed his clothes into grey sweat shorts and an old Stanford University T-shirt that clung nicely to his body and he smelled really good, not like cologne, just very clean, like soap mixed with maybe a little bit of aftershave and deodorant. She couldn't help but notice, as her fingers spread flat across his chest to catch herself, he was very toned underneath his faded crimson T-shirt. His arms came instinctively around her in an attempt to catch her from falling. She leaned against him a little longer than she should have before beginning her recovery; she didn't know why. Ava didn't particularly care for his arrogance or attitude but did like the feeling of him holding her and realized how much she missed being held by a man. Her reaction to him surprised her. Grabbing his bicep with one hand to steady herself, she stood up straight. To her chagrin, he got even better looking when he smiled. He hadn't actually smiled, it was more like a smirk, but it still showed the dimple on the right side of his cheek, and the crinkle lines in the corners of his blue eyes.

"Well, hello there," he said, amused at her unceremonious entry back into the house. Brad had said those same words to her earlier that evening.

She took a step to the side and smoothed her hair. "I--I couldn't find a plunger."

He raised one eyebrow. "I can see that." Ava looked down to see towels laying on the floor, soaking up the overflowed toilet water. "Fortunately for you, I brought one with me."

"You did?" she asked with wide eyes. "But why?"

He shrugged his shoulders. "You looked like you could use a little help."

She wanted to hug him. Okay, maybe kiss him too. At the very least smell him again. Although smelling him probably wouldn't be very sophisticated--she might be hopeless in that department. In an attempt to maintain some semblance of dignity and self-respect, she added to her thought process that she still believed he was an ass and smelling nice didn't change that.

"Can I use it?"

"Use what? The plunger? Already took care of it."

"Wait. You mean to tell me, you went home, changed your clothes, came back, plunged the toilet, *and* put towels on the floor, all while I was looking for the plunger?"

"Yeah. You were in the garage a long time. What exactly were you doing in there?" He teasingly looked over her shoulder as if to search for evidence of some wrongdoing she had been committing.

*Reminiscing.* She couldn't tell him that, instead she giggled at his attempt to tease her and acted mockingly indignant at his accusation. "I really was looking for a plunger!"

"Uh huh." He grinned and winked at her.

Her stomach did a little flip. Was he bi-polar? Was she? What happened to the attitude? She was starting to like Mr. Gorgeous and No Longer Grouchy and she was not happy about it. Awkwardly, she thrust out her hand. "I'm Ava."

He looked at her outstretched hand, amused. "Travis. *Just* Travis. That's my first name." She blushed at the memory of calling him Mr. Travis earlier. He must think she was such a moron. He wiped his hands on his shorts. "You'll forgive me if I don't shake your hand. I haven't had time to wash up."

She felt foolish for trying to be so formal, given the circumstances. *Yes, I am definitely unsophisticated.* "Come on, let me help you get cleaned up." She led him back through the trashed kitchen and out to the pool area. Three more teenagers approached for keys and she ran them through the field sobriety tests she'd seen on cop shows. Satisfied, she found their keys and handed them over.

Travis was grinning at her. "Are you qualified to do that?"

She shrugged. "No, but it eases my conscience, so..."

He looked at the patio furniture sitting at the bottom of the pool, the cups strewn about, her sister and friends snoring on the loungers, and motioned to the bar on the other side of the pool. "Thirsty?" The sides of his mouth were turned up, but she couldn't tell if he was teasing again or if he was serious. She crinkled her nose. "I just had half a beer. It was gross."

He started walking toward the bar. "Do you think there's anything else left?" She followed him, and as he rounded the bar, he said loudly, "What have we got here?" Ava hoped he was talking about alcohol and not another mess. She was surprised to find a sleeping young man in swim trunks lying between the cases of soda and water, and using a towel for a pillow.

"Good grief. Where did he come from? I thought I had accounted for everyone." She had gone around and matched the number of remaining keys in the bag to the number of kids that were still there. She instinctively felt for an extra key in her pocket, but only found hers. "He must have been a passenger."

Travis nodded as though in agreement, and she guessed that he knew all too well about passengers, as one was probably passed out in his guest room.

"Oh snap! Jill!" She had left the poor girl sleeping in the chair. "I'll be right back!" Ava ran into the house.

She found Gracie's best friend right where she had left her and nudged the sleeping teen, rousing her just enough to get her up out of the chair. Ava put her arm around Jill's waist and cautiously walked the girl over the soaked towels, into the living room, and onto the couch. Ava took Jill's shoes off, helped her lie down, and put the throw blanket that had been hanging over the back of the couch around her.

"Sleep tight, kid. You're going to have a helluva headache tomorrow."

Back to the other sleeping beauty behind the bar. And the beauty who was still awake.

She walked out the French doors to find Travis helping the young man in almost the same exact manner she had helped Jill. Smiling at him, she exclaimed, "I just did the same thing in there," and jerked her head towards the house. Ava retrieved the towel the boy had been using as a pillow from behind the bar and covered him with it. The teen stirred a little and woke up, looking confused. Ava recognized him as someone she used to babysit and patted him on the chest. "Go back to sleep, Dillon."

Dillon rolled to his side and with his eyes closed, mumbled, "Ava, I'm sorry about the furniture in the pool."

Leaning down, she whispered, "It's okay. You can take care of it tomorrow."

She looked up to find Travis observing her exchange with Dillon with an almost tender look on his face.

*Who is this guy?* More importantly, was he interested in her? *Is that why he's decided to be helpful now?* He had certainly changed his tune from when he first arrived. As quickly as the thought entered her mind, she pushed it out. No, he wasn't interested in her; he was far too distinguished for that. He looked like he had been on a date and was probably surly in the beginning because he was going to score and had been interrupted. But then why was he being nice to her now? Maybe he was trying to salvage his night by getting lucky with her? The thought made her almost laugh out loud, but then she acknowledged it was also quite appealing. Maybe he could be her first step in Operation Sex Kitten. The idea was fine in theory, but in reality, so out of her character.

She caught a glimpse of her reflection in the French doors. *Yeah, no. That definitely wasn't why he was being nice.* She had no makeup on and her pony tail, shorts, and tank top made her look like she was sixteen, not twenty-nine. She guessed he was at least thirty-eight, and he had an air about him that said he was used to worldly, experienced women. She was neither. *Unsophisticated.*

He was looking at her while pouring a tall shot of whiskey from a bottle that had miraculously been untouched by the partygoers. When he caught her eye, he gestured if she wanted one. She was about to shake her head, then thought, *why not?* Ava shrugged her shoulders and nodded her head yes.

He grinned at her. "Atta girl."

When he brought it to her, she took one sip and then started coughing. "Smooth," she said between hacks. "I think

I'm going to need to mix this." She turned to head to the pool house. He followed her as though he was intrigued. She giggled at the idea he was probably more used to the one being followed, not the other way around.

Ava walked in and switched on the light. It seemed very bright, having come in from the muted outdoor lighting by the pool, and she immediately dimmed the switch. *Much better.*

His six-two presence made the room feel ten times smaller than normal. He had a commanding persona. Not to mention his broad chest and shoulders. His legs in those shorts weren't bad either.

As she went around the counter to the other side of the kitchenette, she patted a bar stool, gesturing for him to sit at the tall counter facing the tiny U-shaped kitchen. Instead, Travis went over to look at the frames on the wall. He swirled his drink as he perused her diplomas hanging on display. She kept meaning to take those to her office.

When he got to her framed and matted doctorate degree, he turned to her with raised eyebrows and asked with an incredulous tone, "You're *Doctor* Ava Ericson?"

"In the flesh." She tried to sound cheerful and not the least bit insulted as she put ice and Diet Coke in her bar glass.

He was watching her every move, as if to size her up to see if she was lying about her credentials. A smile came to his beautiful face. "I had no idea Frannie and Robert had such an educated daughter."

Only people who were friends with her mother would ever call her Frannie. She was either Mrs. Ericson, Francine or Fran to strangers and acquaintances, but once you became Francine Ericson's friend, she insisted you call her Frannie.

"It's probably because they only brag about their son, who is a real doctor. He has his MD." She was teasing. She knew her parents were as proud of her accomplishments as her brother's. "How do you know my parents?" Ava gulped her new concoction. It still tasted terrible but at least she didn't choke this time.

He continued staring at her, as though trying to put pieces together in his head. "Oh, just charity events and the like. I've done business with your father."

That meant one of three things. One, he was a criminal who'd been in her dad's court. *Not likely.* At least she hoped not, since they were now alone behind closed doors, not to mention he was so freaking handsome. *That'd be such a shame.* The shallowness of the thought made her embarrassed. Two, he was a fellow judge. *Again, not likely.* He wasn't quite old enough to have earned the credentials. Three, he was an attorney. *Bingo.*

"What kind of law do you practice?" Ava inquired.

"Who said I practiced law?" Travis teasingly raised his eyebrows and gave her a smirk. She was starting to like it when he teased her. It made her feel more comfortable for some reason. That is, until she started imagining him teasing her in other ways.

*Good God, girl, get it together!*

Operation Sex Kitten might have its first mission. He definitely could teach her a thing or two, at least enough to win Brad back.

"Your demeanor said it for you."

"Is that so?" He took a seat on the sectional that had been custom-made to fit the space. As if he were emphasizing his charming demeanor, he threw his right arm casually over the back cushion, while his left hand continued swirling his drink. He was watching her every move, his eyes intently following her as she walked toward him on the couch. His smile was... almost flirtatious?

*You wish.* This guy only dated sexy, sophisticated women, she was certain of that. Still, she couldn't deny the idea made her toes tingle a bit.

As she sat down on the other end of the couch, Ava suddenly became self-conscious. She remembered her appearance, not to mention her total lack of experience in the s-e-x department. She wasn't a virgin, but Brad had been her only partner, and she knew their lovemaking was pretty vanilla. Still, Travis might be just the guy to practice her moves on for getting Brad back. Then the self-doubt started to creep in. Maybe hot sex was just made up--something that only occurred in works of fiction or when the participants were being paid. Then, she eyed the delicious man sitting next to her and didn't have a hard time imagining it would be anything but vanilla with him.

She looked at his chiseled features, not to mention that chest, that hair, those muscles, his eyes... Which were still watching her, no longer intently but now with amusement, and she felt her face go red when she realized he witnessed her totally checking him out. She gulped down the rest of her drink and sprang from the couch.

"Ready for another?" Her voice sounded way too high pitched and phony.

He shot back the remaining whiskey in his glass. "Sit down, I'll get it." As he rose from the couch, he smiled, winked again, and took her glass. Her knees got weak, and she sat back down. He was on his way back from the pool bar before she was able to regain her composure.

Instead of coming back to the couch, he went to the mini fridge, then stopped and furrowed his brow, as if remembering something, and went to the sink to wash his hands before returning to the fridge for an ice tray and soda. *Oh yeah, cleaning up. That was the whole premise for bringing him out here.* Ava giggled. *Whoops!*

He looked over at her with an inquisitive look. "What's so funny?"

She went over and hopped on the barstool on the other side of the counter from where he was standing. Watching him finish making her drink, she felt the liquid courage starting to affect her. It didn't take much. She was five feet four, a hundred and ten pounds and hadn't eaten since her early dinner. Plus, she rarely drank. "I was thinking I didn't like you very much when you first showed up."

"Oh yeah?" He came around the counter and got in her personal space as he handed her the drink. "And now?"

Even though she was sitting on the barstool, she still had to look up at him. When she did, she found him smirking at her. Ava was rattled, but determined to appear sexy, so she pulled the hair tie out of her hair and shook her blonde mane out.

"Well now," she took a big drink and swallowed hard, "now, I find you sexy." Still holding her glass, she ran her index finger along his arm, trying to be seductive, and trying not to spill all over him.

*Oh. My. God. Did I really just say that?!*

Yeah, she did. Strangely, she wasn't embarrassed. She knew she should be, but she was tired of being cautious, reserved, the girl who didn't throw things in the kitchen when she'd been dumped. The girl who wasn't sexy. She wanted to be the girl who threw caution to the wind. She wanted to be a sex kitten.

Looking for his reaction through lowered eyelids, she was hoping to find his face full of desire, ready to put his mouth on hers and whisk her off to bed. Instead, she found the corners of his mouth turned up, his eyes twinkling. He must really find her entertaining. And not in a sexy, I-want-to-take-you-to-bed way, more like a court-jester kind of way.

# Chapter 3

*Travis*

Travis Sterling didn't know what to do with this enchanting creature in front of him. When he first arrived at the Ericson estate tonight, he was surprised to find an adult at the Teenager-Gone-Wild party. He knew the woman had to be related to Francine; she was her spitting image. At first, he was pissed, thinking Judge Ericson's beautiful daughter had supplied underage kids with alcohol. It didn't take any time for him to realize that wasn't the case, but he was still annoyed he had been forced to end his evening in a way that wasn't on his terms. Although, he wasn't particularly upset at having to end his date early--the company wasn't that great to begin with--he liked being the one who called the shots. Once he'd calmed down, he understood her rationale for keeping his nephew and then felt like an ass for being such a jerk to her. He needed to help her; it was obvious she was in over her head. Plus, he greatly admired her father and adored her mother. Not to mention she was hot as hell. Not glamorous hot, naturally hot. She didn't have a stitch of makeup on, her hair was pulled up in a high ponytail, and still she was stunning. And her body. Those perky tits and tight ass at the end of those tiny but muscular legs gave him a little rise. When she fell into him as he opened the garage door, then introduced herself as Ava, he could have taken her right back into the garage and done her on the hood of her father's Mercedes. He was actually plotting how to make that happen when it became all too apparent she was about the cutest thing ever. Damn it. Why did she have to be so fucking sweet too? He liked it better when she was feisty and his fantasy woman.

About a year ago, at the request of her mother, he had fired off a letter on Ava's behalf to the apartment complex that wouldn't let her break her lease when her schmuck of a boyfriend dumped her right before they moved in together. He had also helped her mother when Ava bought her condominium. Discreetly, of course. Mrs. Ericson couldn't stress enough her daughter was not to know he was looking over the paperwork. He had to say, he had been fascinated. She had managed some pretty incredible terms in the contract, ones he wasn't sure even he'd be able to negotiate. He wanted to meet this woman. He just couldn't figure out how to arrange that with her mother without sounding like a lech. He had to be a good ten years older than she was. Plus, her mother would make sure his intentions were pure before ever agreeing to introduce him, and that wasn't going to happen. So he let his imagination run a little wild instead. If she looked like her mother and had her father's brains, he might have met his match. Meeting her in person tonight, he realized he might have been closer to the truth than he cared to admit.

It quickly became obvious she wasn't the temptress he had first thought/hoped she might be. When she single-handedly dealt with his idiot nephew and his friend with ease, he was impressed, and that attitude of hers had intrigued him, enough to come back and plunge a damn toilet. But then she started accounting for drunk kids, and tucking in passed-out teenagers, even after all the shit they'd put her through tonight. And Frannie never mentioned her daughter was

*Doctor* Ericson. When she started to clumsily flirt with him it was too much. She was such an innocent nerd.

Hell if that didn't make him want her even more.

Except.

Except, this was Judge Ericson and Francine Ericson's oldest daughter. Shagging their sweet little girl an hour after first meeting her would probably be about the worst career decision of his life. But hell, here she was coming on to him, in that tight tank top that hugged her body, and little shorts that emphasized her great ass. Not to mention she was a little tipsy, so that made her a little bolder than he was sure she had ever been in her life. She was fucking adorable.

When she looked up and saw him smiling as she was giving him her best moves, that didn't go over well. What the hell was he going to do now?

She couldn't be further from his type, and yet he really, really wanted to kiss her.

He looked down again to see her bottom lip starting to quiver, and he couldn't help himself. He tilted her chin towards him and softly kissed her. It took great restraint to be gentle with her. He wanted to grab a handful of silk hair and pull her head back so he could put his mouth hard on hers. He knew that would probably be a bit much for her, so he wasn't prepared when she hungrily returned his kiss, forcefully pulling him closer to her, clinging to his back, and straining to be against him. Their kisses quickly got deeper and more frenzied, and soon he was coming up for air before going right back to exploring her mouth with his tongue. *This is not a good idea!* His brain was screaming at him to stop but he was no longer able to think rationally.

He held her face in both hands and continued kissing her passionately. She was utterly intoxicating. Seated on the bar stool, her hips were at perfect height with his. While she sat on the edge of the seat with her legs apart, he stood between her thighs and pressed his erection against her, right where it belonged. She wrapped her legs around him, and drew him as close to her as she could.

His career be damned. Maybe he could become a plumber.

He murmured against her mouth, "I don't have anything with me."

"I do," she panted as she dragged her lips across his.

They began moving their hips in rhythm and he was clawing to get her tank off of her. He'd rip the damn thing if he had to.

He didn't have to.

Ava pulled away from him and slid off the barstool, staring into his eyes. She took a step back and pulled the tank over her head, but didn't rush back to him, instead letting him take her in with his eyes. Without breaking eye contact, she removed her bra and stood there topless. Her tits were perfect and her nipples erect. Letting out a groan, he picked her up in his arms and carried her to the bedroom.

Gently lowering her down on the bed, he positioned himself alongside of her. As he did, she arched against him. He rubbed and squeezed her left breast, delighting in watching her throw her head back in ecstasy before cupping her right one in his hand and lowering his mouth to gently suck and tug on her nipple with his teeth. She let out a gasp and grabbed a handful of his black hair. Ava clung to him as though her life depended on it, curving herself off the bed as he lustfully pleasured her.

He was still fully dressed while she lay there, half naked. She jerked his T-shirt over his head, then wrapped her arms around his neck to pull him back towards her on the bed; bringing the weight of his body directly on top of her. He moaned when his warm chest came down on her cool flesh, relishing the feel of his skin next to hers and basking in the scent of her. She tugged at his shorts while pressing her hips against his as though she wanted him to take her now, but he wasn't done taking pleasure exploring every curve of her body.

He laced her fingers between his and brought her wrists to his mouth, leisurely nibbling and kissing them while she gasped at the sensation. He then took both her wrists in his left hand and brought her hands over her head, pinning them there while he traced her bottom lip with his right index finger, all the while scanning her face, searching for her reaction. When she looked longingly at him, he groaned while biting down on her bottom lip; he had never seen so much lust and want in a woman's eyes before and God, he wanted her just as much. He moved on to her neck, nuzzling below her right ear. Sucking on her earlobe, he thrust his clothed hard-on against the dampening mound between her legs, then lightly licked the skin from her neck and returned to her perfect tits. He focused again on her nipples, squeezing each round breast while sucking and flicking his tongue back and forth over each one, as to not neglect either. Letting go of her wrists, he ran his tongue down her stomach and along the inside of her thighs, purposefully not removing her shorts, even though she was eagerly lifting her hips for him to.

Instead, he slid his hand between her legs and rubbed her up and down through her clothes, then continued licking her thighs, moving up past the bottom of her shorts, but stopping at her panties. She was pressing hard against his hand, her breathing ragged.

When she began tearing at his shorts like she couldn't take it anymore, he brought his head up and smiled at her before helping her remove them. She seemed in awe at the sight of his penis as she gingerly gripped it and he wondered how much experience she had. But as she stroked his shaft she didn't care; he was hypnotized by how soft and delicate her hands felt against his cock. She started to lower her head to his lap and he let out a low growl while leaning back on his elbows, watching her take his tip in her mouth. It was his turn to gasp when she began to rhythmically move her mouth up and down before pausing to explore his balls. She seemed timid as she circled her tongue around them, as though she was trying to be extra careful. He moaned in appreciation and she cautiously put an entire one in her mouth and gently sucked while massaging the other.

He was in ecstasy and was almost disappointed when she stopped to return to his raging erection. His disappointment quickly subsided as he whispered, "Oh my God!" when she took every inch of him in her mouth and held him there while his cock pulsed reflexively against the back of her throat. That proved to be too much for him, and he sat up before flipping her over on to her back.

He couldn't get her shorts and panties off quickly enough and almost fell on the floor when he found her completely waxed. She started reaching for the nightstand and he grabbed her hand. He couldn't pass up the opportunity--her freshly waxed pussy was practically an engraved invitation to lick it. He slid down between her knees and spread her legs wide open, loving how they trembled as he did so. She whimpered when he put his hot breath on the inside of her thighs, and he dragged his tongue firmly up her mound, savoring the smoothness of her skin and the taste of her juices as he lapped them up. After licking her thoroughly from her lips to her ass, he turned his attention to her clit before sliding a finger in and out of her. She gasped when he started flicking his tongue over her knot. When her breathing quickened and he felt her getting wetter, he knew she was already close to climaxing. He began to finger her faster and faster while licking and sucking her harder before replacing his mouth with two fingers and rubbing rapidly over her clit as if he were polishing it. Just then, he felt her entire body stiffen and then shudder with release as she yelled out, "Yes!" over and over. He felt immense satisfaction as she writhed against him in total ecstasy.

He wiped his mouth on the sheet before lying down beside her, propped up on one elbow and watching her face, relishing the final effects of what he had done to her. She kept her eyes closed until her breathing lessened, then smiled before opening them. His cock jumped when she turned to him and whispered breathlessly in his ear, "Your turn."

She pushed him down on his back and straddled him, rubbing slowly and purposefully up and down against his cock, but didn't put him inside her. Reaching out toward the nightstand while trying to remain on top of him, she pulled a condom from the drawer and slowly opened it while starting to grind against him again.

She was apparently enjoying torturing him, but he was not. He took the package from her, ripped it open, and put it on, then grabbed her hips and tried to position himself to penetrate her without her help or guidance. He finally situated himself right under her and started to press himself into her. She was so tight he knew he'd have to go slow. When he was fully inside her, he reached up with his left hand and smoothed her hair from her face. "Are you okay?" he whispered softly.

She answered him by placing her hands on his stomach, arching her body back and thrusting against him in a rhythm that made him sure he wasn't going to last long, regardless of the latex barrier between them. He loved watching her move up and down on him, especially as her boobs bounced when she came down hard. He grabbed her underneath her perfect ass and flipped her over onto her back. He needed to be in control or she was going to make him come in a matter of thirty seconds, and he was enjoying this way too much to let that happen. Slowing the pace, he watched her with her eyes closed. When she opened them, he gazed down at her, overwhelmed with passion. Reaching up, she pulled his mouth to hers. Knowing she could taste herself on his lips and the fact she continued to kiss him long and deep turned him on even more, if that were possible.

He began to increase the intensity of their lovemaking and when he started to grunt as he pushed into her, she cried out breathlessly, "Oh yes! I want you to come!"

That was all it took. He let out a guttural moan and forcefully thrust into her three more times before tensing up, then relaxed as he released inside her.

After he regained his composure, he gazed at her tenderly before gently kissing her lips. "You are so beautiful," he said softly, then slowly slid out of her and went into the bathroom to clean up. When he returned to bed, he grabbed her hips and rolled her so she was on top of him again. She laid her head against his chest, and he heard her sigh before he dozed off, stroking her hair and holding her tight against him, utterly sexually satisfied and content with the feeling of her body on his.

# Chapter 4

*Ava*

Ava woke to the smell of coffee. She opened her eyes and could see the dawn's light starting to shine through her blinds. Taking a delicious full body stretch, hands above her head, and letting out an *mmm* as she finished, she wouldn't have been able to wipe the smile off her face if her life depended on it. She'd finally had movie sex.

She looked over to see Travis in the doorway with a cup of coffee, clad only in his boxers, smiling back at her.

"Morning," he said with a low voice.

"Good morning!" she replied back with a smile. Ava stretched again, only this time the sheet covering her naked body slipped down to her waist. She watched his eyes dance with delight when she didn't rush to drape it back over her and instead laid there, enjoying being naked in front of him.

Sitting down on the bed next to her, he leaned in and asked, "Regrets?" while tucking her hair behind her ear.

Ava flipped over onto her stomach, hugging her pillow, facing him, her ass only half covered by the sheet. Last night had been incredible. She'd gained some of the experience she was searching for and put some of her theories into practice, with mind-blowing results. At least for her.

"Not a single, solitary one," she purred. "You?"

"Are you kidding? I had you, naked, in my arms all night. My only regret is I can't lie in bed naked with you all day."

"Mmm, you're right, that would be lovely." She slid over and put her head in his lap and closed her eyes while picturing what that would actually be like.

He stroked her hair for a minute before speaking. "I think it's best if I go before anyone wakes up around here and sees me sneaking out of your place like a tomcat. I have two boys I'm sure are still sawing logs in my guest room, but I need to get back before they know I was gone."

She knew he was right, of course, but would have loved to have a round two of last night before he left. *What has gotten into me?* She grinned. Travis had gotten into her-- literally.

"I'm only thinking of your reputation, darling," he drawled when she didn't move her head so he could leave.

She sighed. *That damn reputation.*

She got out of bed and put on the tattered robe she had left there after she moved into her condo. Travis slipped his shorts on and T-shirt back over his head and met her at the door leading out to the pool. Having never had a one-night stand before, she wasn't sure what to expect next. Operation Sex Kitten had just gotten underway; this was all new to her. Do they exchange numbers, promising to call, but both knowing that's not going to happen? Or do they leave it as it is, no empty promises, nothing more than a goodbye with a kiss?

Those thoughts were swirling around Ava's head as she stood there, hand on the doorknob, ready to open it and send him on his way, so what he said next confused her a little.

"When can I see you again, Ava?"

*Wait, what? Is that just something he's supposed to say or did he really mean it?* She was at a loss for words. *More importantly, do I want to see him again?*

He brushed the hair away from her face. "I can see you again, can't I?"

He towered over her in her bare feet by almost a foot and was so close to her she had to strain to tilt her head far back enough to look at his face. She let go of the doorknob and leaned her head against his chest. His arms came around her, holding her close.

"I'd love to see you again," she murmured. She was sure there was a lot more she could learn from him.

"Then why the hesitation?" He took a step back and tilted her chin towards him. *My God, he has a commanding presence.*

"I guess I wasn't sure this was more than a one-time thing," she answered as she dropped her eyes from his.

"Is that what you want?" He almost seemed hurt at the thought.

"No. I've just--I've just never done something like this before so I'm unsure of the protocol."

He laughed at her use of the word *protocol.* "Well, the protocol in this situation is you have dinner with me tonight."

She tried not to smile too widely when she told him, "I'd like that."

"I'll be in touch later today then with the details." He leaned down and gently kissed her while opening the door. "Last night was incredible," he murmured against her lips.

He hadn't taken three steps out the door when Ava called after him. "Travis?"

He swung around and waited.

She held her right palm facing up in a questioning manner. "Um, what's your last name?" She was a little ashamed to be asking at this point. She was sure even sex kittens learned last names first.

He grinned at her. "Sterling," he responded, then turned on his heel and quickly made his way to the pool gate that led to the driveway before anyone else saw him.

After he quietly and gingerly closed the gate behind him, he put his hand up to wave goodbye to her as she watched him from her doorway. Ava walked back in the pool house and slumped down on the couch.

*Holy shit. I just slept with Travis Sterling.*

# Chapter 5

*Ava*

Travis Sterling was notorious for two things: being the best real estate attorney in the state and being a perpetual bachelor. And Frannie Ericson adored him. She'd met him many years ago when she was chairing the ball benefitting the Wounded Warrior Project, WWP. Travis was the biggest supporter of the event and had remained so over the years. Her mother often gushed about how kind and generous he was and whoever ended up with him was going to be one lucky girl. One time, right after the inaugural ball, Francine had sighed wistfully and remarked to her husband, in front of Ava, she knew Travis was destined for great things, and she wished he would wait for their oldest daughter. Ava was twenty at the time and had barely had her first kiss. Robert Ericson grumbled he wasn't sure he felt the same way. Travis, although plenty likeable as far as her father was concerned, was already becoming known as quite the ladies' man. Judge Ericson wanted more for his Ava Bear.

Over the years, she'd heard Travis' name mentioned off and on, in the newspaper, social situations, or around the dinner table. She didn't pay much attention, but when she heard mention of him, she'd recognize he was the lawyer her mother thought so highly of. Her mother could always count on Sterling and his firm's support for whatever charity function she was involved in, and she continued working on the WWP, in various capacities, as her time permitted. This year, Mrs. Ericson was again chairing the ball which had become an annual event. This was the first one Ava was going to actually attend as a guest and she was looking forward to seeing her mother in her element. Ava had gone in previous years, acting as a coat-check girl, running items up to the stage for the live auction, or taking people's money for raffle tickets, and was always in awe at how graceful her mother was. How she was able to pull the evening off without a hitch. The upcoming ball was in six weeks, and she and Frannie were supposed to go dress shopping when her parents returned from their vacation. She thought her mother was more excited than Ava was about buying Ava a new dress. While excited to see her mother's success, balls and formals weren't her favorite thing.

After Ava got her real estate license, she heard a lot more stories about Travis. She would overhear female realtors after meeting him swoon about how devastatingly handsome he was and how he oozed charm and masculinity. She'd also heard about his arrogance and impatience and his ability to go for the jugular without remorse if crossed. His reputation as a lawyer was simple; if you wanted the best and could pony up the dough, you hired Travis Sterling. He took no prisoners and if his case ended up actually going to court, he almost always won. Nine times out of ten, the case didn't go to court; nobody wanted to chance going up against him. Which made him in high demand and very wealthy and, Ava concluded, probably accounted for some of his arrogance.

Rich, gorgeous, successful, and virile meant he was quite the catch. From what Ava had gathered, Travis was the elusive Great White Whale of the dating world. Everyone desired him but no one could reel him in. He was linked to everyone from heiresses, to models, to successful businesswomen.

What on earth did he want with Ava? She hadn't felt at all embarrassed or ashamed about what happened between them, but after learning who he was and realizing all the beautiful, sexy women he'd been with, she felt very inadequate. She wasn't putting a lot of stock in actually seeing him tonight, or ever again, other than maybe at a social function--and definitely not as his date. While she was suddenly very self-conscious about her performance last night, she was still tingling from his. Yet remained with no regrets, whether she saw him again or not. He had opened her eyes to what it meant to have passion and desire in bed, and she was glad for that.

The doorbell to the Ericson home rang around ten-thirty that morning. Grace and her friends had been up and cleaning since around nine-fifteen, and they were struggling. Being hungover was not conducive to bending over a lot or mopping up old beer. They had a long day in store, and Ava was not about to help. *Serves them right.* Besides, she had to meet with clients later today. Ava answered the door, bagel in hand. There stood a professional cleaning crew of three men and three women, clad in jumpsuit uniforms with patches that said their names. Their company's van was parked in the drive.

"Can I help you?" Ava asked Sandy, the woman who appeared to be in charge, as she was the only one of the six holding a clipboard.

"Mr. Sterling sent us," the lady replied, and handed Ava an envelope addressed to her.

Ava pulled out a notecard with *TS* embossed in black at the top. The letters intertwined.

*Good grief, the man has his own brand.*

On the card in neat, handwritten block letters it read:
*Thought Grace could use a little help today.*
*Hope you are still able to show the house this afternoon.*
*Looking forward to this evening.*
*-TS*

*Seriously? First he plunges my parents' toilet, then he has mind blowing sex with me, and now this?* She had to give it to him; he was pretty impressive.

Suddenly, she was glad she was wrong--apparently she was going to see him again.

He included a card that had his personal cell number on it and *call at your convenience* on the back in the same handwriting as the card.

She had to fight the urge to rush in and call him immediately. *Play it cool, Ava.* He didn't seem the type to like clingy or needy women, although he certainly liked coming to their rescue. But she got the impression that definitely had to be on his terms and as he saw fit.

**

Ava was able to hold out calling Travis until after she met with her clients. At around two p.m., she was finally back at her condo--free of distractions and noise--and dialed his number with trembling fingers, sitting down on her bed. She didn't realize she was holding her breath until he answered and when she began to speak, was embarrassed to be out of breath.

"Hi, it's Ava." She held the receiver to her ear but lifted the speaking portion over her head and took a deep breath.

"Hi there. I'm so glad to hear from you!" He genuinely sounded glad. "Are we still on for tonight?"

"I hope so," she replied in her best flirting tone. "What do you have in mind?"

He chuckled. "I thought we'd start with dinner at Evangeline's and go from there."

She started to ask him how on earth he thought he was going to get a reservation at Evangeline's on such short notice, but then remembered who she was talking to. *Of course he can get into Evangeline's without a reservation. Either that or he has a standing one.*

"That sounds nice. What time were you thinking?" She was trying to sound sexy, yet nonchalant, but even to her own ears, she wasn't buying it.

"Seven o'clock too late? I've got some work to finish up before I can head out."

*That means I have to wait five more hours!*

Instead, she replied, "Seven works great," this time trying to use a husky, seductive voice. Except she thought her voice came out like an eighty-year-old woman who'd smoked all her life. She swore if he asked her if she was coming down with something, she was going to die from embarrassment.

Luckily, all he asked was, "Do you want me to pick you up or do you want to meet at the restaurant?"

*Well yes, I want you to pick me up.* But since he offered an alternative, she wasn't sure what she was supposed to choose. She didn't understand the rules of whatever this was that was happening between them.

She must have hesitated too long because he made the decision for her. "Should I pick you up at your parents' or at your place?"

"My place." She'd swing by her parents' house later to make sure Grace wasn't up to any mischief tonight. "I'll text you the address."

"See you then." He wasn't the type to chitchat.

"Yes, see you then," Ava replied, having given up on trying to conjure up the voice of a siren.

She was about to hang up when she heard him say her name.

"Ava?" He didn't wait for her to answer him. "I am looking forward to seeing you." He hung up the phone.

That made her almost giddy. The man was charming. Dangerously charming. She knew she needed to keep things light between them and remember what she was doing this for: to get Brad back. Besides, Travis was the Great White Whale. Unobtainable. So she was just going to have fun and enjoy tonight, and hopefully a repeat performance of last night.

What the heck was she going to wear?!

\*\*

Ava ransacked her closet looking for just the right thing to put on. Classy but sexy, revealing but not too slutty. She had nothing that fit that description. Time to call in reinforcements.

She dialed the phone to Face Time her best friend, Anne.

Annie answered with, "What's up, Buttercup?" Her friend had an old sweatshirt on and her hair piled on her head in a very messy bun. It looked like she was eating ice cream; she had one of the long plastic red spoons in her mouth.

Ava tried to look as desperate as she could so her friend would take pity on her. "I need help. I'm having dinner at Evangeline's tonight and I have nothing to wear. Really. Nothing."

She wasn't lying. Her closet consisted of conservative clothes for work, sensible shoes--it didn't make sense to wear ridiculously high heels when taking people out to look at homes--jeans, yoga pants, sweatshirts, T-shirts, her lab coats from when she worked at the university, and gowns she had worn to formals in college.

"Evangeline's, huh? Ooh la la. Who's the lucky guy?"

"Just a client."

"Meet me at the mall in twenty!" Annie giggled and sat up on her knees. "We're going to find something *hawt* for you to wear on your Saturday night date with your client!" She gestured air quotations when she said *client*, and with that, signed off.

Ava knew she hadn't fooled her friend, but she wasn't ready to divulge she was going to dinner with Travis Sterling. Not yet. Besides, that would lead to more questions, which would lead to her breaking down and spilling her guts about last night. Her friend would freak out if she knew she had slept with him after just meeting him. *Ava* should be freaking out. Last night had been completely out of character for her.

*Isn't that the point of OSK? To become a sex goddess and win Brad back?*

Even in college, she had the reputation of being the square in her sorority. Guys dated her, thinking they would be *the one* she would sleep with. When it didn't happen after a few dates, they moved on. The longest boyfriend she'd had before Brad lasted seven dates. She met Brad at the end of the third year in her doctoral program. She was twenty-six years-old and still a virgin. He was a typical California boy--tan, bleached blond hair, and athletic with boyish good looks and a happy-go-lucky attitude. He was a law student at her university and she had seen him around campus, while he noticed Ava at a graduation party for one of their mutual friends and immediately began pursuing her.

Her naïveté and inexperience was something Brad used to his advantage. He wined and dined her, pulling out all the stops with flowers, cards, *thinking of you* texts and calls, and he didn't push her to be intimate. He had been a perfect gentleman, up until almost the end of their relationship. He thought their pairing was ideal. He was a future lawyer from a respectable family, she was educated and the daughter of a judge and a socialite--a real socialite, not the trampy definition that has become associated with the term.

Ava thought his persistence was charming and the fact he stuck around after their seventh date was telling. Eventually she found herself in love with him and one night, when he tried to escalate their make-out session on the couch, she surprised him by not pushing him away like she normally did. His perseverance had paid off.

He started hinting about marriage after he graduated from law school and was studying for the bar. She had graduated from school and foregone going into the corporate world, where the money was--much to her father's chagrin--instead jumping into academia and started earning a modest living so she could help support her future husband during the lean years of being a new lawyer. Brad had taken the bar a second time and was waiting on the results when he suggested they move in together. It wasn't exactly the marriage proposal she was hoping for, but she knew that was just around the corner. She told herself it was the natural progression of things in this day and age.

On a sunny Saturday afternoon, Ava was unloading boxes at their new apartment when Brad arrived with a group of friends on their way to a baseball game. He had told her the day before when they signed their lease he needed to blow off steam with his friends, something he had been doing a lot lately. Ava chalked it up to being nervous about the bar results; once he learned he'd passed, he'd settle back down. She was standing at her open trunk when the carload of people pulled up next to her--Brad's roommates and some girls she knew, some she didn't. She waved to the group as Brad got out of the car, thinking it strange his friends didn't wave back and yell something obnoxious about her not wanting to go with them, like they always did. Instead, they looked away, almost seeming embarrassed. Brad took the box she had retrieved from the back of her little sedan and started walking towards the new apartment. Following behind with a lamp and admiring his tan, athletic legs as he walked quickly up the steps, she didn't understand why he was there, but as she looked at the back of his bleached blond head, she smiled at the thought he wanted to stop and see her on his way to the stadium. She soon discovered why he was really there when he stood in their practically empty kitchen and announced, quite matter-of-factly, he wasn't going to be moving in after all--he had received the results from the bar exam, and he had passed. Learning he was now officially able to practice law created some *opportunities* he didn't know were available, and he no longer wanted to be tied down. As he put it, he had "a lot of living to do before getting married."

She didn't remember much after that, just him kissing the top of her head and walking out the door.

Almost in a trance, she showed up at her parents' door, finally breaking down when she was trying to explain to her mother what had just happened. Her mom let her stay curled up in her childhood bed for three days before opening her blinds one morning and declaring it was time her daughter got on with her life. Ava sighed and agreed; she didn't have any tears left to cry anyway. First thing they did was finish packing her old apartment up. Her lease was expiring and the management company had already rented her apartment so she needed to be out. Unfortunately, when she walked into her new apartment, tears instantly started to stream down her face. She still didn't understand why Brad had chosen to end their relationship, although the more Ava thought about it, the more she suspected it might have had something to do with the short-haired brunette in the red, white, and blue sequined bikini top that was sitting in the back seat next to him when he showed up at the apartment. She had never seen her before that day.

Mrs. Ericson stopped her daughter from putting down the box she was carrying. "There's no way you can live here," her mother told her gently. Before Ava could protest--she had signed a lease after all--her mom continued, "Don't worry about the lease. You'll be able to get out of it. You can stay with us until you get your bearings. We'll put your things in storage." Her mother, although gentle and beautiful, was not one to take no for an answer.

They boxed what little had been unpacked at her new apartment before going to the rental office to argue with the manager about what he was going to charge her for breaking her new lease. He said he was only charging her for her half, but it was an exorbitant half. Her mom tried appealing to the man's sense of decency. "She hasn't even moved in! You won't even need to clean it!" Followed by, "You need to be charging Brad Miller for the entire amount, he's the one who has caused this. This girl is broken hearted! Look at her!" At first, Ava was a little offended at the insinuation she looked pathetic, but then she had to admit, she'd looked better. When that didn't work, Mrs. Ericson gave him the card of her well-known real estate lawyer and informed him all future correspondence would be done through her attorney. With that, she turned, head held high, and summoned her daughter. "We're leaving." Two weeks later, when Ava opened her mail and found a check for her full deposit, she thought, "He is one amazing attorney." She secretly hoped the apartment manager still went after Brad for his share.

**

It took all of twenty seconds after seeing her friend in person for Ava to confess she had slept with someone new.

Anne squealed and wanted every horny detail.

"All I will tell you is he's older and..."

"Ew, how much older?" her friend interrupted.

"Not old like that. Gross. Late thirties, maybe forty."

"Okay, I can work with that." Anne gestured for Ava to continue.

Ava shot her a look and continued. "All I can say is in addition to being older, he's freaking gorgeous, makes a lot of money, and..."

"Is he big?" her friend interrupted again.

Ava hadn't really thought about that. She liked how his dick looked and how it felt and what he did with it but if she had to assess size...

"I think the length is average and the girth above average."

Anne nodded. "Nice."

"But you have to remember, I haven't had a lot to compare it to."

"You'd know if it was too small," her friend stated like she was an authority on the subject. "Or too big."

"Ouch." Both girls winced at the thought of being with someone whose penis was too big.

"Anyway, you were saying?"

"He's got a really nice body."

Anne narrowed her eyes and asked suspiciously, "What's wrong with him? Nobody is that perfect."

"Nothing is wrong with him. At least not that I know of." Ava thought about it and added, "Well, he can be a bit of a prick, I suppose." She paused. "And I've heard he takes no prisoners at work." She paused again. "Like, you don't want to cross him kinda thing."

"Oh, so he's a bully."

Ava shook her head. "No. At least I don't see that." She gave it a little thought. No, she wouldn't classify him as a bully.

She continued, "Besides, it's not like I'm interested in him. He is simply part of my plan to get Brad back."

Anne glared at her. "Ugh. Okay, number one. Why would you want Brad back? Number two, how is sleeping with someone else going to get him back? Number three, why aren't you interested in the mystery man?"

"It's part of my Operation Sex Kitten, or OSK for short. I'm going to get some sexual experience, then be seen with this other man out in public so Brad knows I'm dating him and gets jealous. When he tries to get me back, I'll play hard to get before giving in and then--bam! Knock his socks off in bed with my new skills! There's no way he wouldn't want to be with me after that!"

Anne shook her head, dumbfounded. "You truly are just an inexperienced little school girl at heart, aren't you?" Getting serious, she continued, "Again, even if this hair-brained 'operation' worked, why would you even want him back, Ava, after the way he treated you?"

"I don't know. I guess because he was my first love? And maybe to prove there's nothing wrong with me. I am desirable."

"Okay, let me get this straight. You're boning this gorgeous, rich guy who just happens to be a jerk with a nice body but yet, you don't think you're desirable? Sister, what more do you want?"

Ava shook her head. "I don't know."

"Yeah, well I think you're being greedy. And stupid. But what do I know? I haven't been laid in five months."

Yes, she could always count on Anne to be straight with her, but she was wrong this time. *Keep your eye on the prize.*

Ava wouldn't let Anne come home with her to help her get ready. She knew her friend was only trying to catch a glimpse of her mystery man and had no intention of actually helping her prepare for her date. It didn't take much to convince her to go home once Ava lied and told her she was meeting him at the restaurant.

"See ya later, gorgeous! I want the deets tomorrow!" her friend yelled as she walked to her car in the mall parking lot.

"I don't kiss and tell!" Ava called back as she got into her car.

"Then I'll beat it out of you!"

Earlier in the mall, they had found not one, but two perfect dresses. Ava bought them both. She had purchased her attire for the evening, complete with four-inch heels-- CFM shoes she called them, short for Come Fuck Me (her date was almost a foot taller than she was, it was a justified buy!)--and sat in the waiting area of the dressing rooms while Anne tried on a couple of outfits herself. Ava passed the time while her girlfriend changed clothes by picking up the city's daily paper and was happy to find it was that day's issue. *They still actually print these?* At the moment, she was glad they did and started flipping through the pages looking for the gossip section on page six. It was fun to see if there was anyone she knew now that she was a grownup. She used to read the *Out and About* section religiously in college, and they had usually included a photo or two. She didn't read it much anymore, but recalled the first time she actually knew someone featured. It was a girl she went to high school with, Sharon Edison. Sharon had hosted an event the ambassador of Finland attended. There hadn't been a picture, but the write-up sounded like it had been a fun evening. She'd also seen Travis' name on occasion; that's how she knew he'd been linked to models, socialites, and powerful women. There was one reporter in particular, Tom Jensen, who seemed to write about the various conquests of Travis Sterling. In his paragraphs, the writer would discuss where the couple had been spotted and if they appeared romantic. If there were even the slightest bit of touching, it would send Jensen into a speculation frenzy, often asking if this one was, in fact, *the future Mrs. Sterling*. So far, the reporter was about 0 for 50.

Ava got to the *Out and About* section on page six and found Travis Sterling's photo staring right at her. He looked good. He was wearing the outfit he'd had on when he first showed up last night except it included the tie and jacket she had imagined he had worn when he appeared in her parents' kitchen with no tie and his sleeves rolled up. On his arm was the beautiful Victoria Thornapple, of the famous Thornapple cereal family. She was a dark haired, voluptuous heiress with perfectly pouty lips and a rack to envy.

Ava doubted the lips or the boobs were real.

She chided herself. *You catty bitch!*

Apparently the two were seen leaving the theater after having watched *Les Miserables. Blech, I hate that play*. She knew that made her highly uncultured; after all, everyone she knew that had seen it gushed over what a great production *Les Miz* was. Friends, co-workers, critics, her parents... and now, apparently, Travis. Strangely enough, the reporter did not hypothesize about the likelihood of Ms. Thornapple becoming Mrs. Sterling. *Trav must be losing his touch.* Ava giggled to herself. No, she could vouch that was most definitely not the case.

Ava thought about the picture of Travis in the paper the whole drive home. She wasn't necessarily jealous, per se. It reminded her he really was unobtainable and she was right about Brad being the goal at the end of this. Last night, Travis had been out on a date with one woman, and three hours later, he was in bed with Ava. The two women's roles could just as easily have been reversed, which wasn't necessarily a bad thing if she was going to remain focused and gain some experience to get Brad back.

She finished getting ready and by the time she was done, she was even impressed herself. The dress was a sleeveless, periwinkle blue number that came three inches above her knee and revealed a little bit of cleavage, which the necklace she was wearing drew attention to. The fabric was a heavy silk that hugged her curves just right. She hesitated to use the word *curves* to describe herself because she didn't think her body qualified as curvy. Well, except her butt. She did have what one could call a *booty*; it was probably her best asset. Her breasts were nothing special, a little small for her liking but she always fixed that with the right bra. If she were braver she'd have a boob job, but was too scared of it getting botched, not to mention she didn't like pain. Her face was pretty enough, she supposed. She'd been told her whole life she looked like her mother, and she thought her mother was beautiful. There was nothing special about her medium length blonde hair. She tried to keep up with the latest hair trends, but oftentimes found she was actually behind the times. She liked to keep her hair long enough that she could pull it up in a ponytail, and she wore a lot of ponytails and yoga pants when she wasn't working. Tonight, after curling and styling her hair, it turned out pretty, if she did say so herself. That surprised her; usually when she wanted her 'do to look good, it wouldn't cooperate. The hair gods were on her side tonight, for once. She put a spritz of her favorite cologne on followed by her makeup--eyeliner, mascara, and a shade of light pink lipstick. At the last minute, she added a brush swipe of blush over her cheeks, although she didn't see a difference. *That's okay.* She was pleased with how she looked so far.

Right when she thought that, she was sure he was going to stand her up. Her look had come together too easily; there had to be a catch.

It was only six forty-five; she was way ahead of schedule. No need to panic that he wasn't here yet. She put her sexy CFM shoes on and tried to get used to walking in them before deciding to have a glass of wine to calm her nerves. Pouring herself a small glass and sitting down at the kitchen table, she started thinking more about the photo from the paper, then pulled the electronic edition up on her phone to zoom in on Victoria Thornapple. She really was a pretty woman. At least the man had good taste.

Would their picture be in tomorrow's paper? Ava could see the caption now. *Travis Sterling and unidentified woman leaving Evangeline's.* Would someone else be zooming in on her photo? All of a sudden, she wasn't interested in going to a fancy restaurant. If she wasn't ready to share she was dating him with Anne, she certainly wasn't ready for the rest of the world to find out. There was also the idea that she didn't want to be considered a flavor of the week by people she knew. When they did inevitably move on to other people, if she hadn't gotten Brad back, she'd be the object of people's pity and her mother would be devastated. No, she surely didn't want to go to dinner tonight at the city's hippest restaurant and get her picture taken by the press for Brad and the rest of the world to see. At least not yet.

# Chapter 6

*Travis*

Looking at Ava's text with her address made him chuckle. He already knew where she lived thanks to her mother requesting he look at the purchase contract when she bought her condo. Of course, Ava knew nothing about that, but that was when his interest in her was piqued. He imagined she was a master negotiator, cool and collected, able to get people to do whatever she wanted, and he was just the man for the siren's challenge. Now that he'd met her in real life, he had no idea what to make of her. But he was still up for the challenge.

Driving above the speed limit having left the office late-- a common occurrence for him--he would have to get ready in a hurry. Fortunately, her condo was not far from his place. He literally did live right around the corner from the Ericsons. He'd moved into his house about three years ago and loved it. It was his fortress of solitude, dogs and all, and he became very disagreeable when his privacy was invaded, like by his nephew, Patrick, and his friend last night. Luckily for Patrick, he wasn't home last night to bask in his solitude. He chuckled again. No, he most certainly was not home last night.

He had been thinking about Ava all day. He had tried to be charming and impress her by sending those workers over this morning to help clean up. He didn't think he needed to bribe her to make sure she went out with him tonight, but it couldn't hurt. The fact she occupied his thoughts all day was disturbing. He never thought about women at work. To be honest, he was too busy to think much about them at all, except when he was actually with them. Not that he didn't enjoy their company when that occurred. It just didn't take a lot of work anymore to make that happen. There were benefits that came with being considered one of the city's most eligible bachelors. Women pursued him now. He didn't think he had asked a woman on a date in over five years, right around the time a local magazine did its *Top Ten Available Men* article. He was number three. Since then, he had plenty of women chasing him. Some were successful in catching him, but never for very long. One thing for sure, he never lacked for companionship when he wanted it.

So what was it about Ava that had him so distracted and wanting to make the effort?

If he had to venture a guess, he found her naïveté refreshing. He had no doubt last night's lovemaking session also played a part. It really was incredible. She had tried to be bold and display a sexual prowess he knew damn well was an act. He could tell she wasn't that experienced, but it didn't matter. She made him feel desire he hadn't had in a long time. If he were to be honest with himself, he'd never felt passion and connection like that before, ever. He'd thought he had once when he had started practicing law, but it turned out to not be what he had originally thought. Ava had been so willing to trust him and be a hundred percent there in the moment with him. That was not at all like the women he currently dated. He got hard just thinking about her. Actually, he'd had that problem several times today. Reliving the feeling of her body on his was pretty stirring. He was glad it was Saturday and there was no one else in the office.

Travis meant it when he told her he wanted to be naked with her all day today. He honestly didn't want to leave her this morning. He had no idea what to expect when she woke up and feared she'd be instantly filled with shame and guilt and want nothing more to do with him. Or the reverse, she'd be madly in love with him and want to marry him next week. Both instances had happened to him a time or two or three in the past. A girl he had only taken to dinner twice turned into a stalker, and that's when he decided to start dating women who were as in demand as he was. They weren't interested in anything more than dinner, getting their picture in the paper, and maybe a roll in the hay. What they lacked in substance, they made up for with looks and sexual experience. Damned if Ava didn't have substance and looks (not to mention a feisty side, and an amazing ass). He hoped to help her in the sexual experience department.

But, it wasn't just that.

It was all of it. The whole package. She was kind and caring, authentically so, and her nerdy innocence was so goddamn endearing. Then there was the matter of her intelligence. Sweet Mary and Joseph, a PhD? How had Frannie never mentioned that in all her chatter about her daughter? And to top it all off, she was hot. Smokin' hot.

Shit. This could be a problem.

*It'll wear off; it always does.* Yet, from where he was sitting at the moment, he wasn't in a hurry for that to happen any time soon.

*We'll see how tonight goes. I'll probably be sick of her by tomorrow.*

He showered quickly and had time for a shave before dressing in his favorite tailor-made blue suit. All his suits were custom made--he knew he had made it when he bought his first suit made specifically for him. The navy ensemble had a matching vest and he liked how it looked when he took his jacket off. He picked out a starched white shirt and his newest designer tie, then ran a quick cloth over his shoes to make sure they were pristine.

Dabbing some cologne on his neck and putting on his favorite TAG watch, he gave himself a once-over in the mirror, then was out the door. He had just enough time to spare to stop and pick up flowers. He expected his efforts wouldn't go unnoticed and had a feeling with her, they wouldn't.

Knocking on her door at six fifty-five, he hoped she didn't mind he was a few minutes early.

****

*Ava*

The knock on the door startled Ava. She looked at the clock. *Of course he's punctual.* She teetered to the door in her ridiculously high heels, took a deep breath, and opened the door with a smile. Travis was standing there with red roses. *Did he ever stop with the charm?*

Travis looked her up and down. "You look amazing."

*He smells amazing.*

"Thank you," she replied as she moved to the side of the doorway, signaling for him to come in.

He handed her the bouquet. "These are for you." Then he leaned over and kissed her cheek. *The cheek?*

She smiled and told him thank you again, but instead of taking the flowers, put her hands on each side of his face and kissed him on the mouth. There was something empowering about knowing she was only a temporary thing for him and she didn't have to worry about where this was going. She could be herself, only braver and more adventurous.

The kiss was simply meant to be a more appropriate greeting than the cheek, given their intimacy last night, but it heated up very quickly.

Travis broke away and said, "If we keep doing this, we're going to miss our reservation."

That brought Ava back to reality. "About that... Can we talk for a second?" She stepped carefully toward the kitchen while trying not to trip and fall in front of him.

Travis looked at her as if wary about where this might be headed. "Anytime a woman asks if we can talk, it has never ended well." He handed her the flowers. "You might want to put those in water."

Ava motioned for him to sit at the table while she looked through her cupboards for something to put the flowers in.

"Do you want something to drink? I just opened a bottle of wine," she asked over her shoulder as she opened up one cupboard door after another until finding what she was looking for in the cabinets above the refrigerator.

"No, I'm good for now. What do you want to talk about?"

She was now at the sink, filling a vase with water. Shutting the faucet off, Ava took a deep breath, then blurted out, "Is it okay if we don't go to Evangeline's tonight?" Then she busily started cutting the stems of the roses and putting them one at a time in the water, glancing at him only out of the corner of her eye.

Travis replied slowly. "Yeah, that'd be okay. Mind telling me why?"

She stopped after haphazardly cutting a stem, still not looking directly at him, and gestured with the scissors still in

67

her hand. "It's just, you know, I--I don't know if we should be seen together, like, on a date. I don't think I'm ready for that yet, you know?"

She was saying *you know* a lot. She didn't like it.

He seemed to be absorbing what she was saying. She looked over at him and saw he was nodding with some uncertainty, staring straight ahead at nothing. With a teasing grin he looked over at her and asked, "Are you ashamed of me?"

The ridiculousness of the question made her burst out laughing. "No, of course not!" She hadn't caught on he was joking. "I just don't--I'm not ready to be in the *Out and About* section of the paper yet."

He got up and went to where Ava was still cutting flowers. Putting his arms around her waist and his chin on her shoulder, he murmured into her ear, "I'm sorry you saw that today."

She turned around to face him, scissors still in hand. "You don't owe me an apology. But if you don't mind, I think I'd like to keep things between us under the radar. My poor mother would have a heart attack if she knew we were..." She chose her next words carefully, "spending time together."

He grabbed her shoulders and held her at arms' length. She stumbled a little in her shoes. "Tell you what. We'll keep things just between us, for now. If we're still..." He paused then emphasized the next three words, "*spending time together*, we'll allow ourselves to be seen together at the Wounded Warrior Project ball."

It was a statement, not a question.

The ball was six weeks away. That should be enough time for her to be ready for Brad to see her and Travis at a public appearance together. "I can agree to that." She held out her hand for him to shake it, as if to seal the deal.

He gave her an amused grin as he took her hand and shook it.

She placed the last rose in the crystal container, then pointed to her dress and asked, "Should I change?"

"As drop-dead gorgeous as you are in that outfit, and as much as I would love to see you in absolutely nothing but those shoes later tonight, I can't imagine they're very comfortable. Yes, go put on a pair of jeans."

She was gingerly walking to her bedroom when he yelled after her. "And some comfortable shoes!"

It only took a minute for her to kick off her hooker heels and step out of her dress, leaving it in a heap on her closet floor while trying to find the most flattering pair of jeans she had. *Darn it, they're in the dirty clothes hamper.* She found a pair that ran a close second in the accentuating her features department and slid them on.

She had no idea what they were going to do now that they weren't eating out at a fancy restaurant. Poking her head out of her closet, she called out to him as she zipped up her jeans. "Where are we going?"

She paused, waiting for him to respond. No answer. She yelled his name.

After a few seconds, he appeared at her bedroom door.

"Did you call me, luv?" he asked, then, with a thud, leaned against the door jamb, grinning as he admired the view of her standing there in only a pair of tight jeans and push-up bra.

"I asked where we are going. I need to know what kind of top to wear. Should I dress it up or simply put on a T-shirt?"

He gave her an evil grin. "I think you should go just like that."

"Come on, I'm serious!"

He crossed the room in three strides, grabbed her around the waist, and pulled her into him. "So was I." She had noticeably shrunk since the last time he kissed her, *sans* her high heels. He gently started caressing her lips with his. It didn't take long for their make-out session to heat up again. She knew she should stop it soon before things went too far and he thought she was too easy and decided not to sleep with her again. That would be ironic.

*Oohh but this feels so good! Just a little more...*

When he slid his hand under her bra, she knew she had to hit the brakes and abruptly pulled away from him, gasping for air.

"We need to stop or we'll never get out of here! Aren't you hungry? I'm starving!" She pretended to start looking for a top while he stepped back to the closet doorway. She glanced over at him. He was standing there, hands in his pockets, watching her with that grin on his face again.

"I mean it! What kind of top?" She was unnerved, being in such close quarters with him and embarrassed that he just stood there in silence, blatantly admiring her.

*And damn, he smells so good.*

Getting back into her personal space, he seemed to purposefully reach across her, brushing her chest as he took an emerald green tee off its hanger. Handing it to her, he said softly, "This one. It will match your eyes."

"This one it is. Now, go!" He was now openly leering at her while she made a shooing motion with her hands.

He started to walk toward the kitchen, then stopped and turned around.

"Why don't you pack an overnight bag too." He gave her a wink and headed out the bedroom door.

Again, it wasn't a question, it was a statement.

And that damn wink.

He didn't have to ask--okay, tell--her twice. Ava slipped the green shirt over her head before finding a weekend bag and stuffing items in it.

*I think I like him.*

*Crap.*

*Remember to keep it casual, girl. He is out of your league. Keep your eye on the prize.*

She suddenly had a thought and stopped her packing to walk to the bedroom doorway and call out to him. "Do you want to go change? I mean, well, look at you and look at me now." She gestured to him then back to herself. She realized at that moment she hadn't commented on his attire yet. "You look very handsome, by the way."

"We'll stop by my place after this." He added teasingly, "Thank you. I was beginning to wonder if you'd noticed."

She started back toward the bedroom to finish grabbing her things. "Oh, I noticed."

Overnight bag in hand, they were walking out the front door when she remembered she hadn't packed her toothbrush. She handed him the heavy bag and said, "I'll be right back!"

"Good grief, how long are you planning on staying?" he called after her.

After fifteen seconds, she appeared again at the door, toothbrush in hand. *"This—--"* She gestured up and down her body with her free hand, "—doesn't just happen, ya know," and closed the door behind her.

"I saw you last night without any of *that*—" He made the same gesture up and down her body as she had, "—and I loved it. You are beautiful, with or without the pizazz."

She smiled at him, stood on her tiptoes, and put her hands around his neck. "That's... very kind... of you... to say." She kissed him in between whispering the words.

Putting his forehead against hers, he whispered back, "It's the truth."

She was having fun flirting with him without worrying if she looked stupid. Not that she *wanted* to look stupid; she just wasn't concerned about it and could be herself. If he didn't call after tomorrow, it wouldn't be a big deal. The goal was Operation Sex Kitten—putting theory into practice and gaining new experiences to win her ex-boyfriend back, or at least make him sorry he dumped her.

She locked her door and then nonchalantly declared over her shoulder as she spun around and started prancing toward the parking lot, "I brought the shoes."

# Chapter 7

*Travis*

Travis watched Ava practically skip to the parking lot. He knew he was in trouble. He was smitten and it'd been less than twenty-four hours since he first met her.

Starting after her, he smiled. *This is going to be interesting.*

She immediately walked over to the passenger door of his black BMW M5 and waited for him to catch up.

His first thought was, 'How does she know which car is mine?' but it didn't take but a second to recognize there probably weren't a lot of $95,000 cars in the visitor parking at her condominium complex on a regular basis.

He made a lot of money. A lot. And he worked his ass off for every cent so he didn't feel guilty for buying expensive things but also made sure he gave back. He had a few pet projects he was personally a big supporter of—Wounded Warrior Project probably being the one he gave the most money to by far—but he was still a big donor to two local animal rescues that regularly saved dogs and cats who were scheduled to be euthanized. He was also the anonymous donor that supplied college tuition scholarships for five single mothers going back into the workforce. In addition, he made sure his firm contributed to any local causes whenever they were approached for a donation. Frannie Ericson knew that and always used it to her advantage. Ava's mother was involved with a multitude of causes and charities that she gave as much of her time to as she would a full-time job.

How Travis came to support the Wounded Warrior Project and the tuition scholarships went hand-in-hand. His childhood best friend, Todd Campbell, had been wounded in Afghanistan while serving in the Marines. Travis was appalled at the lack of care his buddy received when he came back home. Unfortunately, Travis was still studying for the bar, so he couldn't offer much in terms of financial support. When he started his law career and was making a little bit of money, he tried to offer as much assistance to his friend as he could afford. Within a few years of returning home from combat, Todd died due to complications from his injuries. It destroyed Travis he couldn't do more for his friend so when three years later, Todd's widower decided to return to school at the local community college, he wanted to help her. He was in a better financial position to do so but knew she would refuse his money, so he created a scholarship where he could remain anonymous as the donor. In order to get the school's help in getting her to apply for the endowment, he created two. When he read the heartfelt letters of thanks from the women he helped and the difference an education made in their lives, he had no problem keeping it going year after year, even expanding it to five scholarships once he made partner. Francine approached him the first year she was chairing the ball benefitting a little known charity at the time called the Wounded Warrior Project. Travis jumped at the chance to honor his friend and became the title sponsor from the very first year even though it was a strain on his budget at the time.

The animal rescues came about because of his secretary, Kelli, who was very involved in helping animals. She was also the reason he ended up with Fred and Ginger, his two miniature poodles. Yes, he had miniature poodles and as much as he pretended they were a pain, he loved how happy they were to see him every night. Fred and Ginger's elderly owner had passed away and when Kelli found out it broke her heart thinking of them going to the shelter where they might possibly be separated. She was visibly distraught about it one afternoon, and he made the mistake of asking what was wrong. When she asked him if he would be interested in taking them, he cited he was never home, which she of all people should know. When Kelli said she would make all the arrangements to hire a twice-daily dog walker who would also groom, feed, and pick up after them, he reluctantly agreed, if for no other reason than to keep the woman who took care of him at work happy. Basically, she promised, he would be providing them a place to live and attention when he was home. Not to mention provide an income for one lucky dog walker, he mused. Within the first week of them arriving, he had a contractor out to fence off part of his yard and put in a doggie door. Soon, Kelli was telling him about different animals' plights, and he promised to write a check every month to her two favorite animal rescues if she swore to never tell him another sad dog story again. She happily took the deal.

He insisted most of his personal contributions be anonymous to the public, the only exception being the WWP. He had the reputation of being a son-of-a-bitch to uphold. Not that it was hard; frankly, he was a son-of-a-bitch when it came to his profession. That's what made him a partner in his firm by age thirty-four, and he didn't apologize for it. People made the assumption that persona carried over into his private life, although, he had to admit, sometimes that assumption was warranted. Maybe not the being an s.o.b. part, but he knew he was arrogant and could be demanding. He was forty years old and wasn't going to change now.

Travis opened Ava's car door and got her situated before going round and sliding into the driver's seat.

"Nice ride." She smiled as he started the engine.

"Thanks, it's one of my favorites."

\*\*\*\*

*Ava*

She understood what he meant by *one of* as they drove up his driveway. He had a three-car garage attached to his house and an entire free-standing six-car garage off to the side.

"Is that full of cars?" she asked with wide eyes.

"Nah." He winked. "I've got a truck and boat in there too."

"Seriously, how many cars do you own?"

"Six, including the truck," he replied matter-of-factly. As if to say, *doesn't everyone own six vehicles?*

He parked in the circular drive in front of the house, rather than in the garage, indicating they weren't staying long. His home and grounds were beautiful, yet understated. An L-shaped single level Craftsman, probably built in the 1960s, that had recently undergone a complete renovation. He unlocked the front door using his thumb print instead of keys and escorted her inside. There were lots of floor-to-ceiling windows with bright, open space--it was quite the contrast to her parents' Tudor with dark wood. The house was tastefully decorated with white walls and furniture and perfectly placed colored accent pieces--professionally done, she was sure. He led her through the formal living room, past the dining area, and into the kitchen. The first thing she noticed when she stepped into his gourmet area was how large and clean it was. It flowed into the great room, and the entire back wall was made of windows that faced the pool. The second thing she noticed was the sound of little dogs barking. Travis opened a door that appeared to lead to a laundry room the size of her condo, and out ran two little white fluffy dogs. They danced and twirled at the sight of their master, and Ava couldn't believe it when the six-feet-two-inch man in front of her started talking sweetly to them. She never would have pegged him for the poodle type; Dobermans or Rottweilers seemed to be more his style. He reached down and picked up one in each hand, then laughed when they kissed him like they hadn't seen him in a month.

"You saw me an hour ago!" he playfully chided them.

He set them back down and after a couple of pirouettes at his feet, they ran to investigate the intruder their owner had brought into the house with him. They approached Ava and immediately reared up on their back legs, prompting her to kneel down to let them smell her. When they decided she was okay, they kissed her like she was a long-lost relative.

"What are their names?" She giggled and hugged them close in order to keep them from kissing her face anymore.

"Fred and Ginger."

She stood up and raised her eyebrows. "As in Fred Astaire and Ginger Rogers?"

"The very same."

She gave him a look that conveyed what she was thinking. *Who is this guy?*

"Don't look at me. Their former owner, an elderly gentleman, named them. I'm told because of their dancing skills."

"That makes sense." She smiled as the pair pranced back to Travis, who had opened a drawer and pulled out little rawhide sticks. Fred and Ginger politely sat until he gave them the treats and then scurried back to the laundry room to devour them.

"Make yourself at home while I go get changed. There's a nice selection of wines in the wine fridge. The opener is in the drawer to the left of it, and wine glasses are in the cupboard above. There's soda, juice, and water in the big refrigerator."

"Thanks," she replied and watched him go back the way they came in. She assumed that eventually led to his bedroom.

She walked over to look at his wine selection but wasn't actually comprehending what the labels said as she was lost in thought about Travis Sterling, trying to reconcile everything she'd heard about him with everything she'd seen personally. She understood how he could have the reputation he had, yet her mother had nothing but adoration for the man. When she first met him last night, he was an ass and still, somehow, she ended up in bed with him for what she thought was her first one-night stand. Then he laid on the charm with his wonderful gestures of a cleaning crew, roses, and dinner at Evangeline's. Now here she stood in his kitchen looking at his wine selection.

*Eye on the prize.*

She jumped when she heard his voice asking, "Did you pick a wine?"

She grabbed the closest white to her and pulled it out of the rack. "How about this one?" she asked, having no idea what she had grabbed, and turned around to face him. He was dressed now in a simple black T-shirt that emphasized his broad chest and muscular arms and was tucked into a pair of faded Levi's with a black leather belt. His black Chuck Taylor's made him look like he was twenty-eight years old. *Doesn't he know he's too old to wear those?* She had to admit, though, he could pull it off.

She walked over to the kitchen island where he was standing with his hands on the counter. He took the bottle from her, examined it, and raised his eyebrows. "You want this?"

Having no idea how to explain why she didn't have a clue about what she had handed him, she went with, "To be honest, I'd rather have a vodka and orange juice, if you have it."

One corner of his mouth lifted, revealing that adorable dimple. "Yeah, I have that." He went around to the other side of the kitchen island where she had come from. He put the wine back and went about getting a rocks glass from a glass-fronted cupboard, then knelt down to a lower cabinet next to the wine refrigerator and pulled out a tray with a large metal container, the kind her milkshakes were brought in when she went to her favorite diner. He opened up a cupboard below the island counter, and she heard shelves sliding before he appeared again with sherbet vodka, one of many he had offered as an option. He went about theatrically adding ice, vodka, and orange juice from the big refrigerator, then took the metal container's twin and twisted the two together so he could shake the ingredients without spilling, smiling at her the entire time like he had a secret. He unscrewed the container and was about to empty the contents when Ava asked, "Do you have a tall glass?" She had seen how much vodka he had added.

Smirking, he added more orange juice and repeated the mixing process before pouring the liquid into a tall glass. He handed her the drink across the black marble counter and waited, watching her as she tasted it. It was delicious.

"Wow, this tastes yummy," she said as she eyed him over the glass and took another sip.

He came around to where she was standing and put his arms around her, placing his hands underneath her butt and pulling her close to him. "Yummy, huh? I don't think anyone's ever described my concoctions that way."

"Maybe you've just been making them for the wrong people," she said with a seductive smile.

He took her glass and set it back on the counter.

"Maybe I have," he murmured as he brought his mouth over hers and slid his hands up her back, grabbing a handful of her hair and tugging a little. She let out a little moan as he fully enveloped her mouth with his. Soon he was tugging her shirt over her head and pulling her bra haphazardly down below her boobs to free them from being constricted in the garment.

He stared appreciatively at her perky round globes while uttering, "You have the most amazing tits," and then cupped one in each hand before leaning over and sucking on her stiff nipples. He swirled his tongue around one then gently sucked on the other before finding her lips again with his. He didn't let go of her breasts and started massaging them harder as he put more pressure on her mouth. Ava had never been touched liked this before. Brad usually just squeezed her tits like they were stress balls before climbing on top of her.

Travis was steering her backwards while still kissing her, and it took her a second to realize that what she was bumping against was the sectional in the adjoining family room. The lovers pulled apart long enough to get their bearings on the sofa. She removed her bra as she watched him pull his T-shirt over his head to reveal that well-sculpted core of his. It was like she was making out with a model from a cologne advertisement in the mall. The realization turned her on and made her feel self-conscious all at the same time. Fortunately, she didn't have time to dwell on the idea she was inadequate as he had pushed her onto the couch and pressed his bare chest against hers while resuming their passionate make-out session. The feel of his skin against hers sent shivers down her spine and the scent of him only added to her arousal. Soon she found herself grinding her hips against his, and they started moving in a rhythm that, had they not had jeans on, would have led to at least one of them having an orgasm. Who was she kidding? At this pace, she could have an orgasm with or without the jeans on.

Mouth still on hers, he reached down and started unbuckling his belt, followed by unbuttoning his jeans and she followed suit, lifting her butt up and shimmying out of her tight denim. She had left her underwear on, which he immediately dispatched the minute he felt them against his erection.

Then, all of a sudden, he stopped. "Damn," he muttered as he pulled himself off of her. "I'll be right back."

She sat up and watched his bare ass retreat, not running, but walking very fast toward the kitchen exit. He was back in record time with a little purple square package he flung on the mahogany coffee table before sitting next to her naked body and putting his arm around her shoulder.

"Where were we?" he inquired and began nuzzling her neck. She was happy to notice he hadn't lost his erection during the interruption.

"I think right about there," she answered.

Sliding his hand between her legs, he started to rub her wet pussy. Watching her face as he began to explore her folds, he asked, "Are you sure we weren't here?"

She drew a sharp breath in, closed her eyes, and starting moving against his hand. "Mmm, I think you might be right."

He plunged two fingers deep inside her, and she gasped again. "No, you're right, that's definitely where we were."

She surprised herself at how eagerly and shamelessly she spread her legs for him, and he began to finger her while continuing to explore her mouth with his, his index and middle fingers going deep inside then slowly sliding out before deliberately reentering her deeply again. She was making quiet moaning noises with her eyes closed. He continued to thrust his digits in and out of her before sliding his hand up to her clit. When she instinctively closed her legs a little, he authoritatively pulled them back open.

"Oh my God," she moaned. He had pulled the skin right above her hood back with his left hand while his right hand expertly rubbed her erect nub. She was starting to gasp and moan when he urgently pulled her onto his lap so he could move his hands about more freely. She was facing away from him, her thighs dangling over his so he could easily open her legs simply by spreading his. With his left hand he started fucking her again with two fingers, and with his right started rubbing her clit fast and hard. She pulled the skin above her hood back for him—she'd liked how that felt—and was gasping for air and making little whimpering noises of 'yeah', which made him finger bang her faster.

He slowed his hands down and started dipping his fingers into her slowly and deeply again while rubbing her sensitive button in small circles. When he pulled his fingers out of her, he whispered roughly in her ear, "Your pussy is so wet. You must love it when I fuck your tight little hole with my fingers."

She moaned. "Oh yes, I love it!"

*Holy fuck! Brad never talked to me like that! Kersplash!*

He plunged them back inside her. "You love it because you're a naughty, dirty girl."

She whimpered again, feeling herself get instantly wetter as he continued.

"Look at you with your legs spread wide open, letting me do whatever I want to you."

She was genuinely soaked. He gradually started to pick up the pace with his hands again.

"My fingers are so deep inside you. Listen to how wet and sloppy you are."

He started rubbing and banging her faster and harder, her juices making a sloshing sound against his hands.

She started to moan louder and tried to close her legs as she was getting close to losing control, but he widened his legs underneath hers, causing her to spread hers back open, and hugged her around her middle with his arms as he continued.

"Are you a dirty girl?"

"Yes!" She was close. She was whimpering and moaning and he was buffing her clit fast.

"Say it! Say 'I'm a naughty, dirty girl'!"

She was gasping when she whispered, "I'm a naughty, dirty girl." His slid a third finger inside her.

His voice got rougher and he said, "What are you? Tell me!"

Louder this time, she did as he commanded and breathlessly cried, "I'm a dirty, bad girl." She was grinding hard against his hand.

He asked, louder and more urgently, "Are you my nasty girl?"

She whimpered and nodded and he ordered her, "Tell me whose little dirty girl you are."

This time she let out a loud "I'mmmm yoooooouuur dirrrrrrrtyyyyy girlllll" as she started to come hard on his hands while her body writhed uncontrollably.

She tried to close her legs again, but he held them open and continued penetrating her until she finished her orgasm, then she forcefully closed them at the knees and pushed his hands away.

Rolling off his lap and breathing hard, she gasped, "What the hell was that?"

"Too much?" he asked sheepishly.

She took a few gulps of air. "At the risk of sounding like a whore, oh my God, no! That was awesome!"

\*\*\*\*

*Travis*

He grinned smugly. *The doctor has a naughty side.*

"I know I should let you recover but all that talk got me really worked up, so..." He pushed her down onto the couch, opened the little purple packet, and slipped the condom on his cock before shoving it inside her. He effortlessly slid right in. He knew the sensation of him in her pussy was heightened from her orgasm when she eagerly moved her hips to meet him with each push. They were perfectly in sync with each other, meeting in the middle with every thrust. It was like they fit together.

"Oh my God, your wet pussy feels amazing!" he uttered as he rammed himself deep inside her again.

"I love it when you fuck me with your hard cock."

*Holy titties, Batman, did she just say what I think she said?*

"Fuck me deeper."

*Yep, she did and she's going to make me come. Dammit.*

He was going to pull out for a break to regain his composure and keep himself from climaxing but found he couldn't stop fucking her. It was too delicious--warm, wet, and mesmerizing. He decided to just go with it, not caring that it'd only been five minutes, and started thrusting inside her fast and hard until he rammed into her as deep as he could and held her hips still for a few seconds, his cock spasming while he filled his condom.

He kissed her deeply before pulling out and escaping to a bathroom to dispose of his latex protection.

He came back rubbing his junk with a hand towel and tossed her a clean one as well.

"Woman, I don't know what you just did to me but whatever it was, you need to do it again."

"Right now?" she asked with raised, worried eyebrows.

Laughing, he answered, "I'm probably not ready to right now. I'm not eighteen anymore, but I would definitely not say no to later tonight." He leaned over and kissed her gently while sliding his hands back between her slit. "And tomorrow morning. And tomorrow afternoon. And tomorrow night."

Making a face, she concluded, "I think I might get sore with all that."

He laughed again. "Okay, tonight, tomorrow morning, and tomorrow night."

She grinned at him seductively. "Okay, I think I can manage that. I'll probably have to give you a hand job for one of those though."

*She's getting this flirting thing down.*

There was no longer any doubt in his mind; he was in trouble.

# Chapter 8

*Ava*

Ava asked if they could stop and check on Grace before going to dinner.

Travis said he thought that was a good idea and mused as they pulled into the driveway, "Patrick better not be here again."

"How was Patrick this morning?" She laughed.

"Very sorry he called me." He chuckled. "I was going to send them over here to help clean up, but then I thought that'd probably only add to your burden rather than actually be of any assistance, so I sent the cleaning crew instead and gave the boys some chores around my place to do. Which I let them get started on as soon as I got home this morning."

"I was nicer. I didn't get everyone up until eight." She smiled at him. "Thanks again for sending that team to help. They saved Grace's ass."

Grabbing her butt as they walked to the front door of her parents' home, he murmured in her ear, "It wasn't Grace's ass that I was thinking about."

He seemed amazed at how good the Ericson home looked compared to the night before. They found Jill, Grace, and a few other friends who had slept over the previous night sitting on the couch in the family room watching a movie.

"I'm just making sure I won't be getting a call tonight from Mrs. Marsten!" Ava announced as she walked through the doorway. Grace wasn't looking at her; she was much more interested in who had followed her sister into the room.

"This is Travis Sterling. He had the pleasure of picking up his nephew Patrick and his friend from your soirée last night. You all should be thanking him--he's the one who sent the cleaning crew to help you today."

"Hey, thanks a lot," they all murmured in some form or another then Grace bluntly asked, in a way only an eighteen-year-old girl who was the youngest child of the family can, "That was really cool of you to do, but why did you do that?"

Travis didn't flinch, although Ava squirmed a little. "I saw what this place looked like when I picked up my nephew last night. Your mother is someone I adore, the very idea of how upset she would be to come back from vacation to her beautiful home in that condition --and my nephew played a part in that--bothered me. Francine has helped me with so many projects, I would be lost without her expertise. So let's just say, I wanted to stay on her good side."

Grace nodded as though she could understand that reasoning. She then squinted her eyes and asked, "But why are you here with my sister now?"

Ava wondered how he was going to handle this one. She had no idea how to answer and firmly kept her mouth shut.

"I met your sister last night, thought she was hot, and asked her on a date. She said yes. I'm hoping to take her back to my place after dinner."

Grace's eyes flew to Ava's face looking for verification that what this gorgeous man had told her was true.

Ava started laughing. "He's teasing you, Gracie. We're having dinner to talk about a project we might be working on together." She was going to kill him. She continued dismissively, "It's not a date. He's got a girlfriend."

She hoped that was enough to satisfy the young girl's curiosity. Her younger sister seemed genuinely disappointed her older sister wasn't really on a date with this hottie and shook her head. "Oh. That's too bad. You'd make a cute couple."

An explosion scene in the movie drew the group's attention back to the screen, and Ava saw it as her chance to escape. "We're going to go now! Behave yourselves, I mean it!"

A few of them gave her a half-hearted, "Bye! We will!" without looking away from the TV, and Grace called out, "Thank you again, Travis!" as they headed towards the front door.

Ava slugged him once they got outside while he laughed and seemed quite pleased with himself. She tried to be mad at him but couldn't help but see the humor in the situation, yet still said indignantly, "It's not funny!" while starting to giggle. "Payback's a bitch!" she warned. For some odd reason, she got the distinct feeling he wasn't worried.

**

They ended up eating at Figurino's, a small, family-owned Italian restaurant that both Ava and Travis were connected to. She used to babysit the Italian immigrant owners' twins, Marco and Maria, and he had represented them (and won) in a case against their realtor who had been negligent in his representation of them during their purchase of the restaurant location.

Ava walked through the door first and Mrs. Figurino rushed to grab her hands the second she recognized her.

"Bella! It's so wonderful to see you!" she exclaimed while still holding her hands. "Tony! Come quick and see who it is!"

She was so busy gushing over Ava she hadn't taken the time to look at Travis, but when she finally gestured to him with, "And who is this?" she realized who he was and put her head in her hands.

"Mr. Sterling!" She chattered in Italian as she grabbed his face in both her hands and kissed him on each cheek. Motioning for them to follow, she said, "Come, come! I give you our best table!" She then called over her shoulder again. "Antonio!"

It was a small restaurant but very popular with the locals, and it was Saturday night. The place was packed, and there was an obvious waiting list to be seated.

Mrs. Figurino quickly arrived back at their table with a decanter of Chianti. "On the house!" she proclaimed and shouted again, "Tony!"

Ava and Travis smiled at each other over the fuss she was making. Travis grabbed the older lady's hand to slow her down. "Have Tony come out when the kitchen has calmed down. We're going to be here a while, there's no rush."

She grabbed his cheek and started sputtering in Italian. Ava guessed it had to do with how good looking he was.

Ava politely asked her, "How are Maria and Marco?"

Mrs. Figurino crossed herself then looked up and kissed the side of the knuckle on her index finger. "Maria starts Stanford in two months, and she is driving me crazy! Marco is getting shipped out for boot camp next month! My boy! A marine!" She was very proud.

Travis smiled. "I graduated from Stanford Law School. Maria is going to love going to school there. And a Marine! That has to make you proud."

The older woman's eyes grew wide, "Ohhhh, you were a Cardinal too? That's wonderful! Yes, we are proud. Worried but proud." She stood there looking at them, her eyes shining, then made a gesture insinuating she approved of the pairing of the two.

Ava got the feeling Mrs. Figurino would have stayed at their table all night, had the restaurant been slower, but she soon realized she was being derelict in her duties and excused herself. Every time she walked by their table, however, her eyes twinkled, and she would say phrases with 'amour' in them and sigh, clasping her hands to her chest.

"I think she might be worse than the paparazzi at Evangeline's," Travis leaned over and whispered in her ear. She thought she heard him utter something about apple blossoms when he pulled away.

Ava giggled and said quietly, "I think so!"

"We had better drink this wine or she will be back trying to give us something else," he said as he lifted the bottle and poured two glasses. Ava disliked red wine but politely sipped it in between bites of bread sticks that masked the taste.

Travis caught on to what she was doing and laughed. "Way to take one for the team."

They ended up having a terrific night, laughing and talking about their lives. Ava never believed she'd ever meet a man she thought was as smart as her father. Travis came pretty close. She loved how warm he was with the Figurinos, and how he reciprocated the wife's loving gestures toward him. And every time he looked at her and smiled, showing that dimple, her stomach did flip-flops. Oh how she hoped he was serious about having sex again tonight! She was excited about all the things she knew he could teach her, things she didn't even know she wanted to try--like the naughty talk he said to her on his couch. She knew she should be embarrassed by how she'd responded, but strangely, she wasn't. Just like she wasn't about their sleeping together last night. She didn't know if it was how he made her feel, or if she had simply gotten more comfortable with her sexuality. Perhaps it was both.

Maybe if she'd been more confident sexually then Brad would have never left her. If she had conveyed she was willing to try new things, he might have been more willing to initiate new adventures and spice up their vanilla sex life. She had a running list in her head of things she wanted to try, things she wanted to learn before getting Brad back into her bed, and knew the wonderful smelling man next to her could be an amazing teacher.

She grabbed the bill when it came. Travis in no uncertain terms made it crystal clear he was paying for dinner and would always pay for dinner, and to even suggest otherwise was an insult. She noticed he tipped their waiter almost one hundred percent. When he saw her curious look at how much cash he left on the table, he shrugged and said, "They didn't charge me for the wine."

She smiled. Keeping her eye on the prize might prove more difficult than she originally thought.

When they strolled arm-in-arm down the walkway that led to the parking lot, he pulled her over to a fountain that was apparently doubling as a wishing well. He reached in his pocket, pulled out a quarter, and handed it to her.

"Make a wish," he urged.

Ava took the coin, closed her eyes, kissed it, held her breath, and then threw it into the water.

He smiled and leaned down to kiss her, his hands still in his pockets. "Just in case that was what you wished for."

No, what she wished for was to get out of this with her heart still in one piece.

"Now you!" she eagerly suggested.

Travis fished around his pocket and found another coin. He didn't close his eyes or do any of the theatrics Ava believed were instrumental in making your wish come true. He simply thought for a moment and tossed in the quarter with purpose. She leaned over and offered up her lips to his.

After their gentle kiss, she smiled and murmured, "Just in case that was what you wished for."

"How did you know?" he teased, his lips brushing against hers.

\*\*\*\*

*Travis*

If Travis thought for a second he was going to be sick of her by tomorrow, he knew that theory had long been disproved. In addition to being hot as hell, she was genuine, insightful and witty. Her laugh was contagious and dammit, she continued to be kind.

He kept secretly hoping at some point in the evening she'd become annoyed with Mrs. Figurino and start pouting and force him to leave. Instead she encouraged the woman, laughing and joining her in teasing him.

Maybe she would find something to complain about, and he could become irritated with her whining and want to take her home. Perhaps she wouldn't eat the food or just stick with a salad. No, she seemed to love everything about the place, including the food, and even drank the wine she clearly didn't like without ever saying a word.

Or possibly they'd run out of things to talk about, and the night would drag on. No such luck. The conversation flowed nonstop and the time flew by; he had actually been surprised to learn it was as late as it was. They had closed the place.

He couldn't think of one thing he hadn't enjoyed about their evening. And those wine stained lips--he kept picturing them wrapped around his cock later. Her performance on his couch made him wonder if she was more experienced than he had thought she was last night.

He had patiently waited until they were outside to kiss her, although he'd been wanting to all night every time she smiled. Which was a lot. He had better find a flaw of hers and fast.

This was scary new territory for him. The women he dated were beautiful but superficial. The kind that exhausted him by the end of the night. The type he didn't wake up next to or bring to his home. He realized he'd never brought a woman to his current house who wasn't a relative or employee of his. Here he was, date number two and not only had he brought her to his house, he'd fucked her within thirty minutes of being there, and he was looking forward to waking up to her in his bed tomorrow morning.

*Somebody hit the brakes!*

Except he didn't and he might have shoved anyone who tried out of the way.

****

*Ava*

They walked into his kitchen and said hello to Fred and Ginger. Her glass of vodka and orange juice still sat on the counter, half full. He dumped it out and asked if she wanted another. She shook her head, and he grabbed a beer from the fridge. Finding a bottle opener, he gestured to the beautifully lit pool area. "Wanna sit in the hot tub?"

"I didn't bring my suit."

Shooting her a look that said *whatever*, he growled, "Do you think I'd let you wear it even if you had?"

She laughed and conceded, "Probably not."

He took her hand and escorted her to his back patio. The little dogs ran through their doggy door and followed the two to the raised gazebo with a modern twist where his hot tub was. A bar and fire pit sat close by.

She looked around and smiled up at him. "Wow, this is really beautiful."

"Thanks. The pool was built twenty years ago and hadn't included a spa, so I added this area when I had the house remodeled."

Benches lined the enclosure that provided privacy from the rest of the yard. Travis set his beer in a cup holder on one of the tub's corners and began flipping switches and pushing buttons. Soon, the jets were roaring to life while colored lights under the water came on, and music started playing as the gazebo lit up.

Travis began to strip, and Ava stood enjoying the view. He had gotten down to his boxers and she'd only managed to kick her shoes off. The wine had taken its toll, regardless if she didn't like it, and she was having a hard time concentrating on anything but her gorgeous date's half-naked body in front of her. She was in awe of how attractive she found him. All of a sudden a little voice popped into her head that screamed, "Why the hell is he not out with Victoria Thornapple instead of you tonight?"

"I'm going to grab a water," she said as she turned to run back to the house.

Getting a bottle of water from the fridge, she started letting the doubts creep in. She'd been doing such a good job keeping them at bay and then realized that she liked him. Really liked him. *Poof.* Hello, insecurities.

Twisting the cap off, she then took a swig and found some gumption. *Who knows why he's out with me tonight instead of some heiress or model, but he is, so stop second-guessing, and accept it for what it is! We've been having a great time. Why wouldn't he want to be out with me? I'm cute, smart, funny, and apparently good enough to fuck twice so stop with the doubting, get out there, and take advantage of the fact I am the one with him tonight. This is my golden opportunity to learn things--don't blow it! I might not have another chance, so I need to get my ass in that hot tub and not squander another second worrying he'd rather be with someone else!*

Her pep talk was interrupted with Travis standing in the doorway in his boxers as the poodles ran past him and stood at her feet, staring at her. "Is everything all right?" He seemed genuinely concerned.

She hoped she'd actually only been saying the words in her head and not out loud for him to overhear and think she was a lunatic who talked to herself.

"The wine hit me all of a sudden and I needed some water. I'm okay now." She smiled and took another drink from the bottle before scratching Ginger behind her ears and rubbing Fred's face. Satisfied with her affection, they laid down on the floor as she walked past Travis and made her way back to the bubbling hot water. He followed her and got in the water while her back was turned. His boxers were on the bench, and he was leaning on the side, his chest against the wall and his arms draped over the edge. His chin resting on his hands, he made a point of letting her know the act of her undressing was going to be a show for him.

*To hell with it, I'm going to have fun and not worry about it. If he wants a show, I'll give him a show.*

She turned away from him as she unbuttoned her jeans, then slid them down, bending all the way over while she did, blatantly drawing attention to her best asset. Then she ran her hands up her thighs as she stood back up, flipping her hair over her head like she imagined a stripper would do. She turned around to face him and slid one arm out of the green T-shirt he had picked out for her earlier. Sliding out of one side of her bra, then putting her arm back in the shirt, she repeated the process with her other arm. She made a production over the fact she was no longer wearing her bra when she held it in her outstretched hand and deliberately dropped it.

He was shifting around in his seat, watching as if he were mesmerized by the show. The show that was even surprising her.

She ran her hands over her body and squeezed her tits together over her shirt and stared at him. Theatrically, she squeezed and twisted her nipples while widening her stance before lifting her shirt a little. Instead of pulling it off, she put it back down then changed her mind and quickly lifted it back up to flash him her bare tits, shifting her hips back and forth before pulling it all the way over her head. Sucking on the tip of her index finger, she then traced it down her middle until she reached her underwear. She stretched the fabric away from her and looked down at herself, then back at him with a surprised look on her face. Putting her hand to her mouth as it snapped back into place, she bent at the knees and stuck her ass out, Betty Boop style. Turning back around, she pulled her panties to right under her ass where she used them to make her round booty jiggle up and down. She looked over her shoulder at him, smiled, then bent all the way down as she slid her panties to the ground. This time when she came back up, she brought her hand through her legs and slid her middle finger up and down her ass crack before slowly sliding it through her legs. Continuing to run her hands up the sides of her body, Ava shimmied until they came to rest on her tits. When she turned around, her hands were full of boobs, and she maintained eye contact with him while dramatically taking a wide step, intimating her pussy was spread and ready.

Travis stood up, exposing a raging hard-on, and sat on the side of hot tub, growling, "Get that gorgeous ass over here now and give me a lap dance."

A lap dance!? She had no idea where this spontaneous striptease came from, or if she'd even been any good at it. She didn't have a clue about how to give a lap dance!

*Screw it, I've come this far.* She tried to think of any movies she'd watched that had a scene in a strip club. *I can do this.* She felt incredibly sexy and desirable simply by him having an erection while watching her and wanting her to continue her performance.

She boldly walked up the steps and deliberately swung one leg over the side and paused to give a little peek of her pink pussy before swinging the other leg over. Walking along the water on the tub's bench to where he was seated, she stepped down and dunked in the water, then slithered her wet body up his before straddling one of his legs.

*Okay, now what?*

Shoving her boobs in his face and squishing them together with his nose in her cleavage, she massaged his face with her tits. When he went to suck on her nipple, she pulled away and wagged her finger at him. Sliding back down his body, she briefly titty-fucked his cock before turning around and rubbing her ass up and down his engorged member. He reached around and placed both hands on her breasts, squeezing them and jiggling them in his hand.

Putting her legs together, she slowly sat down on his throbbing erection. She was so wet that he slid right in her pussy, and she proceeded to move up and down on his cock by sitting then standing back up. This helped her grab his dick with her pelvic muscles as she rose off him. As she took control, he draped his arms over the side of the tub, closed his eyes, and threw his head back. She was feeling smug that she had him so excited when the realization he didn't have a condom on hit her. Although she was on the pill, she knew he was quite the ladies' man, so she stood all the way up and off him.

She didn't know what to do. She had gotten him worked up, but they were a long way away from a little purple square package, and Ava didn't want to be a tease. Turning back around, she started to titty-fuck him again. As she massaged her boobs up and down his shaft, he seemed to understand her dilemma and started to slowly move his hips with her. She shoved her tits together and held still while he fucked them, then dropped her boobs and started sucking his dick, moving her hand up and down to lubricate him before wrapping her tits back around him so he could resume fucking them.

She felt something cold hit her boobs and saw he was squeezing oil onto his erection and into her cleavage. Where he got the oil, she had no idea, but as he glided with ease between her mashed-together breasts, she didn't care.

She could tell he was getting close and felt unsure what to do. Their playtime earlier had been a little naughty, but she knew he was too much of a gentleman to blast her in the face with his load without her permission. Letting him off the hook, she whispered, "I want you to come on my tits. Come all over them!" He happily obliged her by glazing them with more cum than she thought he was going to have, considering he'd already orgasmed twice in the last twenty-four hours. She was a champ and smeared it all over her oily breasts like a porn star.

"You are so fucking amazing," he said in appreciation. She felt amazing. Being the object of his lustful desire not only emboldened her, it turned her on.

He reached between her legs and felt how wet she was, then gestured to her cum covered boobs. "Do you want to clean off first?"

"No, I kinda like it." *Good grief, what must he think of me?*

He gave her a sexy smile. "It's a good look for you."

He started stroking her up and down the entire length of her labia. "You are the sexiest woman I've ever laid eyes on."

She knew tomorrow she wouldn't believe he had been telling her the truth, but tonight she was going to accept it.

"You make my cock so fucking hard."

That she knew was the truth.

He found her clit and started working his magic. "Did it turn you on, dancing for me? Knowing your body was driving me crazy?"

She moaned in appreciation and encouragement for what he was doing to her. He dropped to his knees and started fucking her pussy with his mouth while his hand continued pleasuring her magic knot.

"You taste incredible," he said before shoving his tongue back in her.

She gasped at how wonderful that felt. She had been turned on to start with and it only took minutes of him plunging his tongue in and out of her while attentively manhandling her clit before she got that wonderful sensation she was about to climax.

Her noises and breathing must have let him know because he started to plummet his tongue deeper in her with a fury. Soon she came all over his face, and he lapped it up like it was champagne dripping from her pussy.

She grabbed a towel that was hanging nearby and wiped her chest, then between her legs before sitting down into the bubbling water. He sat beside her holding her hand while the water swirled around them. Ava put her head against his shoulder, closed her eyes, and sighed. "This has been the best date I've ever had." She leaned over and kissed him on the cheek while whispering, "Thank you." He held the back of her head and kissed her gently on the mouth before putting his forehead to hers. "Mine too."

For the second night in a row, she fell asleep in his arms feeling satisfied and content. She could get used to this.

# Chapter 9

*Ava*

It took Ava a second to realize where she was when she woke up in the morning. She looked over at Travis sleeping next to her, his arm around her naked waist. For a few minutes, she studied his features and thought about how good looking he was. He had a tiny scar between his nose and mouth, another going vertically through his eyebrow into his forehead, and fine lines around his eyes. His imperfections somehow seemed to make him more perfect to her.

She eased out from under his arm and made her way to the bathroom, where she ran her fingers through her hair and took a tissue to her smudged eye makeup before brushing her teeth. She thought about slipping back into bed and staring at him some more but decided to see about making breakfast for them instead.

Finding their clothes from last night in a giant heap on the floor, Ava grabbed his black T-shirt and placed it over her head. She couldn't seem to locate her panties amongst their garments, so she pulled his underwear from the pile, slid them over her hips, and made her way to the kitchen.

Fred and Ginger heard her rustling around as she filled the coffee pot and came from the laundry room to investigate. Kneeling down to wish them a good morning with a good behind-the-ears scratch for each, she then returned to the task of making breakfast. She opened the fridge, trying to figure out what to make. He had eggs, that was a start. Fishing around, she also found cheese, peppers, and mushrooms.

*What goes with omelets? Toast?*

Opening the pantry, she couldn't find any bread. Maybe there was a breadbox? She surveyed the kitchen and found what she was looking for. Now all the ingredients were out, she just needed to find a frying pan and where the toaster was located, and she'd be in business.

After finding the frying pan, she realized she'd forgotten to get the butter out. Fred and Ginger whined as if to tell her they were concerned about her cooking abilities.

"Hey!" she told them as she opened the refrigerator, "I'm not that bad!" She found the butter and closed the fridge. In the kitchen hallway leading to the laundry room stood a woman, and Ava let out a scream.

She noticed the woman had dog leashes in her hand.

"I am so sorry to startle you!" the woman cried. "It's okay. I'm Kay, I take care of Fred and Ginger for Mr. Sterling. I came to walk and feed them." The poodles dancing at the woman's feet was a good indicator she was telling the truth.

Just then Travis came rushing into the kitchen, tying the belt of his blue terrycloth robe around his waist as he did.

"Are you okay?" he asked Ava, his voice filled with concern. He hadn't noticed his dog walker yet.

Kay spoke up. "I'm afraid I scared her. I had no idea you had company or were even home. I am so sorry."

Travis let out a deep breath after realizing there was no cause for alarm.

"Shit, Kay. I forgot to text you last night. I apologize." He looked over at Ava, who had regained her composure. "Ava, this is my dog walker extraordinaire, Kay. Kay, this is Ava."

Ava noticed he didn't have a title for her. How could he? What would he possibly call her? *One-night stand that has led to an entire weekend? Friend? Lover? Girlfr—*

*Don't go there, Ava.*

"Nice to meet you, Kay. Sorry I screamed."

"I would have done the same thing," the other woman replied.

Ava assessed Kay's age as probably five or six years older than hers. She dressed the part of a dog walker--sweats, sweatshirt, and tennis shoes. With shoulder-length mousy brown hair that had a few stands of gray intermingled throughout and a little bit of makeup, she was attractive in a dowdy sort of way.

Fred and Ginger were impatiently rearing up on their hind legs at Kay. "I better get these two on their walk before they have a heart attack."

She clipped their leashes on and was out the door.

Travis surveyed the ingredients on the counter with raised eyebrows. "What have we got here?"

"Well, it's the makings of omelets and toast," Ava replied.

Travis pulled out a cutting board and started to expertly dice up the vegetables, then went to the fridge and pulled out some other ingredients to add to the eggs. In no time he had everything in the pan over the stove.

"You can make the toast." He winked at her.

They sat down under an umbrella at the patio table and started eating.

"This is really good," Ava complimented him. "Don't take this the wrong way, but I'm impressed."

"Impressed? That I can cook? I'm a forty-year-old bachelor with a gourmet kitchen; of course I can cook." He laughed.

*Of course he can cook. He's freaking Mr. Perfect.*

Kay came out to the patio, and Travis offered her some breakfast which she happily accepted. When he went inside to prepare her a plate, she apologized again to Ava.

"I had no idea there would be anyone here. There wasn't a strange car in the drive, and I've never seen anyone in the kitchen on my morning visits before." She stopped talking when Travis stepped out the door carrying a plate of food and a glass of juice.

"What are you ladies talking about?" he asked as he placed the dishes in front of his dog walker.

"I was telling Ava again how sorry I am. That you never have company so—" At that moment, she realized she had said too much. Travis looked at Ava and smiled.

As they were eating and chatting, they started to watch the dogs chase each other around the yard. They were entertaining. Fred had something in his mouth that Ginger was trying to get, and he was trotting around the area after escaping her attempts to steal it, teasing her.

"What does he have?" Travis asked.

"I'm not sure." Kay whistled and the dog immediately came to her. "What do you have, boy?" She tried to get whatever it was from him, but he resisted her attempts at getting him to drop his new found prize. Finally, Kay pulled it from his mouth and held it up. It was Ava's underpants.

Ava snatched them from her with a mortified, "Oh my God!" She felt her face turning beet red.

Travis started laughing. "Well, that explains why you are wearing mine."

Ava was so embarrassed she wouldn't look up at either of them. Travis leaned over and kissed her cheek and put his hand on top of her hand that was gripping her wadded-up panties. "Babe, if it makes you feel any better, they steal mine all the time too."

That knowledge didn't make her feel better, but his calling her 'babe' did.

Kay watched the tender moment between Travis and Ava before standing up. Balancing her empty plate and glass with one hand, she pushed in her chair with the other and said, "Thanks for breakfast. I'm going to feed the furballs then head out. Do you need me to come back tonight?"

"No, I think we'll be around. We've got it covered, thanks," Travis told her.

*We.* That made Ava's heart skip a beat.

*Keep it casual. Eye on the prize.*

"Okay, I'll be back tomorrow then. Nice meeting you, Ava. Hope to see you again soon without scaring the daylights out of you."

"Nice meeting you too," Ava replied and grinned. "I look forward to it."

Travis and Ava leisurely stayed at the patio table, drinking coffee, laughing, and talking. Every now and then, he would lean over and kiss her briefly or grab her hand. She wondered if he was this attentive to all his dates. He had to be. *One doesn't date the caliber of women he does by being a heel.*

She went inside to refill their coffee mugs, and when she came back, said, "Do you realize it's almost eleven o'clock?"

Travis laughed. "Is it really? Doesn't feel like it. Did you need to be anywhere this morning?"

She shook her head. "No, do you?"

"Just back in bed with you naked in my arms," he teased.

"I think that could be arranged," she said matter-of-factly as she kissed him softly on the mouth.

They did end up back in bed, naked, but they didn't make love. Instead, he held her as they continued their conversation from breakfast.

"Would you rather go on vacation to Las Vegas or New York City?" he asked, rather out of the blue.

She thought about it for a brief second and said, "Vegas. I love to gamble." Then added, "Unless it was at Thanksgiving. I've always wanted to go to the Macy's Day Parade and stay to watch the tree lighting ceremony at Rockefeller Plaza."

"Yeah, that's always sounded like fun," he replied.

"My turn. Summer or winter?"

With no hesitation, he replied, "Summer. Christmas or Halloween?"

She answered, "Oh, Christmas definitely. Football or baseball?"

"Hockey," he countered. "Sight-seeing or sitting by the pool?"

"Hmm. That depends on where I was and how much I had to drink the night before."

That drew a laugh from him, and she continued the game. "Kids or no kids?"

"If it's my sister or brother—kids. If it's strangers—no kids."

That wasn't what she meant, and he knew it. "I'm talking about you, funny guy."

"Oh me?" He feigned misunderstanding. "If it's me, definitely no kids."

Ava didn't know why she was so disappointed with that answer.

He continued the questioning. "Top or bottom?"

"Both." She smiled devilishly. "Hugging or kissing?"

"Well that depends on who I'm hugging and who I'm kissing," he said as he rolled over on top of her. "If it's my secretary, hugging." He gave her a long, sensual kiss. "If it's you, absolutely kissing." He continued kissing her, and their game quickly came to an end so they could start a different kind.

Their intimacy this time was very tender and traditional. He took the lead, staying in the missionary position as he made love to her, looking into her eyes while expertly moving his cock in and out of her pussy. She ran her hands over his shoulders as he brought his lips down to hers, and Ava arched her back in reaction when his mouth moved further down and found her nipples. He brought his hand to her clit as he continued thrusting his hips against hers, bringing her to climax right before he came.

He stayed inside her briefly, kissing her passionately before rolling off to dispatch his condom.

"Just so you know, I'm on the pill," she offered when he walked back in the room. They had shared a great deal of intimacy in the last thirty-six hours. She wanted to show she trusted him and hoped he would trust her.

"Well, that's good for preventing pregnancy," he said as he laid back down beside her. "But there are other things condoms are for."

"I was tested after Brad dumped me," she said. "I had been on the pill so we didn't use anything else. He kinda dumped me out of the blue so I needed to be sure he hadn't given me something. Fortunately for him—and me—everything came back negative."

He bent his arm at the elbow and rested his head in his hand when he asked, "How would you know it was from Brad? Were you tested before you were with him?"

Ava didn't understand what he meant at first. Of course it would be because of Brad, who else would it be? *Ohhh, I get it.*

She sat up straighter, pulling the sheet around her chest. "I was a virgin before Brad. You are the only other man I've been with, besides him."

There was no mistaking the *what the fuck?* look on his face. Did he really not have any idea how inexperienced she was?

Since she was being honest, she might as well continue, so she added shyly, "And you're the only man I've ever had oral sex with."

She gave him a second for that to sink in. The realization that he was also the only man she'd stripped in front of or talked dirty with seemed to slowly dawn on him as he absent-mindedly nodded his head.

"So you had never put a man's dick in your mouth before Friday?" She shook her head. "Or had a man lick your pussy?" She vehemently shook her head, and then looked at him with a grin and said, "I had no idea what I was missing."

"But you definitely know what you're doing." It was more like a question rather than a statement.

"I've been reading a lot of books and watching a lot of movies this past year. I've also... how do I say this? Taught myself what I like." She took a deep breath. "I thought I knew there was more to sex than what Brad showed me, but really had no idea." She paused. "I had no idea how awesome it could be until you showed me. I've experienced things with you I didn't even know I would like!"

"Like lap dances?"

She nodded.

"And dirty talk?"

Her eyes widened, and she said, "I had no idea I would enjoy that so much!"

She pondered what she had revealed to him. "Is that... normal or am I a total deviant?"

He threw his head back and laughed. "Yes, it's normal. And you are beautiful and sexy and adventurous, and I've loved every second of making love to you."

She felt relieved as she nestled close to him. "Good, because I've loved every second of what you've taught me."

**

They fell asleep together, but when Ava woke up, she was alone in the big bed. She looked at the clock on his nightstand. 4:18 p.m. What a glorious, lazy Sunday! She hadn't even showered or dressed yet!

She remedied that by slipping into his shower, then getting herself dressed and ready, complete with perfume, makeup, and styling her hair before going to search for him. Finally locating him in his study working, she quietly said, "Hey," when she walked in.

He looked up from his desk and smiled. Clad in another Stanford tee with black basketball shorts and wearing glasses, he looked so smart and sexy. She walked over to his desk chair and kissed him on top of his head while hugging his shoulders from behind. He pulled on her wrists, drawing her around the chair and onto his lap.

"Hey, sleeping beauty. How was your nap?"

"Wonderful. Sinfully, deliciously wonderful," she purred. "Were you able to sleep at all?"

"I was able to rest for about a half an hour." He caressed her inner thigh. "I have a little bit more to do, then I'm yours for the night. Do you want to go out for dinner or should we order takeout?"

The idea of having him all to herself was too wonderful to pass up. "Let's get takeout."

"Sounds good. Give me a little while longer to finish this up, then we can take the dogs for a walk and go grab something. Or we can have it delivered." He held the back of her head and briefly kissed her on the mouth before reluctantly lifting her off of him. "I promise I'll hurry."

Ava went back to his room and found her phone to catch up on social media and the news before checking her email. She also had five texts from Anne demanding to know how her date went.

She replied to her friend with: *still on it. I'll call you tomorrow.*

It was now five forty-five and she popped her head around the doorjamb of Travis' office. "Is it okay if I take Fred and Ginger for their walk?" She hoped that would spur him on to finish and go with her.

Staring intently at the small piles of paperwork he had spread out all over his desk, he was clearly right in the middle of something, because he just nodded his head without looking at her and answered, "That'd be great."

Ava wanted to kiss him again but knew he was busy so she retreated back to the laundry room to leash up the dogs. She took them on an hour-long walk, past her parents' house to make sure there wasn't a driveway full of cars, before canvassing the rest of the neighborhood. She thought he'd be ready when she returned. Peeking her head into his study, he didn't even notice her. It was almost seven o'clock.

"Hey, I'm going to order takeout."

He looked at his watch. "Shit, babe. I'm sorry. I hit a snag. Can you have it delivered? Get whatever you want."

"How about Chinese?"

He was looking at his paperwork again. "Yeah, can you order me beef teriyaki, white rice, and lo mein noodles?"

The takeout arrived, and she brought in a tray with their dinners already plated and a beer for him and a water for her. He took a break and moved over to the sitting area with red leather furniture in front of the fireplace where she had set the tray on a coffee table. It was too warm at night for a fire, but she imagined it was probably lovely to sit in front of in December.

As they ate, Travis was very apologetic about neglecting her.

"I know you're busy, Travis, don't worry about it."

"Just a little while longer. Can you spend the night or do I need to take you home?"

She actually did want to spend the night but was hesitant about being too available to him. Especially after he'd been unable to break away from his work to spend time with her. She didn't want to be petty; she did understand how busy he had to be, but had selfishly been looking forward to spending some more time with him before the weekend ended and their hectic week began. She should have known every day of his was busy.

"I should probably go home. I have a closing scheduled for tomorrow morning, and I'm sure you have to be to work early." She hoped she didn't sound bitter.

He didn't say anything, and she rose to take the tray back to the kitchen. He stood up and slipped his hand around her waist from behind, nuzzling her ear. "I truly am sorry. I hope you'll let me try to make it up to you."

She smiled. "It really is okay. I'll get this cleaned up, then do you think you can take a break and drive me home?"

He seemed disappointed at the prospect of taking her home.

"Are you sure you can't stay?"

She hesitated, and he pounced.

Kissing her neck, he muttered, "Please?"

When she didn't answer, he started caressing her sides, then took the tray from her and set it down on the table before turning her to face him. While working his way to her cleavage, he murmured, "Pretty please?"

She still didn't answer, and his lips found hers, and he started coaxing her tongue with his until she returned his probing. There he continued until they were both aroused and breathless.

"With sugar on top?" he managed to whisper as he ground his body into hers.

*Damn him.*

"Okay," she conceded, "but you have to stop working and spend time with me."

He grinned happily. "I will. Give me fifteen more minutes."

Fifteen minutes turned into thirty, and Ava stood in the doorway of his den. This time she was naked except for the Come Fuck Me heels she had brought with her. With an arm over her head and one leg bent at the knee against the wall, she asked, "Are you almost done?"

He started to apologize again when he looked up and saw her seductively nude pose. She strode purposefully over to the credenza behind his desk and hopped up to sit on it. Crossing her legs at the knee, she waved a condom package back and forth in between her thumb and index finger. "Or should I give you another fifteen minutes?"

He stared at her for a second, then took his glasses off and threw them on his desk. Without a word, he grabbed a handful of her hair and started forcefully kissing her on the mouth. She stood, her heels making her closer to his height, and he shoved her against the wall while pressing his clothed erection into her naked pelvis. He ripped his T-shirt over his head and pushed his naked flesh against hers as he laced her fingers with his over her head. Ava curled one leg around his hip, and Travis dropped his shorts and underwear, kicking them out of the way. His condom was on in record time, and he held one of her legs under her knee and began to fuck her hard against the wall—so hard that the picture next to them fell, and they both started laughing. He pulled her over to a large, empty desk that sat opposite his. There, he spun her around so her ass was facing him, lifted one of her legs up to the side, and bent her over the empty workspace. Her tits smashed against the cold wood while her pussy was on full display for him. Once again, he started to fuck her hard, pulling her hair as he rammed into her balls deep, over and over. Her pussy lips were smearing the desk with her juices as they made contact every time he thrust up against her, stimulating her clit as she rubbed against the polished grain. His steady rhythm brought her to the brink of orgasm, and she started to moan loudly. "Oh yes!" That provided all the encouragement he needed, and he picked up the pace. She let out a final, "Oh my god, yes!" and felt him spasm as he tried to keep pumping into her in spite of his own impending orgasm, in case she hadn't quite reached the threshold of her climax. He finally grabbed her hips and held her still as he finished depositing his load into his rubber, then collapsed on top of her while they caught their breath.

His hands were around her body on her breasts, and he brought her with him when he stood up and pulled out of her before making his escape to the den's washroom. He came out and handed her a hand towel, which she readily accepted. Looking at the cloth in her hand, he joked, "My housekeeper is going to have a fit with all the towels she's going to have in the laundry this week."

"You don't have extra towels in the laundry every week from when you masturbate?" she teased, trying to catch him off guard.

"Nah, I do that in the shower." Nothing fazed him.

Grabbing her by the hand, he said, "Come on," and pulled her to his bedroom. There he handed her a fluffy white robe while she kicked off her shoes, and he slipped on the blue one he had worn that morning.

Taking her hand again, he led her to the kitchen, where he opened a bottle of white wine and poured them each a glass. Leading her into his living room, they laid on his wide white leather chaise lounge. He opened his robe, and she took hers off before lying next to him, his arms encircling her while she placed her robe over them like a blanket and snuggled into the warmth of his naked body next to hers. She didn't think she could ever get enough of how great his skin felt next to hers or the sexy smell of his chest and neck.

He wanted to know about her education, and why she chose to get her doctorate in organic chemistry, and how she came to the conclusion to sell real estate.

"The grant on the project I was working on ran out and my mother suggested I explore the possibility since I had negotiated my own real estate purchase without anyone's help. My father wasn't so sure. But then, he had paid for the part of my schooling not covered by scholarship over the past eight years. Mom thought I'd be good at it. I had learned a lot about the business, having gone through it and researched every step of the process so I knew I could be successful, but I was torn. I'd spent my entire adult life working to earn my degree in chemistry; it seemed like such a waste to not do something with it. But, I figured I'd do it until I had two years of expenses saved, that way if I was offered a project I believed in, I could do it, regardless of how little it paid."

"What kind of project would that be?" he asked.

"When the writing was on the wall about our grant drying up, I was offered a spot on a team researching a specific protein's role, if any, on accelerating liver cancer. I had to turn it down because it didn't pay enough, and I was already in a contract for my condo. I really wanted to be a part of that team. My grandpa—my mom's father—had liver cancer. I know I could have asked my father for a loan, but he helped pay for eight years of school, and I was living in his pool house at the time. I felt like I'd mooched off him long enough, you know? If I would have had enough money saved to offset the cut in pay, I could have taken that job. So, that's my goal—sell enough houses in the next year or so to build a nest egg big enough to allow me to take an opportunity that speaks to me when it comes along. If the pay is decent, even better. But not having to have salary play a factor in my decision would be ideal. So, here I am, selling houses for a little while."

"Couldn't you make enough to build a nest egg working in your field in the private sector?"

"I could," she agreed. "But most of the corporate jobs are on the east coast or farther north, near San Francisco. I think if I were offered a corporate job here, I might take it, but they are few and far between around this neck of the woods. The money is good so the competition is fierce." She looked at her surroundings and smiled. "Not equity law partner good but still a comfortable salary."

She snuggled against his chest. "But that's not what I want to do. I want to do research that makes a difference in people's lives by more than developing a better bottle for their ketchup."

They laid silently on the lounger for a while, both seeming to be lost in their own thoughts. Ava was reexamining what 'eye on the prize' meant. She knew the prize was no longer Brad. How could it be? He paled in every facet next to the man holding her. But she also knew Travis couldn't be the prize. As a forty-year-old bachelor, he was holding out for someone a lot more amazing than she was. Still, she was thankful she was able to spend time with him, however long that might be. He had made her realize she didn't have to settle for someone like Brad. While it wouldn't be Travis, she had a right to someone as amazing as he was, and he had helped her raise the bar of what she would accept. Not to mention she still had a lot to learn for Operation Sex Kitten. He could help her become more desirable for the next man in her life, and she was going to take full advantage of her time with him and enjoy it while it lasted.

\*\*\*\*

*Travis*

Travis stroked Ava's hair and wondered what the hell he was going to do about this woman lying naked next to him. He'd still been unable to find something he didn't adore about her. She was beautiful, smart, altruistic, and sex with her was amazing. What was the problem?

The problem was he wasn't ready to settle down. Neither was she. She had important things to do, cancer to cure. Their timing just wasn't right. The best he could hope for was to enjoy as much time with her as he could spare before they went their separate ways.

Soon he heard the steady breathing of her sleeping and lifted her up, taking her back to his bedroom, and gingerly tucking her in before heading back to his den. It was going to be a late night, but he didn't care. He would have happily stayed up until noon the next day if it meant a repeat of the night he had spent with her.

*Fuck, fuck, fuck.* He was in trouble.

\*\*\*\*

*Ava*

She heard him come to bed at four a.m. so tried to be quiet when she was up at six. She planned on gathering her belongings, leaving him a note and getting a ride from Uber. He woke when she was dressed and zipping her overnight bag.

"Hey," he said, "give me a minute and I can give you a ride home."

"Don't be silly. I heard what time you came to bed. Stay and get some sleep. I'm going to request a ride from Uber."

She was going to kiss him and tell him what a fun weekend she had, letting him know she didn't expect anything more when he said, "Why don't you take my car? You can bring it back tonight when we have dinner."

*Dinner tonight? Okay, if he insisted.*

"Which car are you talking about? The $100,000 one or the other $100,000 one in your garage?"

"Take the BMW."

"Travis, I drive a Prius. I'm not going to dri—"

He cut her off with a stern, "Ava, take the BMW. Please. For me? The keys are hanging up on the rack by the garage door. I won't be able to fall back asleep knowing some stranger took you home and right now I really need to fall back asleep for at least another ninety minutes."

She knew he needed to sleep so she wasn't going to argue. Instead, she kissed him on the cheek and said she'd see him tonight.

"I'll call you later," he mumbled before dozing back off.

# Chapter 10

*Ava*

Her phone rang at eleven-fifteen while she was in the middle of her client's real estate closing. It was Travis. She silenced it, then sent him a quick text. *In a closing. Call you when I'm done. Hope you got some sleep. xoxo*

Was the xoxo too much? Eh, too late now.

Her phone immediately vibrated with his response. Ok.

Ok? OK?? She guessed it was better than what she usually got from her sisters, which was k.

Her phone buzzed quietly again in her pocket. It was a text from Anne this time. Lunch and deets today? Noon. Baja Grill.

Ava texted her friend back. I'll be there.

How was she going to explain her weekend to her best friend without getting her too excited? Anne was a hopeless romantic. A practical hopeless romantic, but a romantic nonetheless.

She pulled up next to her friend at the restaurant in Travis' car. Ava had debated about driving it but thought it was probably safer at her office and the title company's parking lot than unattended at her condominium. Not that her complex wasn't safe; it just would be Ava's luck it got stolen.

She got out of the car while Anne stood with her mouth gaping open. "Whose car is this?"

Ava slipped her arm through her friend's and steered her into the restaurant. "It's a long story. I think you better sit down."

Ava proceeded to tell her friend the particulars of her weekend—who Travis was, where they went, and how much sex they had while managing to leave out the most intimate details.

"Oh. My. God. I cannot believe this! Do you like him?"

Ava replied indignantly, "Well of course I like him. I spent the weekend with him, didn't I?"

"No, I mean do you like him, like him? Do you want to see him again?"

"Yeah, I think I do. I mean, I know it's nothing serious, but Operation Sex Kitten is now in full swing, so why wouldn't I want to see him again?" She couldn't let her friend know he was so much more to her now than some silly, hairbrained project.

"Seriously, sister? Still with the sex kitten thing? Did you not prove how damn desirable you are by spending an entire weekend with this man?"

"I know, but I've still got a lot to learn. I think he can teach me."

"But once your lessons are complete, you don't honestly want Brad back, do you?"

She wasn't sure what kept her from telling Anne the truth. "I don't know. Maybe. I mean, I know I'm just having a fling with Travis. I guess Brad is in the back of my mind."

Actually, Brad is the furthest thing from my mind.

Her lunch date looked at her somberly. "As long as you're having fun and being careful."

Ava didn't know if Anne meant careful as in practicing safe sex, or careful as in protecting her heart. She guessed it didn't matter; the answer was the same either way. "I'm having a great time, and I'm definitely being careful."

Her friend squeezed her hand and gave a little squeal. "Oh, this is so exciting! I cannot believe my little girl's all grown up and having a torrid love affair."

"I don't know if I'd call it a love affair. But I would consider it an affair, even though technically neither of us is cheating on anyone. So you still need to keep this quiet. Don't tell anyone, I mean it! I don't want people to find out, which is why we didn't go to Evangeline's on Saturday."

"I wondered why I didn't see you in yesterday's paper. Okay, you can count on me. Mum's the word."

"Thanks, friend. I appreciate that."

"No problem." Anne grinned. "But you're buying lunch."

Ava accepted the terms of her friend's silence and picked up the check. "A small price to pay."

**

Ava was back in her office when she looked down at her phone. *Two missed calls and one text from Travis, how did that happen?* She'd forgotten to take her phone off vibrate after the closing and hadn't heard it in her purse while in the restaurant.

She had called Travis while she was driving to lunch, but he was on the other line so his phone automatically forwarded to his secretary, who she left a message with. He had apparently tried to return her call.

His text to her read, *Hey! Sorry I missed your call. Are you available for lunch?*

She was about to text him back, then realized it would be easier to call him and explain. He answered after the first ring.

"Hello, beautiful."

*What a nice way to be greeted.* "Well hello to you too." She giggled. "I am so sorry I missed your call. I put my phone on vibrate at the title company and forgot to take it off."

"Have you had lunch?"

"Unfortunately I did with my girlfriend, Anne. I mean, it's not unfortunate that I had lunch with her; it's unfortunate I didn't get to go with you. Not that you were necessarily asking me." She was babbling.

Hearing him laugh brought a smile to her face, and he continued, "Actually, I was going to ask you. Maybe next time. But we're still on for dinner, right?"

She suspiciously asked, "What did you have in mind?" She didn't want to go somewhere where people would know them or their picture would be taken. This really was starting to feel like a secret affair.

"How about I pick us up something from the barbecue place around the corner from my house and we stay in?"

She knew what restaurant he was talking about. She ate there a lot when she was staying in the pool house.

"Danny's Homemade BBQ? I love that place!" she replied enthusiastically.

"Great, I'll see you tonight around seven-thirty?"

****

*Travis*

She was looking at her phone and leaning against the BMW's bumper in his garage when he pulled in at a quarter to eight. He'd only been a few minutes late leaving the office, something that was easily remedied by exceeding the speed limit, but Danny's was packed, and he hadn't thought to call his order in until he was almost to the restaurant.

He met her by the house door, briefcase in one hand, takeout bag in the other, and still managed to put his thumb up to the reader that unlocked the door.

"Babe, I am so sorry to keep you waiting. Danny's line was out the door. I hope you got my text?"

"It's no big deal. I texted you back."

"Did you? I guess I didn't hear it. The restaurant was pretty loud."

She pushed the button to close the garage door for him since his hands were full, and they walked into the house. Fred and Ginger were doing their happy dance when she let them out of the laundry room.

"Hi guys!" she cheerfully exclaimed before picking them up and bringing them to the kitchen to get a treat from the cupboard. Travis put the food on the counter, set his briefcase on the floor next to the island, then reached for his phone. "Oh, there's your text," he said with a smile before taking her in his arms and kissing her soundly.

"Hi there," he whispered as he looked into her eyes and brushed the hair across her forehead.

She was smiling like she was drunk when she whispered back, "Hi yourself." Ava stared at him for a few minutes before telling him, "You look tired."

He confessed, "I'd be lying if I said I wasn't."

"You need to get to bed early."

"That's the plan," he said then released her and turned to the food on the counter. "Let's eat! I'm starving!"

Travis let her do most of the talking through dinner. He was tired and preoccupied but was still glad she was there.

He smiled appreciatively at her when she started to put containers in the refrigerator and their dishes in the dishwasher.

When he yawned, she asked, "You ready to take me home?"

He was surprised at the question and walked to where she was standing.

"Nope," he said as he scooped her up in his arms and carried her to his room.

She didn't protest as he carried her effortlessly through the house to his bedroom, but he noticed her brow was furrowed and gave her an inquisitive look.

"Travis, I know you're tired. Why don't we call it a night?"

He laid her on his bed next to him and started kissing her. "I thought about these lips all day long," he confided.

"I thought about you a time or two, I guess," she teased.

He threw his head back and laughed, then rolled on his back, pulling her on top of him and started nuzzling her hair, which smelled like apple blossoms. When she wiggled up against him, he sighed, enjoying how she felt in his arms. Soon they were both fast asleep.

**

Travis woke up at four fifty-five in the morning, exactly the same time he woke up almost every day, five minutes before his alarm went off. The woman who he had shared a bed with four nights in a row was sound asleep with her head on his chest. He had to admit, he liked waking up next to her.

Gingerly rolling her over, he slid out of bed and shut the alarm on his phone off before it had a chance to ring and wake her up. He grabbed his workout shorts and shoes and headed off to his home gym. He hadn't worked out since Friday but surprisingly, he felt pretty good, not like he normally did if he missed too many workouts in a row. He laughed. *I guess there's more than one good way to blow off steam.*

He tried not to think too much about Ava or how he was feeling about her, instead focusing on his workout. Every time she entered his thoughts, he pushed himself to run a little harder or do another set of reps. After the best workout he'd had in years, he showered in the bathroom adjoining the gym and slipped on a thin robe he kept on a hook right outside his steam room before padding to the kitchen to start coffee. It was six-fifteen and he expected she would be making her way to the kitchen soon.

As he leaned against the island counter looking at his phone, something outside caught his eye. Fred and Ginger were running up and down the length of the pool as Ava swam laps. Naked. With a fresh cup of coffee, he went outside and straddled a lounger while watching, mesmerized by her graceful body. And that ass. Man, that ass.

When she finished, she dunked her head under water again to pull her hair off her face. Fred and Ginger were looking down at her, and she laughed as she stood up.

"You two are quite the cheerleaders!' she told them as she walked up the pool steps.

They licked her wet calves and feet while she toweled off, not yet having noticed him. When she finally did see him, she jumped and gave a startled gasp.

"Oh my goodness, I didn't see you there!"

He gave an amused look and held up his mug. "Coffee?"

Instead of answering, Ava wrapped her towel around her and walked over to straddle the same lounger he was in, putting her hands on his shoulders as she swung one leg over the chair in front of him.

Hair dripping wet, she looked down at him and asked with an authoritative tone, "What's so funny, mister?"

Travis reached under her towel and grabbed a handful of the ass he had been admiring. "Not a thing, miss," he said as he pulled her down so she was now straddling him. Her arms came around his neck as his mouth met hers. She tasted like mouthwash.

Fred and Ginger decided they weren't going to get any more attention at the moment and began a game of tug-of-war with a rope toy in the grass area.

His arms started to move more urgently up and down her back as their mouths stayed busy with each other. She was pressing her naked pubis against the tent under his robe. When she bit his bottom lip, he slid the flimsy fabric open and with both hands under her butt, lifted her on to his rock hard cock.

Travis moaned. She felt fucking amazing.

Ava held his head tight to her chest as they swayed back and forth with him inside her. Soon he was holding her hips and pulling her down hard as she bucked up and down on his cock. When she arched her back with her hands on his thighs and began pressing against him, he took that as an invitation to circle her clit with his thumb.

He knew exactly how to touch her and within minutes after he started rubbing her magic button, she was moaning his name as she orgasmed. He pushed her onto her back and began thrusting into her hard and deep.

He had a sudden realization why she felt so exceptionally fucking amazing. "Shit! Shit! Shit!" he muttered and pulled out of her.

"What's wrong? Did I hurt you?"

"No, I don't have—"

She seemed to realize the problem without him having to say it. *A condom.*

Without missing a beat, she grabbed the back of his ass and pulled his groin to her face. He knew she could taste herself as she began to lick and slurp his erect cock before getting down to the business of sucking and stroking it with her hand at the same time. Her technique was excellent and before long, he was starting to move his hips rhythmically against her face.

"Baby, I'm going to come," he whispered breathlessly.

She kept stroking and sucking him as he was trying to push her head away from his cock. Keeping her mouth on his dick, she started jerking his shaft fast.

He gave one last attempt to push her head away before he released his warm cum in her mouth. He smiled when she pulled her towel to her mouth and spit before putting him back in her mouth to lick him clean.

While staring into her eyes as she got every last drop of cum off his cock, he shuddered and grabbed her chin. "What the hell am I going to do with you?"

She grinned, his cock still on her lips. "What you've been doing so far works for me."

Travis looked down at her and wiped some cum from the side of her mouth with his thumb. "I think I've turned you into a slut."

Ava drew her head away from him and frowned. "Is that a bad thing?"

He pulled her naked body up next to his and held her tight. "Oh God no, baby. That's an amazing thing. *You're* amazing. You blow my fucking mind," Travis whispered as he scanned her eyes with his. The last thing he meant it as was an insult.

Leaning her head against his chest, she whispered, "You have no idea what you do to me."

"Well, let me tell you what you do to me. Today will be the second day in a row I've been late for work. And I'm rarely late for work. Ever." He kissed her softly before adding, "And I couldn't give a damn less."

They continued to make out, naked, on the patio until Fred poked Travis' knee with his cold nose. It was past their breakfast time, and they had been patient long enough.

"Okay, boy, I'll feed you in a second." Reluctantly, he pulled away from Ava. As he headed to the laundry room, she headed to his bedroom. "I'm going to hop in the shower," she called over her shoulder.

Travis came to molest her one more time as she was blow-drying her hair. Fortunately, he was dressed. Unfortunately for him, she was not. Ava was so fucking hot it took every ounce of his willpower not to take her back to his bed and fuck her senseless all morning. He pawed her naked breasts and said in her neck as he was kissing it, "I have to get going. Just take my car again."

"You better be careful, you might not get it back," she warned.

"I know where you live." He winked and turned to walk out of the bathroom, watching her face in the mirror as she checked him out.

"Hey, Travis!" she called after him. He turned around and waited for her to finish her thought. She could have been reciting her ABCs for all he noticed; he was only concentrating on the way her hips swayed back and forth as she crossed the room to him.

"You look really hot in that suit," she murmured as she threw her hand around his neck. "Good enough to eat." He groaned when she started rubbing his crotch with her other hand and brought his mouth down hard on hers. They kissed for a few minutes, and when he was rock hard against her hand, he broke away and snarled, "Goddammit, woman. I'm already late!"

He tweaked her nipple and bolted out the door before turning right back around to suck on her tits for a few seconds more.

"Fuuuuck, I gotta go!" he cried.

He didn't really want to go and had she put forth any more effort, he could have been persuaded to stay a little while longer. Luckily for his career, she simply grinned as he leered at her a little longer.

"Would you leave already? I don't know what you're still doing here!" she teased.

Just then the dogs started barking, and Kay's voice yelled out, "Hello?"

He shot her a look that indicated they would continue what they were doing later.

# Chapter 11

*Travis*

Travis knew he needed to gather some perspective. Ava Ericson had bewitched him, and he had to figure out what to do about it. On one hand, he was a selfish bastard and knew he was going to continue fucking her, but on the other he was worried he was falling for her, and that wasn't something he was prepared for. And he was always prepared. He didn't want to see a future with her. She had things to do with her life: cure cancer, get married, have babies. Still, the thought of her doing that with anyone else gave him a twinge in his stomach. He chalked it up to the old 'I don't want her, but I don't want anyone else to have her' credo men were famous for. Funny thing was, he'd never experienced that feeling before with any of the other desirable women he had dated.

Yes, he definitely needed perspective.

Calling Ava that afternoon, he smiled at her warm greeting when she answered the phone.

"Hello, you sexy, gorgeous man," she purred into the phone.

This might be more difficult than he thought. "Hi yourself, beautiful."

When he started making chitchat with her, he shook his head. She had to know something was up. He finally got around to it.

"I am slammed at work right now. For some reason, ahem, I've been neglecting my responsibilities."

She giggled. "I know you're trying to make me feel guilty about that, Mr. Sterling, but unfortunately, I don't. Not in the slightest."

"Oh, I'm not trying to make you feel guilty. I never want you to feel guilty for what you do to me. But what I am trying to tell you is I'm not going to be able to spare any time for the rest of the week."

Her disappointed "Oh" made him strangely happy. She was let down about not seeing him and his ego loved it.

"Can we have dinner on Friday?" he asked.

"I'm sorry. I have plans for Friday."

He was a little taken aback. He had assumed she'd be jumping at the chance to see him whenever he was next available.

"How about Saturday then?"

"What did you have in mind?" she asked cautiously.

"I have tickets to the symphony."

He had no sooner gotten the words out when she adamantly responded, "Nope."

"What do you mean, *nope*?" he asked in an irritated voice.

"Travis, do you have any idea how many of my parents' friends go to the symphony? Or how many stupid photographers there will be waiting outside like vultures to get a picture of you and your new flavor of the week? I understand what this is between us. It's temporary. I'm okay with that arrangement. I just don't want the world to know I had an affair with Travis Sterling."

Travis would never consider her a flavor of the week, but he understood why she might think that way. Yet, her not wanting to be seen with him in public was the polar opposite of the women he usually dated. They wanted to get their picture with him published. It was like bragging rights.

"Well then, what did you have in mind?"

"I don't know. Dinner somewhere low-key? A movie? Game night?"

"Saturday then. Why don't you drive the Beemer here around seven, and we'll go from there."

"Um, no. I am not keeping your car until Saturday. I will get it back to you tonight."

Travis didn't argue. "I'll talk to you later this week, okay?"

**

His heart skipped a beat when he arrived home that night around ten p.m. His BMW was in the driveway, and he hoped maybe she was too. He opened the door to the car she had been driving. It smelled like her, but she was nowhere to be found. There was a card with his name sitting in the driver's seat on top of a box of caramels. His car key was inside the envelope, and the card read:

*Something yummy to thank you for letting me use your car.*

*'Til Saturday.*

*Ava*

It had her lipstick kiss and smelled like her perfume. It was all he could do to not drive to her place. Saturday was a long way away.

**

The week dragged for him. The highlights were the random texts she would send and the few times they talked on the phone. Thursday night found them texting for an hour after he got home. She had sent him a text around ten-thirty p.m. asking if he was home, and when he replied he was, their text conversation went from there. She was flirting, and he kicked it up a notch when he told her what he was going to do to her Saturday night.

She replied with, *Promises, promises* and an emoji of a pair of luscious lips.

****

*Ava*

A dozen roses arrived at her office the next day with a card that had the same lips emoji and *A fact, not a promise.* written on it. Ava walked around smiling for the rest of the afternoon.

*This is temporary! Get it together, girl!*

She simply grinned and thought, *It may be temporary, but I'm going to enjoy the hell out of it while it lasts.*

She had called her best friend on Wednesday to ask her to dinner on Friday. Since she had told Travis she had plans, it made sense to really make some; that way she wasn't a total liar. Her dinner date with Anne included a lot of wine, a lot of laughter, and delicious desserts. Ava and her friend were both suckers for wine and sugar.

After getting grilled by Anne about what was happening with Travis, Ava confessed, "The sex is so amazing. It's like movie sex."

Anne let out a little exasperated sigh. "Okay, great sex—check. And you of all people are deserving of that, but I'm talking about other stuff! Do you have anything in common?

Anything to talk about when you're not fucking each other's brains out?"

"Oh, yeah! Of course. He's probably one of the most fascinating men I've ever met. We have so much fun and always have things to talk about."

"So then explain to me why you keep insisting this is only temporary?"

"Annie, it just is. I'm having fun until this runs its course. And it will run its course. When it does, I'll definitely be ready for whoever comes along after. Whether it be Brad or someone new. I seriously had no idea sex could be this awesome!"

*Or simply spending time with a man.* She decided to keep that thought to herself.

"I get it, he's great in the sack. So there's no chance you're going to fall in love and live happily ever after with this guy?"

Ava smiled and shook her head. "It's just a fling!"

She thought maybe if she kept saying it, she'd make herself believe it. She knew any other line of thinking was a set up for heartbreak. If she thought getting over Brad was tough, it would pale in comparison to how destroyed she could be trying to get over Travis. *If* she fell for him. Which she was *not* going to do.

*That's why you have to keep it light!*

**

Saturday night finally arrived, and Ava showed up at Travis' door in a pale pink sleeveless sundress and a pair of strappy heels that were higher than she was used to wearing. He seemed to appreciate her in high heels so she had picked up a couple of pairs to wear when they were together. When Travis opened the door barefoot, in a pair of Levi's and an untucked white button down rolled at the sleeves that showed off his tan, her heart started beating a bit faster. There was a dishtowel over his shoulder. He was cooking them dinner, and he let out an appreciative "Wow!" as he looked her up and down.

Ava blushed a little and stepped inside. "It smells amazing!"

"You look amazing!" he countered and motioned toward the kitchen.

Walking in front of him, Ava said over her shoulder, "I picked up a pie for dessert. I wasn't sure what kind you'd like so I hope you like Oreo cream.

They hadn't made it out of the living room when he spun her around and put his mouth on hers.

*Oh my god, he tastes so good!*

She clung to him with one hand while trying to balance the pie in the other. He was kissing her throat when he pulled back and started chuckling. Taking the pie from her as she composed herself, he said, "Sorry, you just look so damn sexy."

She always felt sexy with him. She didn't know how he did it, but he never left a doubt in her mind that he desired her, which seemed to leave her perpetually wet between her legs whenever she was around him.

The fact he was fucking gorgeous didn't hurt either. She could suck on his beautiful lips all night. While riding his hard cock, of course.

She wondered how she was going to make it through dinner without jumping him. She knew he was thinking the same thing about her; the look he was giving her suggested he wanted her as the main course. Instead, they both put their game faces on and headed to where the wonderful smells were coming from.

"Where are Fred and Ginger?" Ava asked when she didn't see or hear them.

"Kay went to visit her mom this week and took them with her. She does that when she knows I'm working a lot," he replied as he poured her a glass of white wine.

Sitting on an island stool, she took the glass with both hands and gulped down a few swallows before daring to look at him again. It seemed whenever their eyes met, there was electricity in the air, and she wanted to get through dinner with her clothes on.

He was staring at her from across the center island. "Do you have any idea how badly I want to make love to you right now?"

Ava nodded as she took another drink of wine. "Maybe about half as much as I want you to," she replied boldly.

Travis started to take a step toward her when she continued, "But! You've made this delicious meal and we have all night to do that." Teasing, she added, "We need to show some restraint. What are we, animals?"

Travis cocked his head as if pondering that, then smirked. Coming around the island, he grabbed her face in his hands and muttered "Yes" before smothering her mouth with his. His tongue sought hers out while he slid his hands up and down her back.

"I've missed this ass all week," he growled as he beckoned her to stand so he could grab it in his hands.

She hungrily returned his kiss and wrapped her arms around his head as she stood up. Right when she started to press against him, the stove timer went off, indicating the dinner in the oven was ready. He groaned and pulled away from her so he could take the dish out.

It looked as good as it smelled and tasted even better.

They managed to make it through the meal with only mild petting and the occasional kiss. He was a fantastic cook, and she enjoyed the food, and the company, immensely. After clearing their plates, she started to open the pie container when he came around behind her and started kissing her neck.

"Why don't we go have dessert before having that?" he softly asked in her ear.

Ava set the knife on the counter and leaned against him with her eyes closed as he continued nuzzling her neck. She reached up behind her and ran her fingers through his hair while enjoying his touch and with her other hand she started to massage the bulge through his pants. Soon, she was rubbing her ass up and down against him as he was pressing into her while fondling her breasts over her dress. Tilting her head to the side, she offered her mouth, and he quickly claimed it with his.

Ava could sense his urgency and took his hand to lead him to the bedroom. Standing before the bed, she began to unbutton his shirt, kissing down his chest and stomach with each button she undid. She still couldn't believe the man was as magnificent as he was. He looked Photoshopped. He didn't need to touch her to turn her on; all she had to do was look at him. She kissed him thoroughly all over his rock solid core, enjoying not only the sight and touch of him, but also the smell and taste too. He sat down on the bed and pulled her to him. They were almost at eye level as she stood between his legs, and for a moment they just looked into each other's eyes, each searching for answers to unspoken questions. Tentatively, she leaned in and kissed him softly. He groaned and drew her onto his lap, kissing her roughly and urgently. She knew teasing time was over.

He had her dress unzipped and off her in what seemed like one motion. As Ava stood before him, clad only in her new lacy underwear and bra and high heels, he paused momentarily to look her over before running his hands up her thighs, over her hips, and all the way to her breasts, where he reached around and undid her bra. Lowering his head, he cupped her tit so he could eagerly suck on her nipple while squeezing her other breast in his free hand. He quickly moved his mouth to her other nipple—he was always careful to balance his affections toward her two boobs evenly, like he didn't want to leave one out.

One of his hands began to wander to her pretty lace panties. In the back of her mind she hoped he made a note he should take them off, not rip them off, since they were obviously new. As he massaged her firmly over the thin fabric, he looked at her and smiled. She knew the garment was thoroughly soaked. Sliding them to the side, he began to rub her up and down with his palm as he slipped a finger inside her. Her hands pressed the back of his head harder into her as she became more excited.

She could hear how wet she was. Funny, she didn't recall ever hearing sloshing noises with Brad. *But let's face it, sex with Brad compared to sex with Travis was like crackers and a gourmet meal. No comparison.*

As usual, he knew exactly how to touch her to bring her to orgasm, but this time he didn't let her finish before he stopped. She wasn't worried; she knew he had something in store for her when he positioned her on all fours with her legs together. Kneeling behind her, he began stroking his protected cock up and down her ass crack. He grabbed both of her hands and placed them on her ass and helped her spread her cheeks apart to expose her pussy and her asshole. Rubbing his cock inside her slit to lube himself, he returned to caressing his member up and down her spread cheeks until he eventually got to her pussy entrance. There, he circled his cock all around her opening before finally pushing himself inside her. It felt incredible. Ava dropped her hands on the bed and grabbed two handfuls of sheets. The sensation was so tight and somehow keeping her legs together stimulated her in a new way. He hovered over her as he buried himself hard and deep inside her pussy, pulling himself almost all the way out before plunging back in. Bringing his arm around her neck, he pushed her chin up to tilt her head back so he could kiss her as he fucked her firmly and slowly from behind. She wondered if he knew by her breathing and her noises that she was close; she just needed a little push. She got her answer when he started to pump her harder while reaching under her to burrow his fingers into her folds until he found what he was looking for. Giving her clit the attention it needed while ramming her with his cock, he growled in her ear, "Let go and come for me, baby." Ava happily accommodated his request and allowed herself to feel nothing but the pleasure he was giving her. She came rather unexpectedly, gasping and moaning as her body shuddered.

He leaned back to the kneeling position so he could continue to penetrate her. She knew he was admiring the scenery when he grabbed a handful of her flesh and groaned, "God I love this ass!"

Pulling out of her, he buried his face between her cheeks, licking and kissing her sensitive pussy then running his tongue along her crack before resuming fucking her brains out. He pulled her to the edge of the bed, where he kept her in the position of all fours, legs together. Standing this time, he mounted her again and firmly fucked her hard, the sound of his balls slapping against her ass exciting them both. He furiously pounded into her over and over.

This was something new for her and the raw, primal lust was hot. She wondered what he would be like if they hadn't seen each other for a whole week.

She heard him breathing faster, and he started to grunt as he slammed short, quick strokes into her. She could tell he came, and he laid on top of her, sweaty and breathing hard from his sexual workout.

"Oh my God babe, that was amazing!" he panted.

When he had recovered, he pulled out to make his usual trek to the bathroom to get rid of his condom and clean off. She so wished they didn't have to use one, but she appreciated his reasoning. He'd never responded when she told him that she had been tested after dating Brad, and that he had been her only other partner.

He gathered her up in his lap, where they kissed and caressed each other while talking about their respective weeks. Travis was considering taking a pretty big case that was going to keep him busy, but he assured her as he kissed her hair that he would make time for her. The thought made her happier than it should for someone who was 'keeping it light.'

They ventured back into the kitchen for the pie they had skipped earlier. She fed him bites of the creamy dessert as she proceeded to tell him about the two sales she'd made that week, and how excited she was about the possibility of those clients referring her to their friends.

They talked well into the night. Having not seen each other since Tuesday, they had some catching up to do. It surprised neither to find it was in the middle of the night when they decided they should probably try to sleep. Although Ava loved lying on his broad chest and listening to his heartbeat with his arms around her—she felt so safe that way—tonight she backed up into him so they could spoon. Unfortunately for their sleeping needs, that led to her feeling his growing erection against her backside.

Feeling him starting to get hard turned her on, and she let out a soft moan as she started to slowly and rhythmically rock her hips. Her ass was grinding against him and soon he was rock hard again. He slipped a condom on as she lifted up her top leg behind her, his cock sliding inside as he began to fuck her sideways with long, slow strokes. Like earlier, this was a new position, and she loved the sensation. Bending forward, she grabbed onto the side of the bed and began pushing back against him as the intensity of his thrusts increased. He felt so good inside her she hoped they would go a while. This might be her new favorite position.

He was an amazing lover, very in tune and attentive to her needs. When he reached around and began to play with her clit, she groaned at how wonderful the sensation was. She wanted it to go on and on, that's how incredible it felt.

Unfortunately, he was too much of an expert on her sexual desires, and she had to stop him from making her come.

"You're too good at that! I want to have you inside of me a little longer because it feels so good."

He nuzzled her hair as he whispered in her ear, "You're really good for my ego."

She could tell he was grinning.

He resumed his long, slow strokes into her but it wasn't long after he resumed fucking her that she heard his breathing change. He reached around again to rub her hard and fast to match the tempo his cock had increased to thrusting in and out of her. Fortunately for her and his ego, he brought her to orgasm just before his own. As she lay there, basking in her fulfillment, she hoped she satisfied him half as much as he did her.

When he came back to bed, she decided it was safer to crawl on top of his chest and fall asleep there. Once his arms were around her, it didn't take long for her to sink into a peaceful, contented slumber. She adored this man, and no matter what happened tomorrow, next week, or next month, she was in his arms tonight and that was good enough for now.

# Chapter 12

*Ava*

On Sunday morning, Ava took advantage of his pool to swim laps while he was working out in his gym. They met up in the kitchen for breakfast, and Travis looked at her inquisitively, then said, "Do you want to go to the Farmers' Market?"

"I love farmers' markets! That sounds like fun!"

When they went to leave the house, he held her hand as they walked out the side door and over to the car garage. He wasn't lying when he told her there was a truck and boat in there along with three other high-end cars.

"Any particular one you want to take out today?" he asked her.

Ava was torn between the blue Porsche 911 convertible and the cherry red Corvette with T-tops. How could they go wrong with either one? She told him what she had it narrowed down to, and he said, "Let's take the Porsche. I haven't had it out in a while."

He asked her if she wanted to drive, and she shook her head no. Truth was, she was dying to drive it but was a little rusty on her clutch work and wasn't about to embarrass herself by stalling that gorgeous machine in front of him. Being a passenger was more than sufficient for the time being.

He was sexy as hell driving it. There's nothing quite like a man who can shift gears seamlessly in his $125,000 sports car to get a girl's heart pumping. Ava, however, was wishing she'd been able to channel her favorite 1950s actress and magically pull a scarf out of her purse to cover her head. She was quite certain her windblown hair was not going to be sexy once they stopped.

*Oh well, he's seen me with bedhead.*

As they pulled up to their destination, they received a lot of admiring looks from both men and women. The men she was certain were admiring the car, while she had her suspicions the women were admiring her companion. Who could blame them?

She checked her appearance in the visor mirror and ran her fingers through her hair, trying to smooth it. Travis came round and helped her out her seat. She was appreciative because she was not going to make a graceful exit out of the low-to-the-ground car without his assistance.

They were able to walk around hand-in-hand and began to behave like a couple. More than once, he pulled her to the side of a tent or building to kiss her thoroughly, and they laughed when a passerby told them to get a room. All-in-all, it was a fun day for both of them.

\*\*\*\*

*Travis*

It felt very natural to act like a couple with her, and he was certain she felt the same way. He needed to make sure she knew his intentions and didn't get any ideas of a future with him. If he were being honest, he was also trying to tell himself he couldn't see a future with her.

During their drive home, he began the conversation. "Ava, I love spending time with you, but I need you to know I am not boyfriend material. I'm not interested in settling down or getting married."

He was certain she already knew that, but she winced slightly when he said it out loud.

"Travis, I am well aware this is temporary between us. I love spending time with you too, but I know this is a fling. Which is part of why I don't want to be seen with you in public where people know us. If and when we do eventually make an appearance together, we'll be able to truthfully say we're friends. Because honestly, you have become a dear friend to me, and I hope we will continue to be friends long after we stop sleeping with each other."

He was both happy and disappointed with her reply. Maybe he had read too much into how he thought she felt about him. His ego took a minor blow, but it helped him with the perspective he had been seeking even if it wasn't what he expected her to say.

They stopped by her condo so she could drop off her purchases. As he sat at her kitchen table, she came around the counter and gave him a thoughtful look. "Do you realize we've never made love at my place?"

That needed to be remedied.

He reached out and grabbed her hand as he pulled her toward him. She straddled him while putting her arms around his neck and gently kissing his mouth. He let her set the pace, so she slowly and tenderly began sucking on his lips before lightly seeking his tongue out with hers. She softly pressed against his hips with hers and dug her fingers into his hair before increasing the pressure of her mouth on his.

He began to kiss her throat as his hands were firmly planted on her back. She closed her eyes and tilted her head back while she enjoyed what he was doing to her. Soon, his mouth was back on hers, and he had taken over their make-out session. He didn't mean to; it was just his personality to be in charge. He noticed, however, she didn't put up much of a fight.

Soon they were both naked from the waist up. He loved that she got goosebumps whenever they had skin-on-skin contact and paused against her mouth when she got a shiver down her spine.

Holding her by her ass, he stood up, and she wrapped her legs around him as he carried her to the couch. Undressing her completely, he sat her so she straddled the arm of the sofa and began to caress her body from head to toe. Taking his time to discover her, he watched her reaction to the various ways he touched her. He kissed her a lot, both on her mouth and where his hands had explored, and was incredibly turned on by how intimate and sensual the experience was. But he wanted to taste her before he made love to her again. Sliding her down onto the couch, he spread her legs and began slowly licking her outer lips. She whimpered and tried to move her hips to position his mouth inside her lips.

He pulled back and smiled, loving how she always managed to convey to him what she wanted, but this time he was going to delight in teasing her a little first.

With his mouth against her opening, she gave a sharp gasp when he let out a hot breath against her. He moved down to lick the insides of her thighs to her knees and kissed and sucked back up until he was right where her V started. All the while she moaned in torturous delight. He took his time licking and sucking around the area while taking care not to actually touch her drenched pussy. Finally, she grabbed a handful of his hair and moved his mouth to her slit.

When he plunged his tongue into her folds, she yelled out, "Oh my God!" and began pressing against his face.

He licked her up and down, loving the taste of her. As he moved a finger inside her, he moaned and dragged his lips to circle her clit with his tongue. She was panting and thrusting her hips against him as he expertly moved his mouth around her pussy. He knew her body so well and enjoyed pleasing her, almost as much as he loved being pleased.

He felt her constrict around his finger while she started bucking her hips and panting between moans as he lapped up her cum. He could do that five times a day and love the fifth time as much as the first.

****

*Ava*

Ava remained still, letting the effects of her orgasm subside before she reached up and kissed him on the mouth. She knew it turned him on when she tasted herself on his lips, and she loved kissing him anytime.

Slithering down onto the floor between his legs, it was her turn to tease. She also kissed the crease between his thigh and pelvis, savoring his smell. She acted like she was going to lick his balls, but instead went beneath to the area between them and his ass, where she licked and sucked the skin before focusing her attention back to his testicles. Making wide circles with her tongue over each one, she then put them in her mouth and gently sucked. It was his turn to gasp and moan.

As she ventured toward the head of his cock, she stroked the shaft all over her face. She loved the warmth and smoothness against her cheeks and closed her eyes as she relished the feeling. Moving to his cock's head, she used her tongue and traced all the way around the tip, teasing and sucking slightly before licking him up and down, eventually taking him in her mouth. She sucked him up and down halfway while her hand worked the bottom half of his dick in unison with her mouth to satisfy him. Holding him firmly at the base, she took him as deep as she could. He let out a long groan and grabbed a handful of her hair, using it to guide her mouth up and down on him until she tasted his precum. She started using her hand again as he continued holding her by the hair and directing her mouth as it bobbed up and down his cock. When he pulled her head off him, she began to jerk him fast, keeping her face close. She made it quite clear she wanted him to come on her face, and soon her wish was granted as he glazed her mouth, cheeks, and nose with his white load.

He looked down at her coated in his juice and shuddered as she sucked the last remnants out of him. She was surprised when he leaned over and kissed her.

He must have read her mind because he murmured "Tit for tat" before jumping up to get a towel to clean her face with.

****

*Travis*

It wasn't until they were driving back to his place that he noticed some cum still in her hair and got a little hard thinking about how it got there.

He woke up Monday morning with her snuggled up next to him. Oddly, he seemed to sleep better when she was in his bed. He got up to do his morning workout and she followed suit, doing laps in his pool. He liked their routine and was disappointed thinking about not seeing her again during the week.

It was probably for the best. This was getting too comfortable.

The week following was much like the week before, only they didn't see each other at all until Friday. They relished their weekend nights, and he made it a point to do as little work as possible on Sunday in order to spend as much time as he could with her.

Travis had heard her when she told him she had gotten tested after Brad. He had made it to the doctor later in the week but was disappointed to not have the test results by the time the weekend rolled around again. He was fairly certain everything was fine, but he was waiting for the official results before not taking precautions to keep her safe. He could wait a little longer to be sure.

**

The week after, he sent her a text Wednesday night asking her to have lunch with him the following day. He had gotten his test results back with a clean bill of health and was anxious to share them with her.

She happily agreed on the condition they treat it like a business lunch in case they ran into anyone they knew.

# Chapter 13

*Ava*

Ava arrived at the office building of Carson, Burns, Sterling, and Cooper promptly at eleven twenty-five a.m. Travis had told her he was going to be pressed for time so she wanted to make sure she wasn't late, so as not to waste a minute of his available lunch hour.

*Just a business lunch.* She kept repeating that quietly to herself as she approached the impressive entrance of the glass building. She'd come from the office so she was dressed professionally and conservatively, although she had started wearing sexier high heels, especially on days when there might be a chance she would see him before being able to change.

She walked into the beautiful lobby and started making the long walk across the enormous entryway. The receptionist desk sat in front of the brightly lit letters of the names of the firm's partners while directly facing the entrance doors. The marble floor and high ceiling made her footsteps echo with every step she took. The young girl wearing a headset, and sitting at the raised stainless steel workstation, tried not to look bored as she watched Ava coming towards her.

Ava politely smiled at the girl. "Ava Ericson for Travis Sterling."

"Is he expecting you?" the girl inquired.

"Yes." Ava smiled again.

The girl hit some buttons and said, "Ms. Adamson? Ava Ericson is here for Mr. Sterling."

Pause.

"Okay, I'll tell her." The girl turned to Ava and motioned toward a small sitting area that seemed to get lost in the huge lobby with the soaring ceiling and windows that served as walls. "Please have a seat. Mr. Sterling will be right down."

Ava click-clacked over to the modern styled furniture and sat in the chair with the best view of the elevators that were to the right of the reception area. The chair was orange and seemed to be a cross between a futuristic egg chair and a classic club chair and was surprisingly comfortable. She sat on the edge of the seat cushion, back straight, with her legs tucked to one side, ankles crossed.

"May I offer you something to drink?"

"I'm fine," Ava answered appreciatively.

Just then Charlie Patterson, Brad's roommate, entered the lobby. He gawked at Ava while totally checking her out. When he realized who she was, a smile lit up his face, and he rushed over and grabbed both her hands, holding her at arm's length admiring the view. "Ava Ericson! Look at you! You look amazing!" he gushed.

"Charlie, it's so nice to see you!" Ava hugged him politely.

"Wow, I can't believe it's really you. How have you been?" He sat in the chair opposite hers, as if indicating he wanted to stay a while and hear all about how her life had been since breaking up with Brad. She didn't quite know what to think of it. While Charlie was never rude or mean to her when she would hang out at Brad's, he was never overly friendly. He was more like indifferent.

Ava started to catch Charlie up on what she had been up to over the last year, leaving the details of the last three weeks out, while she patiently waited for Travis to come down in the elevator. She would glance over whenever she heard the *ding* of the elevator arriving at the ground floor to see if the beautiful man was one of the car's passengers.

"So, what's going on with you?" Ava inquired.

"Same old, same old. Loving my job, not dating anyone serious, and still living with that bum," he stated flatly. "He's actually trying to get on with the firm here."

Ava raised her eyebrows and nodded, as she tried to envision the two men living and working together.

A month ago, she would have been painfully obvious while trying to be nonchalant when asking, "Oh, how's that going?" but now found it to be strangely easy not to inquire anything further. Because she really didn't care. She knew he was waiting for her to ask more follow-up questions about how Brad was doing. The liberation she felt not asking, coupled with truly not giving a damn, was empowering.

She knew Charlie was talking but she stopped listening the moment Travis appeared from an elevator car. She smiled when she was able to catch his eye. He gave her a big grin and strode towards them, all six-feet-two inches of him in his custom-tailored suit. *Damn, he is so hot.*

Travis was about ten feet away when Charlie finally stopped talking. He'd noticed she was one hundred percent focused on his boss walking their way. When Ava stood up to greet Travis, Charlie realized the equity partner was not coming over to talk to him.

Ava felt her insides doing flips and was trying hard to wipe the stupid smile off her face. It wasn't happening. *How can I be so happy at just the sight of him?* She took a deep breath. *Just a business lunch.*

Charlie stood up as well, respectfully acknowledging his boss.

"Mr. Sterling!" Ava was practically beaming as she held out her hand.

Travis looked over at Charlie and nodded before he grabbed Ava's hand and held it while he leaned down and kissed her on the cheek.

"Am I interrupting something?" He was still holding her hand but eyeing the associate attorney.

"No, Charlie was keeping me company while I waited for you." She turned to the other man and smiled.

"Yes, we were just catching up. It was good seeing you again, Ava." Then Charlie looked over at Travis and humbly nodded. "Mr. Sterling." He clumsily tried to make a wide circle from where Travis was standing.

Ava stopped him and politely hugged him once more, then looked him in the eye and said, "It was good seeing you again. Take care, Charlie."

She picked her purse up off the stainless steel end table and rejoined Travis, who gestured to the door as if to ask her if she was ready. Travis looked over at the younger man who was observing them while waiting for the elevator car. A small smile escaped Travis' lips when he placed his hand on the small of Ava's back, less than an inch above her ass, and escorted her to the door.

It was a beautiful July day so they decided to walk to Barrio, a restaurant downtown that offered American cuisine. They had walked a block making pleasant chitchat, but while standing behind her as they were waiting for the crosswalk light, he growled in her ear, "Do you know what I'm going to do to you later tonight? Let's just say your panties would come flying off right here if you knew."

She smiled and discreetly reached behind to squeeze the inside of his thigh as she leaned back and said, "What makes you think I'm wearing any?"

He looked a little startled, then quickly regained his composure and said loudly, "Whoa, Ms. Ericson. Slow down! I thought this was just a business lunch!" then gave her a wink.

She needed some kind of armor to protect her knees from going weak every time he winked at her. She was thankful for his strong grip on her elbow that guided her across the street once the light changed.

The restaurant was a charming, upscale café in the city center. The maître d' started making a fuss the minute they walked through the door, and they were seated immediately in a booth in the prominent part of the restaurant, in spite of there being an obvious wait—based on the number of people milling around by the doors. *So this is what it's like to go out with him in public.* No wonder women went gaga over him. She'd caught a taste of it when they went to Figurino's, but she thought she had played a small role in how well they were treated there.

"So how do you know Charlie Patterson?" he asked her once they had ordered.

"How do *you* know Charlie Patterson?" she teased.

"He's a junior associate at my firm," he shot back. "Your turn." He wasn't teasing.

*Was he jealous? And of Charlie Patterson of all people?*

She knew she should diffuse the situation. She never thought she'd ever see the day when he was jealous over her. It was an interesting and odd feeling.

"He is my ex-boyfriend's roommate." Then she couldn't resist adding, "I think he was checking me out before he realized it was me. He was so embarrassed when he figured out who I was."

"Well too bad for him that you're going to be waking up in my bed tomorrow morning," he snarled bluntly.

"I am? I don't recall being invited, Mr. Sterling."

He grabbed her hand and started to suck on her wrist sensually and seductively. "You have an open invitation to my bed, baby. Any time." With his free hand, he reached under the table and slid a hand up her inner thigh beneath her skirt. "Especially if you aren't wearing any underwear." She tried to move away and snatch her hand back, but he held it tight to his lips and squeezed her thigh, all while grinning devilishly at her.

"Stop it!" she hissed, looking around to see if people were watching. They were, of course.

He continued to blatantly snack on her wrist while she tried in vain to discreetly pull away. He was tracing the inside of her thigh. She knew he was trying to move high enough to see if she was lying about her panties. Her skirt was too long to do so without hiking it up, although she wasn't about to put it past him not to do just that. He was embarrassing her as punishment for making him jealous. He finally released her hand but made no attempt to remove his hand from her thigh. She looked around again. People were staring and whispering. She was sure they were wondering *who is this woman being kissed by Travis Sterling?* and she was going to kill him if her picture ended up in the *Out and About* section of tomorrow's paper. She felt her face starting to get red. The arrogant smirk hadn't left Travis' face.

She squeezed his arm and hissed, "I'm afraid I will not be able to go on any more business lunches with you, Mr. Sterling, if you're going to behave like this."

Just then their food arrived, and he casually brought his hand back. *Wow, that was fast.* People who had already been seated when they arrived hadn't even had their orders taken yet. She looked over at him. Special treatment seemed to be second nature to him, expected. When he entered the door, people bowed and scurried - ready to carry out his every demand. She wondered if anyone had ever told him *no* in his life. Watching him prepare to cut his steak, she knew if it happened, it was few and far between. His air of confidence and cockiness was a sexy aphrodisiac, and she was not immune.

"I was serious about you waking up in my bed tomorrow. Come for dinner tonight and I'll make you breakfast in the morning." Her flirtatious man was back.

She almost told him *no* just to see his reaction, but then thought better of it. She didn't want to risk a repeat performance of her wrist, thigh, or any other body parts being molested in public again.

"Aren't you working late again tonight?"

"I'm at a point where I can take a well-deserved break," he replied.

"I was planning on going to the gym after work to swim laps, but I can come by after that. I can probably get there shortly after you do." She knew when he was working normal hours, he usually arrived home a little after seven-thirty p.m.

"Swim laps at my place. I want you there when I get home." He grinned at her. "I'll even pick up some take-out."

It was his usual commanding, not suggesting. Still, Ava had to admit, she liked the idea of swimming by herself at his place better than going to her gym's public pool, so she didn't argue. Instead she smiled and said, "I'll make the salad."

"Perfect."

They finished lunch and strolled back toward his office, stopping at the fountain in the middle of the square. She wanted to kiss him right there as the mist of the spraying water hit them while they sat on the statue's edge. She looked around, needing a distraction to keep her from doing just that, and saw a small anthill a few feet away in the cobblestone bricks of the plaza. She proceeded to point out interesting ant facts she had learned when observing a colony for one of her high school science projects. He was listening with interest and amusement as she animatedly described how ants will care for insects of other species in order to get their sugary honeydew, and he feigned amazement when she continued to explain what the movie *A Bug's Life,* got right and wrong.

Travis raised one eyebrow, indicating he had no idea what *A Bug's Life* was.

"It's a children's movie about an ant colony," she dismissively told him before continuing on enthusiastically about what was accurate and inaccurate about the film. She squatted in front of the anthill and observed the occupants hard at work before she stood up and smiled. He smiled back, having enjoyed the impromptu, but passionate, lesson on tiny insects that could carry fifty times their body weight.

She really was comfortable around him, loving she could be herself, and that he seemed to appreciate her just as she was. It would have been so easy to hold his hand while they walked along the downtown streets and stop occasionally for a romantic peck like lovers do. She savored the feeling she got when she was around him: content, safe, and adored all wrapped up with a happy bow. She knew for sure at that moment she was in love with him and was more than certain it was not going to end well for her. He had been very upfront about his feelings regarding being someone's boyfriend or husband—she had no one to blame but herself. In all fairness, she could blame how good he looked in that suit and the heavenly things he did to her body, but that didn't negate his crystal clear edict on commitment.

He made sure she got to her car safely, gave her the code to the security system at his house, and softly but discreetly kissed her on the mouth. "Next time you come to my building, I don't want you to wait in the lobby for me. Come directly to my office. That way I can kiss you properly behind closed doors."

She liked the idea of that, but suspected kissing her behind closed doors was secondary to making sure she wasn't chatted up by any of his underlings again. "See you tonight," she said quietly.

He told her, "I'll be home around seven-thirty," then shut her door and waited for her to roll the driver's window down. Leaning in through the opening, he reached all the way up her skirt until he felt her panties. Rubbing in circles over the silky garment, he growled, "Liar," before kissing her again, more leisurely this time, then stepping back. She blew him a kiss, then drove off.

*Ava, girl, you need a reality check. Fast.*

\*\*\*\*

*Travis*

Travis was in the lobby of his building waiting for the elevator when Bob Tressinga, one of the more senior attorneys on his staff, approached and pushed the already lit *up* button. "I was jealous of your lunch date, my friend. I don't know how, but I'm fairly certain every girl you're with is prettier than the last. You are my god. You have to teach me how to get women like that."

Travis smiled knowingly. "She's just a friend." He thought about what Ava had said the other night about being able to say they were friends, because they were.

Just then, Stuart Chamberlin joined the waiting group. "Who's just a friend? That little minx you took to lunch today? Man, I'd like to be her *friend*." He seemed to feel safe commenting about his boss' lunch date in that manner, since Travis had made it clear they weren't an item.

The elevator doors opened and as they entered, Travis snarled, "That minx, as you like to call her, is Judge Ericson's daughter, fellas. So wipe your mouths and have some respect." He was annoyed at their openly lusting after the woman he was secretly sleeping with, but played it off as if he was offended out of deference to her father.

****

*Ava*

Ava finished doing laps and went inside to the kitchen, hair damp, and still clad in her bikini. She had forgotten her cover-up, so she had taken one of Travis' dirty dress shirts out of his hamper to use as one. It still smelled liked him.

161

Holding it to her face, she took a deep breath of the material and sighed happily as she inhaled his scent before slipping it on over her.

The dogs were on a playdate at the dog walker's so she had the entire house all to herself. Kay had taken them home after their afternoon walk and left a note saying she'd return them tomorrow. Ava giggled. Only *his* dogs would go on sleepovers.

Still having thirty minutes before Travis would be home, she took her time gathering the ingredients for the salad and placing them on the counter, then decided to listen to the music on her phone while preparing the contents. Putting on her favorite song, she spun around the island, shaking her hips to the beat while looking for a bowl to mix the salad in, along with a knife and cutting board to dice and chop the peppers, cucumbers, and tomatoes. She was bopping around the kitchen, singing along and shimmying, when Travis walked in, twenty-five minutes earlier than expected. She didn't know he was home yet—the dogs were not there to sound their barking alarm to alert her to his presence, and her music was up loud so she hadn't heard the garage door open and close.

\*\*\*\*

*Travis*

He stood there, mesmerized, watching her move around his kitchen with complete abandon and set the bag of takeout down quietly next to his briefcase before loosening his tie. Seemingly out of nowhere, a wall of emotions hit him all at once. He realized he loved every single thing about her. He had loved walking around the city with her today, listening to her talk passionately about ants, of all things—trivial things he would have never given a second thought to before he met her. He loved that the excitement he felt over the thought of coming home to her made him leave work earlier than he had in years. He adored how she was kind to whoever crossed her path and smiled at everyone she met, how she always showed appreciation to anyone who helped her, and how she genuinely cared about others. He loved that, in spite of being flipping brilliant, she often didn't get it when he was teasing her, but she could be feisty as hell and wasn't afraid of him. He was crazy about her goofy sense of humor and how nerdy and naïve she could be, and that she openly adored him and didn't care he knew it. Right now, he couldn't name one place he'd rather be than watching her dance around his kitchen. He did not like Charlie Patterson, Bob, or Stuart—or any other Tom, Dick, or Harry for that matter—thinking they had a shot with her. She was his and his alone. He'd never felt like this about anyone. It was to his inner core, and he suddenly had an animalistic need to claim her as his.

He didn't take his eyes off her as he slowly walked into the kitchen and shut off her music. She jumped with a start and smiled welcomingly at him. He didn't smile back, just continued over to her and immediately started unbuttoning the shirt of his that she had on. The house seemed totally silent. She stood there, completely still, his face inches from hers but staring intently at his task of undoing the last of the buttons on the shirt before pulling it open to reveal her bikini. He looked her up and down before untying her top and pulling her bottoms down around her ankles, placing his shoe on them so she could step out. He looked her over again, this time almost evaluating her with his eyes. She continued standing there, motionless and naked under his shirt, letting him objectify her. She seemed to try to look into his eyes, but he was completely focused on her body. This was different than his usual teasingly leering—it was primal. He still hadn't said a word when he picked her up and put her on the counter. He undid his belt and slid his pants and boxers off, his cock already completely erect. With carnal lust, he took her right there. He wasn't gentle nor did he let her body get used to him being inside her before he started plunging into her, looking at her with a hunger that he could only satisfy by shoving himself into her as deeply he could. With every thrust it was like he was branding her as his. He wasn't interested in her pleasure; he just wanted to take from her. He wanted her to give everything to him until she had nothing left to give to anyone else. She was his. No one else's. His. He started to grunt as he rammed her harder and faster. When he climaxed inside her, he felt pleasure that he had somehow marked her as belonging to him. His cum coating her womb was his stamp.

He finally looked at her again, really looked at her, as the woman he was in love with, not as his possession, and he was overcome by another wave of emotion. She was sitting on the kitchen counter, staring back at him, stripped and completely exposed. She had let him treat her like his property, trusting him enough to let him claim her as his. Fuck her without protection. Knowing he would protect her and care for her because she now belonged to him, body and soul.

Neither had uttered a word yet, and the house remained quiet, except he now noticed the loud ticking of the clock on the wall. It was like they were in a spell that would be broken with a simple word. He began to kiss her passionately, now wanting to give her as much pleasure as he had just taken. Not ready to break the spell, he lifted her up off the counter, still erect and in her. She wrapped her legs around his middle to keep him in place inside her, and without another sound, he carried her to his bedroom. There, he attentively and tenderly made love to her, his cum acting as additional lubricant, although she didn't need any more. He took his time kissing and caressing every inch of her body as if he couldn't get his fill of her. Her response let him know she couldn't get her fill of him either. He came again inside her, and they finally collapsed, entwined in each other's arms, the two still wanting to remain as one even though they were both perfectly satiated.

For the first time in as long as he could remember, he was vulnerable. Vulnerable to what he would do if something were to happen to her or if she grew tired of him. He didn't like knowing she could destroy him if she wanted. Yet, he also knew she was incapable of doing that. He knew she felt the same about him, so why did he have this feeling of panic inside him? He needed to slow things down and get his emotions in check.

As she was drifting off in slumber in her usual position on his chest, Travis murmured, "Oh, Ava Faith," and kissed her head through her hair, holding her tightly against him. She fell asleep with a sigh and a smile. He laid wide awake, loving how she felt in his arms and scared out of his mind. He wasn't in control and that wouldn't do.

# Chapter 14

*Ava*

Ava woke in the middle of the night to the smell of food. After her and Travis' marathon lovemaking session, they had both fallen asleep fairly early and without having eaten dinner.

She padded out to the kitchen in the white robe she had commandeered as hers to find Travis reheating the takeout he had brought home earlier. He smiled when he saw her in the doorway, her hair messed up from not only sleep but from having been thoroughly fucked before going to sleep.

She knew she was going to analyze the evening's earlier events at some point, but right now, she was just going to enjoy the food and the company. Asking him for clarification seemed too risky. If he was feeling anything more for her, her wanting him to label it was a bad idea that she feared would cause him to flee.

"That smells good! I'm starving!" was what she went with instead of, *Hey, what just happened between us?*

They ate in relative silence, chalking it up to being tired and in the middle of the night, but it was much more than that. Ava knew he felt it too. She was happy when he motioned for her to assume her position on his chest in order to fall back asleep.

She woke to the sound of Travis being sick in his bathroom. It probably wasn't the smartest idea to eat food that had been left out for hours. She made it to the guest bath just in time.

Ava was fortunate she could go home and take it easy for the day. Travis did not have quite the same luxury and went in to the office later in the morning, then gathered work to bring home after getting sick again and left mid-afternoon.

They were both feeling better by Friday evening but decided to each stay at home, opting to have breakfast together the next morning instead. Travis was going to be up late working, and Ava was going to try to make sense of what was going on between them. Of course, she didn't tell him that, instead telling him she was going to go to bed early, which she did, but she didn't fall asleep as she went over the events from Thursday in her mind.

Had anything changed between them? She was going to wait and see if he said anything to indicate it had, otherwise she was inclined to leave it alone for now. Why rock the boat?

**

He picked her up the next morning in his Mercedes, asking when he opened her car door for her, "Do you have to be anywhere today?"

"No, I don't have clients today. Why?"

"I thought maybe we could drive up the coast for breakfast and maybe stay until dinner. Or breakfast tomorrow, if we feel like it."

She liked the idea and was happy to find there was only slight uncomfortableness between them, but they soon fell into their usual talking about everything and anything, with the occasional affectionate gesture or kiss. They held hands as they walked into the diner they found. Sliding into a round booth, he threw his arm around her as they looked at the menu options, and she teased him about ordering lunch instead of breakfast.

He feigned to defend his food selection. "I'm finally hungry again! Yesterday was awful," before adding, "I'm sorry about feeding you that."

"It's not your fault. But to be honest, I'm a little apprehensive to eat. I tried again last night and it didn't go so well. But I'm feeling a lot better, so I'm optimistic."

Their meal went fine, and they enjoyed the rest of the day sightseeing, stopping to walk along the beach barefoot. They were unusually quiet as they strolled in the sand, Ava not sure if she should ask questions about their relationship, if they even had a relationship. Travis appeared to be lost in his own thoughts as he slipped his arm around her waist and kissed her hair, still not having said a word.

They found a restaurant on the water to have dinner and watch the sun set into the ocean. The entire restaurant was quiet as the orange ball sank slowly out of sight, and everyone clapped when it finally dropped below the horizon. Ava looked at Travis and found him smiling tenderly at her. She returned the smile as he leaned over to kiss her softly on the mouth, closing her eyes and enjoying the feel of his lips gently on hers while he cupped the side of her face in his hand. She eventually opened them to find him staring at her. She couldn't quite make out the look on his face but knew it was an affectionate one.

They had one more glass of wine before deciding to head out. At the car, before opening her door, he bent over and kissed her again, softly at first, but when she let out a quiet moan and brought her arms around his neck, it began to heat up. She pressed against him, wanting to mold her body to his. Soon, he had her against the car while he pushed his clothed body tightly against hers. There was no way they were going to make it back to town, but the idea of having sex in the car seemed a little too teenager-ish, even as excited as they were. Across the highway was a little motel with bungalows and a neon sign that flashed *vacancy*.

They were given bungalow number thirty-six, although there weren't thirty-six cabins. Ava started to try and figure out their numbering system but quickly realized she didn't really care at the moment.

They were undressing each other within minutes of entering their room. Travis went to remove her panties when he stopped.

"Ava?"

She was confused about why he was no longer undressing her. "What's wrong?"

"I know this is natural, but were you expecting to start your period today?"

Ava frowned. She knew she was about to start the sugar pill week of her birth control, but her period usually came in the middle of the week, not at the beginning or before it. Of course, she'd also been having a lot of sex this last month, so that probably had something to do with it.

"No, I must be a little early. I'm so sorry."

He looked at her oddly. "Babe, why are you sorry? Don't apologize for being a woman."

"I'm sorry because I've ruined our night."

He frowned. "How have you ruined our night? I'm still going to make love to you; we'll just put a towel down."

She felt weird. Brad never wanted anything to do with her the entire week, whether she was actually menstruating or not. He didn't want to risk getting any blood on him. She naturally assumed that was how all men felt and had a little bit of a complex at the idea of continuing.

Travis seemed to be able to immediately tell something was wrong and stopped.

"This doesn't bother me. But if you're uncomfortable, we can just snuggle and kiss tonight."

Ava liked that idea. Of course, his idea of snuggling and her idea of snuggling were two completely different things, as it became quite apparent when he put in his A game make-out session before moving down to spend an extraordinary amount of time attending to her tits and nipples until he had driven her crazy with desire.

She was soon pressing against his erection and grinding her hips against his as she whispered, "I want you," and he happily accommodated her by sliding his cock inside and gently making love to her. There were a lot of unspoken words exchanged between them as they looked into each other's eyes while moving in their perfect rhythm. There were also a lot of questions that were left unanswered.

**

Waking in the morning to Travis walking through the bungalow door with coffee and a grocery bag, Ava stretched and smiled. Last night, she had been relieved to find there had been very little mess and rinsed her panties in the sink after finding a tampon in her purse. In the grocery bag were a box of tampons, a box of pads, a package of underwear, and a bottle of Midol. He obviously was new at being with a girl in the middle of her period and wanted to make sure all his angles were covered. She loved him even more for his attempt.

Once again, the ride home started out awkwardly. Their level of intimacy had increased tenfold over the last three nights. At least she thought so. Last night they had period sex. She didn't think she could have that with just anyone and hoped he felt the same.

****

*Travis*

Travis had been in a state of constant conflict the last three days. Every time he was with her, it was easy and enjoyable, but when he started to think about it being more than just a temporary thing with her, he felt a sense of panic. This morning's run to the store did not help.

*What the fuck am I doing? I bought her tampons, for Christ's sake. I'm not ready for this. I don't want this. How the hell am I going to stop it?*

He appreciated she hadn't asked him to talk or explain what he was feeling because frankly, he didn't know what the hell to think. He knew he loved her and was willing to bet anything she felt the same. He also knew being in love did not change their bad timing in any way, shape, or form. If anything, all it did was make the situation worse and more complicated.

They stepped inside her condo, and he suggested she pack an overnight bag before they went back to his place, but warned her he had a lot of work to do.

"You know what? I think I'm going to stay home tonight," she said with her arms around his neck.

Travis scowled. Despite his misgivings about his earlier purchases for her, he had been looking forward to their Monday morning routine, not to mention holding her again all night. Quite simply put, he wanted her available to him, but on his terms.

"Honey, I'll just be a distraction as I pout that you're not paying attention to me," she teased.

He was pretty sure that was the first time she'd used a term of endearment in place of his name and found it nice.

"It's not that I don't want to pay attention to you. I've just been working like crazy, and it looks like I've got another case I'm going to take."

Actually, he had been on the fence about taking the other case. The client had specifically requested him, but he was worried he might be stretched too thin. However, as he read the particulars of the case, it pissed him off, and he knew he was the best attorney in the firm to handle it. Not to mention it would provide a way to keep him busy and not thinking about what was happening with Ava or what she was doing when she wasn't with him.

For the first time in a month, Ava slept in her own bed on a Sunday night.

# Chapter 15

*Ava*

She was walking into her office on Monday morning when her phone started ringing. Her hands were full so she didn't even look down to see who was calling. Her stomach dropped when she heard Brad on the other end.

"Hi, beautiful. How are you doing?"

Ava was immediately suspicious. What did he want? He hadn't reached out to her in over a year. Something smelled fishy. She was surprised at her attitude.

"Oh hey, Brad. I'm fine thanks."

Silence.

If he was waiting on her to keep the conversation going, he was going to be waiting awhile.

Brad started making chitchat and when he actually started talking about the weather, she cut him off.

"I'm pretty sure you didn't call me to talk about how much rain we need, Brad. What's up?"

He took her hint and got right to the point. "Can we have dinner? I'd really like to catch up. I've missed having you in my life, Ava."

*What. The. Fuck.*

Her first inclination was to tell him not a chance in hell, but then curiosity got the better of her, plus she kind of wanted to see if she could make him sorry he dumped her.

"I don't know, Brad. I'm so busy these days. When did you have in mind?"

"How about Thursday night? I'll see if I can get a reservation at Evangeline's."

*Evangeline's, huh? This should be interesting.*

"Yeah, I can meet you there. Text me what time."

He started to try and make small talk again, and she cut him off. "I've got to go. Thanks for calling." And she hung up.

*Man, that felt good.*

Yeah, Operation Sex Kitten definitely had a new prize and it wasn't Brad Miller. Not spooking the gorgeous Mr. Sterling seemed to now be her focus. She didn't know if sex was the way to make that happen.

Charlie Patterson called her that afternoon and asked her for lunch on Wednesday. *What the hell was going on?*

She also got a call from the broker at Ridgeport Realty, a competing real estate agency, inquiring if she'd be available to meet with him tomorrow. Ava had been the best student in her real estate class, which had caused a lot of brokers to seek her out to come work for them after she passed her licensing exam with flying colors on the first try. The brokers reminded her of the recruiters on campus who came calling each time she was finishing a degree. Women with bachelor's degrees in the sciences are pretty highly sought after, and women with doctoral degrees in the science field make headhunters almost pee their pants. She'd had several successful months with her company, so she wasn't surprised to receive the call. Her father always taught her to at least listen to what other people had to say, so even though Ava was perfectly content with Oceanside Realty, she took the competing broker up on his offer for lunch.

Travis didn't reach out to her all day or that night, nor did he respond when she sent him a text before she went to bed. At the very least, he would always respond to her if he didn't initiate with a text or email. Either he was really busy or he was starting to avoid her, or both.

*So he's taking another case.* She found the timing of that interesting, then thought maybe she was just being paranoid. *Why wouldn't he take another case right now? He's the best in the state; of course he's always busy.* It probably had nothing to do with avoiding spending time with her. She hadn't asked anything of him or even hinted she expected anything other than their status quo. *As far as he's concerned, I'm still content with his 'I'm not boyfriend material' stance. Don't read anything into this, Ava.*

She needed to let him know nothing had changed; she had no expectations of him.

**\*\***

Ava met with Frank Harris, the broker of Ridgeport Realty, at a restaurant downtown near Travis' office building. The meeting left her a little floored and she found herself wanting to talk with her favorite gorgeous attorney.

She dialed his number and was half-expecting him to send her call to his secretary, so she was a little startled when he answered himself.

"Hi, I'm downtown. Can I come by and say hello?"

"Absolutely. I'll let them know to send you right up."

On her elevator ride up to his floor, she realized she'd never seen his office and was wondering what to expect based on the lobby's décor. When the elevator doors opened, she was immediately greeted by a receptionist desk next to a waiting room with lots of beech-colored wood and stainless steel complimenting modern design furniture. To the left were glass doors with a bullpen of cubicles while offices lined the perimeter. To the right were glass doors that led to Travis' office. His secretary, Kelli, met her when she got off the elevator and delivered her to Travis.

His traditional office design was markedly different than the modern look of the rest of the building she had seen. He was on the phone when she walked in, so he smiled and motioned for her to sit in one of the leather chairs opposite his mahogany desk as Kelli stepped out and closed the door behind her. Instead, Ava walked around his desk to him and traced her finger up his thigh, letting her hand linger on his groin while he shot her a look. His office was impressive as his entire corner room had a magnificent view of the city below. Strolling around and looking at his décor led her to the black leather couch in his sitting area.

He was still on the phone when she hiked up her skirt and spread her legs with her heeled feet on his coffee table. He gave her an appreciative grin, and she kept eye contact with him as she started to rub herself over her panties, happy her period had been very short-lived this month.

She slid her underwear to the side and rubbed her slit before taking her fingers out and sucking them as Travis was trying in vain to wrap up his phone call. She heard him say, "I'll get back to you," before quickly hanging up the phone and walking to his office door to lock it.

Without a word, he was seated next to her, kissing her hard as he massaged in between her legs. Arching her back, she ground her pelvis against his hand and began to fondle the bulge in his pants. When they were both thoroughly aroused, she straddled him while unbuckling his belt and unzipping his pants. Sliding his cock out of his boxers, she slipped her panties down so they were only around one ankle and put him inside her. Rhythmically moving her hips back and forth as she fucked him, he pulled her mouth to his and kissed her deeply.

"I missed you last night," she whispered as she looked into his eyes while rubbing her clit against his pubic bone.

He groaned and held her hips as he fucked her hard from underneath. Ava threw her head back and spread her knees wide while he bucked wildly into her. When he slowed down, she took over, bouncing up and down on his cock as he frantically unbuttoned her shirt and pulled her tits out of her bra so he could bite and suck on her nipples. While feasting on her boobs, he reached under her skirt and began to expertly maneuver her clit around until she was in sensory overload and quietly moaning her approval. She slowed her bouncing as the orgasm crept from her toes to her pussy, and she came intensely on his cock. Once she climaxed, he flipped her onto her back, holding her feet together at his chest while he fucked her hard and fast until she felt his hot cum explode within her.

She loved how he felt when he burst inside her. The fact that he'd gotten tested for her so he could do that warmed her heart.

He stayed in her until their breathing calmed, then swiftly grabbed a bar towel from his minibar and cleaned her off before attending to himself. Pulling his pants back up, he sat down without zipping up while she put her panties back on and buttoned her blouse. Ava put her head in his lap and tenderly caressed and kissed his shaft over his underwear while he stroked her hair.

"To what do I owe the pleasure of your visit? Or was that just it?"

She hadn't planned on having sex with him in his office, but was not in the least bit sorry they had.

She smiled and continued fondling his half-erect cock. "Actually, believe it or not, I came here with the best of intentions. But for whatever reason, whenever I see you, getting naked seems to top my list of priorities."

He pulled her up onto his lap and sensuously kissed her before putting his forehead against hers. "You tend to have that effect on me as well."

She was relieved to hear him say the feeling was still mutual.

"I had lunch with a competing broker today. They made me an amazing offer and I was excited to tell you about it."

She proceeded to tell him the terms of what they proposed. Every single thing Travis thought of, she had already addressed and had an answer for.

"I think it's a great offer, Ava. When do you have to have an answer?"

"I told Frank I would let him know by Thursday at noon."

When she said the name *Frank*, he jerked his head and pulled back to look at her.

"Frank? Not Frank Harris?"

She nodded her head. "You know him?"

Travis unceremoniously removed her from his lap and leapt up before tucking his shirt back into his pants and getting himself properly situated. He paced back and forth, as if trying to come up with the right words and struggling, which was very uncharacteristic of him. Finally, he resorted to his tried and true lawyer mode and, unfortunately, that also included prick personality.

"Ava, they're using you. They think if they get the girl I'm sleeping with on their agent roster, I'll go easy on them with this lawsuit I'm about to file."

*Um, fuck you? Pretty sure I've earned this offer they presented and it has nothing to do with you.*

"Travis, they don't even know we're dating—or sleeping together. No one does. I think they asked me to join their team because I'm a damn good agent and would add value to their company."

"Don't be naïve. It wouldn't be that hard to figure out we're dating. Pay a P.I. five hundred bucks and he could probably even get pictures. Why else would they offer such an inexperienced agent that kind of deal?"

Ava stood up, not trying to hide how insulted she was. "Because I'm that fucking good," she said as she looked at him with disdain.

"Ava," he warned, "if you take this offer, we can't see each other until this case is over."

"Well, hopefully you can get it to trial fast then," she sneered as she picked up her purse and walked toward the door. How dare he give her an ultimatum like that?

She paused, giving him one last opportunity to make things right. He didn't, and she gave him her best *your loss* look before walking out the door.

Fortunately, she made it onto the elevator before tears started streaming down her face. Who was she kidding? It was definitely her loss.

# Chapter 16

*Travis*

Travis stood looking at the door Ava had just walked out of. Frankly, he was shocked by what had transpired. He knew he'd been an asshole to her, but never in a million years did he expect her to get up and walk out. He knew damn well that's what he deserved but right now, his pride had taken over all rational thought.

Good, she was starting to take up too much of my time anyway.

Except now thoughts of her were taking up even more of his time, and he slept like shit. He knew he'd made a mistake by letting her leave and not chasing after her, but he wasn't sure if he should try to fix it. He was not going to let her see how much control she had over him. Nor was he going to concede it to himself. Besides, her taking the job after he asked her not to spoke volumes about how she felt about him. He wasn't about to admit he had demanded—not asked—she not take it and almost left her no choice.

****

*Ava*

Ava met Charlie for lunch downtown the following day. She did her best to not look like she had been up all night crying. Travis hadn't come after her nor had he tried to get in touch with her. Not that she expected it; she had just really hoped he would. Maybe she should have told him she wouldn't take the job—left him with no doubt about how much he meant to her. Maybe he was right about the reason they made her such a great offer.

She knew in her heart he gave her the ultimatum so he could cool their relationship. She also knew he was not the reason Ridgeport Realty was trying to recruit her—his arrogance she normally found so incredibly sexy was now like a wet blanket. The reason they wanted her was not about him, and he could piss up a rope if he thought it was. Her anger about that helped her get out of bed and dressed the following morning.

While walking to the restaurant where she was meeting Charlie, she began to wonder why Charlie had wanted to meet with her. She suspected it had something to do with the fact she had lunch with his boss last week, and he wanted to capitalize on that. So when he revealed the real reason he had asked her to lunch, you could have knocked her over with a feather.

"Do you think it'd be weird if we went on an actual date?" he asked her after they'd finished their meal. It had been a pleasant lunch, both seemed to be comfortable and the conversation was lighthearted. Although when he asked her about Travis, she got a little knot in her throat when telling him they were just friends. Could they even consider themselves that anymore? When Charlie was assured of the platonic nature of Ava and Travis' relationship, he took that as a green light to pursue a date.

"Don't you think Trav—I mean Brad would have a problem with that?"

Charlie assured her he wouldn't. "After I saw you last week, I went home and told Brad about running into you.

When he didn't react, I waited until the weekend to ask him if he would mind if I asked you out. He said it was fine."

Ava was thoroughly confused and knew she was missing a big piece to this puzzle.

"Well that is weird because he called me Monday morning and asked me to dinner."

"He did what?" he asked incredulously before shaking his head. "That son-of-a-bitch. He's getting back at me for hitting on a girl he was dating. But in my defense, I didn't know he was dating her at the time. I'm sorry you're being put in the middle of this."

*What the fuck is it with everyone being so sure no one is pursuing me simply because I'm worth being pursued?*

"Well, I'm having dinner with him tomorrow night so I'll let you know if he really isn't okay with you asking me out."

"Are you at all interested in going out with me? I hated how things ended with you and Brad, and that I was even a part of it by being there. I've wanted to reach out to you but didn't think you would want to talk to me. I was so surprised you were happy to see me last Thursday, and it didn't seem like it was only because you wanted to hear about Brad."

No, she didn't want him giving her any updates on Brad. His boss, on the other hand...

She squeezed his hand before patting it. "Is it okay if I think about it?"

"How about this? There is a group of us going to the Wounded Warrior Ball next weekend. Maybe you could hang out with us, and we'll see what happens?"

*Shit.* She had almost forgotten about the ball. That was where she and Travis were going to first be seen officially in public together. She dared even say as a couple. Not anymore.

The thought of what might have been suddenly made her sad. Fortunately the reason they were no longer together continued to piss her off.

"That will be fun. Thank you."

*Now I need to find the perfect dress that says 'Sucks for you, Travis Sterling. I could have been on your arm tonight!'*

Operation Sex Kitten had a new goal and direction. She called her mom while walking to her car after lunch. "We need to go ball gown shopping!"

"Oh Ava, you haven't gotten your dress yet?" her mother scolded. "How many times did I ask you to go only for you to assure me you were going to take care of it on your own?"

"I know, Mom. It completely slipped my mind."

It hadn't really, but she was working so hard during the week to make sure her weekends were free to spend with Travis that she'd neglected to go look for one.

"Can you go later this afternoon? I don't have any clients so I'm free."

"Meet me at Delilah's at four o'clock," her mother replied.

*Come on, Delilah, work your magic!*

She'd gotten almost all of her formal gowns from Delilah's Dresses and had never been disappointed. This time was no exception. She found a beautiful sleeveless royal blue chiffon gown with a mermaid train that hugged her body and accentuated her petite frame. Her mother took a sharp breath in when Ava stepped onto the platform in front of the fitting room mirrors.

"Honey, this is the one. You look stunning. It's the perfect style and the perfect color. It's as if it was designed just for you."

She needed to feel beautiful and confident when she next saw Travis. This dress would help her do just that.

She bought the ideal accent pieces and three-and-a-half-inch heels. She had gotten better with the high heel thing, but she didn't want to push her luck with too high a shoe and fall face first right as she was walking by Travis.

At dinner with her parents that evening, she casually mentioned she was having dinner with Brad the next night. Her mother scowled and asked, "Why?" Her dad didn't react other than his set jaw. She knew he trusted her judgment and that she would not get involved with Brad again.

"He called me out of the blue on Monday and asked me to have dinner. I'm more curious than anything about what he wants." *Besides, it will help keep my mind off what Travis is doing.* Remembering what they were doing a week ago on Thursday, she was dumbfounded to think about how she went from feeling so content and in love to so miserable and alone in less than a week.

*All good things must come to an end.*

She stopped herself. *Why do they have to come to an end? Who the fuck made up that rule?*

Her mother graciously changed the subject. "Robert, your daughter is going to be the belle of the ball. We found her the perfect dress today."

Ava stood up to clear her and her parents' plates, kissing her dad on the cheek. "You better bring your gun, Pops. They're going to be lining up to dance with me," she teased.

Judge Ericson rubbed her upper arm. "I wouldn't doubt it, Bear. You're as beautiful as your mother." He narrowed his eyes at her. "You better be as picky as she is too."

She knew that comment was in direct reference to her having dinner with Brad tomorrow. She loved him for being both bothered by it but still trusting her to make the right choices.

"Don't worry, Dad. I know I deserve someone as wonderful as you. I'm never settling again." She kissed him on the top of his head then took the dishes to the sink.

Frannie didn't look as convinced.

**

Brad had texted her he wasn't able to get a dinner reservation until eight p.m. That actually worked out better for Ava because she had gotten used to eating late while dating Travis, as she stayed at work after hours during the week in order to free up her weekend to be with him.

He was already in the lobby waiting for her when she arrived. She'd taken care to look nice but didn't go all out, especially with the information Charlie had shared with her yesterday. He looked good, his typical California boy shining through. It was obvious from his tanned skin and sun-bleached hair that he'd been spending time surfing. He also knew how to lay on the charm, but it was funny what a different light she now saw it in. She wasn't the least bit interested in him anymore, something she never thought she would have felt just five weeks ago.

Even though he had a reservation, they still waited. She was thinking about how different it was from showing up somewhere with Travis, where people scurried to assist and accommodate him, when Travis and a drop dead gorgeous raven-haired beauty actually walked in. True to form, they were seated immediately. He hadn't even noticed her. She felt a lump in her throat and a pit in her stomach.

Brad noticed Travis, though, and urged Ava to go over and say hello. "Charlie said you two had lunch last week. I'd love an introduction, if you wouldn't mind."

Wild horses couldn't have dragged her over to say hello to Travis, especially when she saw the tender looks he was giving his date. Ava tried not to stare, but the woman was stunning. He had definitely traded up from her, that was for sure.

"He hates to be disturbed when he's eating," was the best reason she could think of to offer why she wasn't going to stop by his table.

As usual, all sorts of thoughts were racing through her head. Had he realized when he was with Ava that maybe he was ready to commit and fall in love, but it needed to be with someone more in his league than she was? Tears stung her eyes at the thought, but she conceded that was just the way the world worked.

Brad took her hand and tried to look into her eyes. "You are more beautiful than ever. I have missed holding you in my arms."

*Really? Those arms don't hold a candle to the ones I was in last week.*

The reality that she wasn't going to have that feeling of being safe and protected in those arms again made her eyes well again with tears. Brad must have thought it was over him because he seemed encouraged. When she gave him the hand squeeze and pat she had given his roommate yesterday instead of leaning in to kiss him, he looked confused.

"Brad, you will always hold a special place in my heart, but I think it's best if we leave things as they are."

"Give me a chance, Ava. Please? Let's go hiking this weekend. Remember how much we loved doing that?"

It was at that moment she realized she hadn't loved doing that—*he* loved doing that. They never did any of the things she loved doing. It was always about making him happy, and she had been a willing and eager participant so she had no one to blame but herself. Those days were gone.

Looking at him like she felt sorry for him, she said, "I really didn't love it. In fact, I haven't gone once since we broke up and don't miss it a bit."

She was leaving him nothing to work with.

"Well, we could go antiquing if you want."

*Antiquing? Where the fuck did he get I like antiquing?*

She wasn't going to give him an ounce of grace and replied in an almost annoyed tone, "I don't like to go antiquing! Why on earth would you think that?"

Damn, she missed how special Travis made her feel. Even if it wasn't real on his part, she'd take it any day over how this oaf was making her feel.

She had another epiphany. She was deserving of someone who made her feel special *and* it was real. A version of Travis Sterling who was in her league, perhaps.

This had been one enlightening, empowering, and depressing evening all rolled into one.

But Brad appeared to have decided he wasn't going down without a fight. When they were standing outside the restaurant about to go their separate ways (Ava realized Travis would never let her walk to her car alone at night), he grabbed her by her arms and kissed her hard on her mouth.

He had always been what she considered a good kisser, but the abruptness and the almost forcing his mouth on hers was not enjoyable, and she vigorously pushed him away.

"What are you doing?" she hissed. She stared at him angrily for a second before shaking her head and saying, "Not cool, Brad." Turning to leave, she was startled to see Travis waiting at the valet with Miss America, watching what had just transpired between her and Brad. Miss America said something to him, and he leaned over, put his arms around her shoulders, and kissed her temple.

*You know what, Travis? You can join Brad in a fuckoff party.*

Head high, she walked to the parking lot alone.

****

*Brad*

Brad stood there as she stormed off. *Well, that wasn't what I was expecting.* He had honestly thought getting her to go out with him again would be a slam-dunk.

He had realized right away there was something different about her. She was a lot more confident and didn't seek his approval. Not to mention, she seemed more beautiful than ever. When Charlie had talked to him about asking her out, he hadn't been the least bit jealous. When Charlie revealed he saw her when she was having lunch with Travis Sterling, Brad suddenly became a lot more interested. He'd been trying to get in with Carson, Burns, Sterling, and Cooper and thought maybe Ava would be able to help. Plus, when he was the one who took her on a few dates instead of his roommate, he could get even with Charlie for hitting on

Marie. Seeing other men in the restaurant appreciating Ava was giving him second thoughts about it being only a few dates. Hell, even Travis Sterling couldn't keep his eyes off her. He needed to figure out how he could best use this to his advantage.

# Chapter 17

*Travis*

Travis had seen Ava the second he walked into Evangeline's. Tara had called and asked him to dinner and, needing the distraction, he didn't think twice before telling her yes. Besides, she said she had something important to tell him and practically left him no choice. He was not expecting to see Ava, and it took his breath away for a second when he did.

She looked great, and the guy she was with seemed to suit her. They were both young, blonde and good looking. Still, it should have been him that was there with her tonight. It was all he could do to not go and beat the shit out of the guy when Travis saw her shoving him away as he kissed her, even though he was secretly thrilled she didn't want to kiss him. The look she gave Travis as she turned around was one he had seen the first night she met him when he was being difficult. Except this time the effect on him was different. Instead of being amused and annoyed like the night at the party, it hurt. Just like seeing her with another man had.

*What the hell am I going to do?*

Unfortunately for him, pride and panic were still the driving forces in his decision-making, but now a new alarming twist set in. *What happens if she finds somebody else?*

*Of course she is going to find someone else, you dumbfuck.*

\*\*\*\*

*Ava*

The night of the ball arrived, and Ava looked like an absolute knockout. She had paid to have her hair and makeup professionally done and was very pleased with how both turned out. As she stood appreciating her appearance in the mirror, she decided tonight she'd consider herself beautiful. That was going to come in handy when she made sure to say hello to the ball's title sponsor.

She met up with Charlie and his group of friends during the cocktail hour. The women were very friendly, and the men were the same, in a non-threatening way. The number of men and women was uneven so she knew they weren't all in pairs. She was trying to get a read on who was coupled with who, if any, and quickly figured out Jeff and Tracey were an item, even as they pretended not to be, and Nicole had the hots for Ryan. The rest of them seemed to just be friends. They were a fun group, but one in particular was being exceptionally attentive to Ava, even more so than Charlie. Matt Poulson was an engineer, and they seemed to have a lot in common as they talked around one of the high-top tables strewn throughout the lobby area where drinks and hors d'oeuvres were being served.

Ava looked at her watch. Ten after six. The bell for the receiving line was going to chime soon so she excused herself to the bathroom to check her hair and makeup. She hadn't seen Travis yet, but having not really mingled outside the small group, she wasn't surprised.

The bell chimed right as she finished reapplying her lipstick. Taking a deep breath in as she gave herself a once-over in the mirror, she thought, *here goes nothing.*

The group had graciously waited for her before making their way to the line. Frannie and Robert would be part of the receiving group, as well as Travis and other large sponsors and their spouses, high-ups in the WWP foundation, a couple of honored guests from the military, and those who had been helped through the project.

The third person in was a very handsome major general from the Marine Corp. When Ava got to him, he quietly sucked in his breath before smiling casually at her as he took her hand. Ron Thompson didn't take his eyes off her and moved his thumb over her hand before letting go. She simply gave him a smile and glanced up under her lashes at him to acknowledge the touch.

Two people over were her mother and father. Judge Ericson leaned over and kissed her cheek. "You look stunning, Bear," he whispered in her ear before pulling back and smiling appreciatively at his oldest daughter.

Frannie kissed her as well and gushed, "I don't think I've seen you look more beautiful."

Ava needed that because they were coming to the end of the line and Travis. With a jolt, she noticed the woman from the restaurant was his companion. Wearing a stunning red dress with thin sequined straps, her long black hair flowed loosely around her shoulders, and her lipstick matched her gown almost perfectly. She was even more beautiful tonight than the first time Ava saw her.

And she was pregnant.

Travis looked very dashing in his tuxedo. He had a red vest underneath his black jacket to match his companion's gown, his wide shoulders filling the suit out nicely.

The couple ahead of her had been making small talk along the entire line, a definite no-no but it had allowed her to chat with people and not be blamed for holding up the process, so Ava didn't care. The couple obviously didn't know Travis, and as he introduced himself, he put his arm around Miss America and introduced her as Tara Whitaker, then patted her belly and said, "and this is Travis Jr."

Ava felt the color drain from her face as she took her turn approaching Travis and Tara. The terrible hurt was written all over her face as she looked at him with tears in her eyes, barely acknowledging his companion. Neither said a word, and Travis seemed rueful when he finally looked her in the eye. Thankfully he was the last person in the line, and she hurried off to the bathroom, feeling like she was going to throw up.

**** 

*Travis*

Tara leaned over and whispered to Travis, "Why do I have a feeling you're going to regret whatever it is you just did, big brother?"

Travis watched Ava with her hand over her mouth walking quickly to the bathroom. "Already do," he muttered as he looked down, upset and ashamed at what he had done.

She had looked so amazing that Travis literally uttered "holy fuck" out loud under his breath when he saw her earlier. Never having seen her dressed up quite like that, he was awestruck at how beautiful she was as she stood alone at a high top table in the lobby where he was mingling with guests. He had been on his way over to say hello when a brown-haired man showed up to deliver a drink to her. The second she smiled at the guy appreciatively, Travis immediately felt a pang in his stomach. He remembered that look—she used to give it to him.

Jealousy had reared its ugly head once he saw her coming down the receiving line with the brown-haired man in tow. He wasn't thinking when he pulled his little stunt, and now he was full of regret.

\*\*\*\*

*Ava*

Ava made it to the restroom just in time before she lost the contents of her stomach. As the tears were streaming down her professionally made-up face, she managed to laugh, "Well, there went a hundred dollars." Her head was spinning. The woman was obviously more than six weeks along, so he must have been with her before he met Ava. Had they been briefly broken up? Was he seeing her while he was dating Ava? She couldn't fathom how he could have been seeing both of them at the same time—she had been with him for entire weekends. Unless he really didn't have those extra cases and was seeing Miss America during the week, he wouldn't have had any other time. That didn't make any sense. No, they must have been broken up, and when he found out about his impending offspring, that's when he decided to cool things with Ava.

She sat down in the little stall and pulled herself together.

Taking a deep breath, she whispered, "Life goes on, Ava dear. You know that as well as anyone."

Walking out of the stall and looking at her tear-streaked face in the mirror, she realized she had sort of ditched Matt as she dashed to the bathroom. Luckily she had refresher makeup in her clutch and was able to do a good job at fixing her face before heading back where the engineer was waiting for her in the lobby.

"Are you okay?" he asked, his voice full of concern.

Managing a meek smile, she said, "I think I might have had too much to drink on an empty stomach. I'm fine now."

They joined their group for dinner and she was determined to enjoy the company of this fun crowd. She pretended not to see Jeff indiscreetly grope Tracey and called Nicole over when Ryan joined the conversation she, Charlie, and Matt were having. The music started, and some of the girls made their way onto the dance floor. It wasn't a song Ava was particularly fond of, so she stayed where she was, talking with Charlie and Matt. It became a little awkward when a slow song came on, and the two men seemed to be in a Mexican standoff about who was going to ask her to dance when Ron Thompson took her elbow and said, "May I?" before leading her to the dance floor.

Ava never thought she could be a sucker for a man in uniform until tonight. The way this man looked in his was hot, and the way he carried himself was even hotter. If she thought Travis oozed masculinity, Ron Thompson was the very definition of it. His whole demeanor shouted he was in charge, and there was nothing he couldn't handle.

She guessed him to be in his early to mid-forties. He was very fit with brown hair, brown eyes, and his nose was a little crooked as if it had been broken one too many times, but it was his smile she found most attractive. It was infectious.

And yet, he wasn't Travis.

*Oh, the Travis who is here with his pregnant girlfriend not ten days after you stopped seeing him? That Travis?*

Ron brought her back to reality.

"I hope your date won't mind I'm dancing with you," he said as he moved her around the floor.

She knew that was his clever way of asking if either Matt or Charlie was her date, so she simply smiled and said, "I'm here with a group of friends."

His face didn't react, but he did seem to hold her a little tighter after her disclosure.

Ava caught sight of Travis and Tara dancing and quickly turned away. She couldn't bear to look at him with the mother of his child. She had never allowed herself to even imagine that with him because of his 'I'm not boyfriend or husband material' bullshit. He was husband, and apparently father, material—just not for her.

Ron glanced over to where she had hastily looked away from.

"Old boyfriend?" he inquired as he brought his gaze back to her.

"Ancient history," she replied grimly.

Ron seemed to be sizing up his dance partner's face after she said that. She knew there was hurt in her eyes that told him it was hardly ancient.

"He's a fool," he whispered in her ear as he pulled her even tighter to him.

Ava managed a weak smile and briefly put her head on his shoulder, as if to silently thank him for the compliment. He smelled nice.

Just then the song ended, and Ron escorted her back to her friends.

"Thank you for the dance," he said before turning and walking away.

If she hadn't been so upset over Travis and the bombshell he dropped, or if she wasn't so damn in love with him, she might have been interested in Ron Thompson, or even Matt Poulson. But right now, no one was ever going to measure up to Travis Sterling. Logically, she knew it was just going to take time to heal her broken heart but emotionally she questioned if getting over him was ever going to be possible.

Yet, what choice did she have?

The next slow song, Matt grabbed her hand before anyone else could and took her to the dance floor. The song wasn't even half over when she heard a deep voice say, "May I cut in?" It was Ron Thompson. Matt was obviously not happy about it, but he also knew it wouldn't be wise to start anything with a high-ranking marine, so he stepped aside.

Ron pulled her off the dance floor and onto the patio.

"I'm sorry to cut in like that, but I have to be going, and I wanted to say goodnight and tell you how much I enjoyed meeting you. And that I'm going to call you."

Ava smiled at his presumptiveness. "You don't even know my phone number."

"That's why you're going to give it to me," he stated rather matter-of-factly.

She paused for a moment and looked at him standing there in his dress uniform. She imagined he looked as good in civilian clothes.

"I don't always look like this, you know, all made up and hair styled. This isn't really me. The real me has her hair in a ponytail and nothing but mascara for makeup," she warned.

He smiled. "I think I'd like you like that even better."

With the caveat given, she gave him her number.

"I'm going to be out of the country for a few weeks, but I'm going to ask you to dinner when I return," he said as he put his phone back in his pocket after having entered her information into it.

She knew any other girl would be swooning at the thought of dinner with him. Yet to Ava, the idea seemed lukewarm at best. Still, she gave a smile as she told him she looked forward to hearing from him. He kissed her on the cheek then accompanied her back into the ballroom.

As he turned to leave, he hesitated and looked back at her. She stared inquisitively at him with her head cocked until he leaned down and kissed her quickly and gently on the mouth before whispering, "Take care."

Watching him walk off, she wondered, *What the hell just happened?*

On her way back to the group, she stopped at her parents' table. Frannie grabbed her hand. "I saw you with General Thompson!"

"Yeah, he said he's going to call me when he gets back in the country," Ava replied, still a little dumbfounded.

"He's a real catch, Bear. Very honorable and respected. He's going to continue to rise through the ranks of the Marine Corp."

Ava thought about their interactions. "He's definitely a gentleman," she conceded as she looked in the direction of his exit.

*Travis*

Frannie wasn't the only one who witnessed the exchange between Ava and Ron. Travis had watched them both leave and return from the patio. He wanted to go scoop her up and carry her away when he saw the general kiss her.

Only he didn't scoop her up. He didn't do anything.

How could he after what he'd done to her? The hurt look on her face as she came through the receiving line practically crushed his soul. How or why he didn't go after her, he'd never know. This was a night he would definitely like to get a do-over for.

He sadly conceded he'd blown it with her. From the Ridgeport Realty ultimatum, to not going after her at the restaurant when she walked to her car alone, to his royal fuckup tonight, he'd lost her. Ron Thompson was someone who deserved his sexy, adorable Ava far more than he did.

****

*Ava*

Ava smiled when she saw Jeff and Tracey making their way back to the table after disappearing for a while. She wasn't sure who they thought they were fooling, but maybe that made it more exciting for them.

As the evening wound down, the group invited her to an after party in one of the hotel suites they had rented. She considered going but decided against it. Both Matt and Charlie had had too much to drink and were starting to get a little handsy with her. Besides, she needed to go sit in her bathtub, listen to sad love songs, and cry.

On her way to her parents' table to say goodnight, she looked over and saw Travis watching her. She returned his gaze, trying to keep an emotionless look on her face, as if to say she had given up on feeling anything more for him.

How she wished that was the case as the tears started to flow down her face during the drive home.

# Chapter 18

*Travis*

Travis was in a particularly foul mood when he met with the other partners the following week and didn't appreciate being called out for not having looked at the curricula vitae of the potential new hires they were meeting that afternoon.

I've been a little fucking busy making money for this place, boys, not to mention losing the girl. Sorry I haven't done HR's job too.

He almost told them to go ahead and meet without him but thought better of it. The last thing he needed was a horrible hire he couldn't bitch about because he had decided to skip the final interviews.

As they sat in their comfortable, high-backed rolling chairs around the large modern glass and stainless steel table in the conference room, the applicants started making their way in, one at a time. Thank God his secretary was incredibly competent and had created files on each one, even if he hadn't bothered to look at them yet.

Contestant number four's name looked familiar. He knew he'd seen it or heard it somewhere before.

Brad Miller, how the fuck do I know that name?

When the good-looking blonde kid walked through the door flashing his million-dollar smile, he understood immediately how he knew that name, and his blood pressure started to rise a little. Through a clenched jaw, Travis managed to offer a condescending smirk when Brad told him specifically how great it was to finally meet him. He let the boy blather on about his credentials and what he could bring to the firm, never saying a word while the other partners nodded and offered encouraging words as Brad answered their questions.

The team looked impressed, and as Brad stood up to leave, Randall Cooper teased with, "I think it's safe to say you'll be hearing from us soon." Brad was smiling broadly, obviously pleased at what he'd just been told.

"We can tell him now," Travis interjected coolly from across the table. Leaning back in his chair with a look that suggested he was annoyed at having had his time wasted even talking to this applicant, he continued without remorse. "We're going to have to pass."

The great thing about the partners' hiring process was they had an unwritten rule—any new hire must be approved unanimously. Travis was going a little out of procedure in that they usually discussed it behind closed doors, sometimes bargaining and making concessions. There was no way he was going to make any compromises regarding Brad Miller, especially when the little prick had the nerve to drop Judge Ericson's name, thinking that would score him points. Apparently he wasn't aware Travis had written a letter on behalf of the judge's daughter when he bailed on her and their apartment lease last year.

When Randall looked surprised and dared say in front of the kid he was vetoing, "I don't understand," Travis didn't hold back.

Bringing up his lack of character, questionable ethics, and unabashed name dropping of a man whose daughter he screwed over a year ago and then almost forced himself on no more than a few weeks earlier, Travis made it crystal clear not only was there not a chance in hell Brad Miller would be working for Carson, Burns, Sterling, and Cooper, but he'd be lucky if he found a job anywhere in San Diego County. The normally tan kid was literally a pasty shade of white when Travis dismissed him from the conference room with a smirk and "Thanks for coming in."

Man, was he glad he hadn't missed today's interviews.

\*\*\*\*

*Ava*

True to his word, General Thompson called Ava two weeks later when he returned stateside. They had a few relatively flirty but nice conversations before he asked her to dinner, and she readily accepted. She was done pining for Travis, the futility of doing so finally having sunk in.

Stopping by her parents' after work on the evening she and Ron were supposed to have a late dinner, she saw Ginger running down the sidewalk, and neither Kay nor Travis were anywhere in sight. Getting out of the car, she called for the pup, who immediately came to her. She had missed those two furballs of his. Cuddling the freshly groomed girl, Ava asked her how she got out and acted as if she expected the dog to respond.

She put the poodle in the car and felt a pit in her stomach when realizing what she had to do next. Ringing Travis' doorbell with Ginger in her arms, she took a deep breath. She hadn't seen nor heard from Travis since the ball and wasn't sure who to expect to answer the door.

He opened the door barefoot and shirtless in a well-worn pair of Levis, and Ava felt her knees get a little weak. *Why the fuck does he have to be so damn gorgeous?*

"Hi," she said trying to sound friendly. "Look who I found wandering down the street!"

Travis had a look of surprise when he saw Ava standing at his door, and it seemed to take him a minute to register why she was there. He took Ginger from her while searching her face. Did he think she was going to yell at him?

"Thanks for bringing her back. I really appreciate it."

They stood there in awkward silence before Ava asked, "Do you know how she got out? Did Fred get out too?"

"I'm not sure." Then his face got an expression as if a lightbulb had gone on. He walked out the front door and over to the side gate that was wide open.

"Shit, I don't know how I could have been so careless," he chided himself. "Let me go see if Fred is in there. Can you come in while I look?"

The familiarity of being in his house was emotionally overwhelming. She missed everything about her time with him, from their conversations to their sexual exploits to how safe she felt when she fell asleep on his chest in his arms. Standing in his entryway brought back all the memories of how comfortable and happy she had been when she was there.

It wasn't fair. She was uncertain about what exactly wasn't fair—the fact that she got to have a taste of how wonderful being in love could be only to have it taken away, or the circumstances of how and why it was taken away. Either way, it was gone.

He came back from the kitchen with a grim look. "He's not here."

Immediately she offered to help look for him. She loved Fred and would be devastated if something happened to that dumb dog.

Why was there was a flash of disappointment on his face when she turned to walk to her car? She motioned with her phone. "I'll call you if I find him. Will you please do the same?"

He nodded. "Will do. Let me just grab a shirt and shoes and I'll head out too."

Sitting in her car for a second, Ava allowed herself to savor the small victory. She had done it! She'd been able to see Travis without crying or getting angry. Maybe there was hope for her yet.

Looking at the clock, she realized she had almost thirty minutes before she needed to go home and start getting ready for her date with General Thompson. Forty-five minutes if she showered fast and didn't shave her legs again.

After ten minutes of driving up and down the street, Ava realized how pointless that endeavor was and parked at her parents' so she could be out on foot looking for him. Finally, she saw him across the street from where she was looking. He was sniffing around a neighbor's yard when she called for him. He lifted his head upon hearing his name and looked around. She knew the second he had recognized her by the wiggle of his butt.

He started to race toward her when she let out a horrified scream as the car zoomed past. Ava felt like the next three seconds were in slow motion—the squeal of the brakes, the yelp of Fred, and her realization of what had happened.

She rushed frantically to the whimpering dog. It appeared he had been hit by the bumper, but not actually run over by the tire. But a bumper could still inflict a lot of damage on such a small dog. Knowing he was in pain and likely to bite anyone who picked him up, she urgently asked the young driver if he had a blanket or towel. Clearly distraught at having hit a dog, the kid silently shook his head no.

Ava stayed calm. She knew she didn't have time to go grab something to wrap Fred in before rushing him to the vet so, out of alternatives, she whipped her shirt over her head and gently placed it around Fred before gingerly picking him up. Running as carefully to her car as she could with him whimpering in her arms, she pleaded, "Hang on, little guy," the whole time until she reached her car.

She tried dialing Travis' number on her way to the nearest emergency vet but was shaking so bad from the adrenaline wearing off that it took her three attempts to hit the right button for him in her phone directory. Hoping she at least made sense and didn't sound like a lunatic, she tried to explain that Fred had been hit by a car, and she was on her way with him to the emergency animal hospital not far from his house.

Travis said he was on the outskirts of the neighborhood, so he could easily make it out the guard gate and into traffic. The red-light gods must have been on his side, because he pulled into the hospital just as Ava was getting Fred out of her car still wrapped in her shirt.

While she was wearing nothing above her waist but a bra.

They both rushed him in, and Ava began the frantic process of trying to explain what had happened before the staff whisked the dog away to be evaluated. The adrenaline had surged again when she was reliving the events while explaining what had happened, so it hadn't hit her yet that she was shirtless in the waiting room until Travis started unbuttoning his shirt.

*What the hell is he doing?*

He pulled it off his body and held it open for her to put her arms in. She wasn't processing why he had taken off his shirt until he gestured she was in nothing but her underwear. Feeling her face burn when she realized she had been in that state of undress the whole time talking to the veterinarian staff, she hoped when they unwrapped Fred they'd at least understand the reason.

With an embarrassed smile, she slid it on. It was still warm and smelled like him. Instantly getting goosebumps, it was all she could do to keep from taking a deep breath of the fabric in. She was still intoxicated by his scent.

And now he was shirtless again. *Goddammit, this isn't fair.*

Thankfully she realized she needed to call Ron and cancel their date, so she was able to temporarily escape by excusing herself to step outside and call him in private.

Unfortunately, that didn't take as much time as Ava had hoped, and she was back within a few minutes. Now the uneasiness set in. She sat in the uncomfortable waiting room chair with her feet not quite reaching the ground, painfully aware of how close her former lover with the naked, amazing chest was to her. As she recognized the pine cleaner and wet dog smell that comes with a vet clinic, she concentrated on the delicious aroma coming from the shirt she had on and began to absent-mindedly kick her feet back and forth under the chair, stopping when she realized what she was doing.

*No, that's not a red flag or anything that I'm uncomfortable.*

Rocking her body a little, she decided to at least attempt civil small talk. *This should be interesting.* Trying to think of a safe topic other than the weather, she came up with, "So, work still busy for you?"

Travis nodded. "More than ever. You?"

"Yes, I'm told it usually starts to slow down after school starts and fall is right around the corner, but I've never been busier."

He politely acknowledged what she said. "That's good." After an awkward hesitation, he asked, "Are you liking your new office?"

She didn't know how to respond. She didn't want to lie, but she also didn't want him knowing she'd turned the Ridgeport offer down, especially in light of recent developments in his procreation area. Thankfully the doctor came out to discuss Fred's condition before she had to answer. The dog was still in the touch-and-go state and was going to need surgery if there was any chance of saving him. Travis listened carefully, and when the tech brought him an estimate of the possible charges, he barely looked at it before signing.

The reality of possibly losing Fred was starting to sink in and she was scared. She didn't know how she would live with herself if he died.

Tears welled up in Ava's eyes, and she softly said, "I should have never called to him before I crossed the street. If he hadn't been racing toward me, he would have never run out in the road and..." She looked over at him, tears now streaming down her face and whispered with a sob, "I am so sorry, Travis."

He gently took her in his arms, holding her tight as she cried.

"Oh Ava. Baby, this isn't your fault. You didn't know." He stroked her hair while kissing the top of her head. "This was just a terrible accident. If anyone is to blame, it's me for leaving the gate open."

For a second, Ava allowed herself the luxury of being in his arms and pretending he meant to call her baby. She hadn't felt that secure since the last time he had held her, and now he was being so kind. The reality of their situation crept into her conscious, and she started to cry for another reason: she missed him. She felt guilty for not pulling away. She no longer belonged in his arms—someone else did—but allowed herself to be nestled there just a little while longer.

With a deep sigh, she moved away and gave him a smile. "Thanks."

He had the most tender look on his face and for a second, she thought he was going to kiss her when Major General Ron Thompson came through the automatic doors. Ava watched Ron as he did a quick assessment of the situation. Travis shirtless, Ava in an obvious men's shirt, her face tear-stained, and their body language screaming attraction.

She got up and greeted him, grabbing him by both hands. "You didn't have to come here! I am so sorry to cancel on you last minute!"

Ron smiled at the warm welcome. "Of course I was going to come. You sounded upset, I wanted to be here." He hugged her and added, "Don't give dinner another thought, we'll do it some other time. How's the dog?" Arms around Ava, he glanced at Travis out of the corner of his eye.

She knew he was wondering what was going on with the shirt situation. "I used my shirt to wrap Fred in. Travis was very kind and offered me his when he got here." As an afterthought, she realized she also needed to explain *why* Travis was there. "Fred is Travis' dog. He's in surgery now."

"Do you know how long he's going to be in surgery? We could quickly go get something to eat next door." With the corners of his mouth turned up, he looked towards Travis and added, "Hopefully they don't have a *no shirt* policy."

The look on Travis' face indicated he would rather give his left nut than go with the two of them to dinner. "You guys go ahead. I'm going to wait here. I'll call you if anything changes."

Ava frowned. "Are you sure? Do you want me to stop and get you a shirt?"

"Yeah, actually I would appreciate that. Do you remember the security code?"

Did she remember the security code? Of course she remembered the code!

"I think so," was her response. "If I don't, I'll call you."

They decided to take care of getting Travis dressed before they grabbed a bite. Ron waited in his four-wheel drive in the loop in front of Travis' house while she ran inside. While locating one of his favorite Stanford shirts, she couldn't help but notice there were no feminine toiletries or clothing anywhere in his bedroom, bathroom, or closet. In fact, it looked exactly like the last time she'd been in it. She was pretty sure that was even her toothbrush still in the cup.

She thought it was odd but was in too big a hurry to dwell on it as she rushed back to the truck.

Ron went into the Chinese restaurant next door while she dashed in to give him his shirt. When she handed it to him and said, "I know it's your favorite," with a smile, he hugged her and kissed her hair, taking his time letting her go. "Thanks."

"Any word?" she asked when he finally released her.

He shook his head, "Not yet."

"I'll be back as soon as I can," she promised as she retreated towards the door. "Call me if he gets out of surgery."

It was a good thing that she was constantly moving because if she would have taken thirty seconds to think about what was happening with her, Ron, and Travis, her head might have started spinning.

"Any news on Fred?" Ron graciously asked as she slid into the booth across from where he had already been seated.

"Not yet." She shook her head and fought back tears again thinking about her little furry friend fighting for his life.

Ron reached across the table and grabbed the top of her hand. "It's going to be all right," he stated authoritatively. The way he said it, she knew he was used to his orders being carried out. Except these weren't orders he was able to give. Still, she appreciated the sentiment and smiled.

"There's one thing I can't figure out though," he said with a cocked head.

Ava looked at him, waiting for him to continue.

"What were you doing with your ex-boyfriend's dog in the first place?"

His confusion was understandable, and she knew she owed him an explanation and proceeded to tell him the story of Travis living around the corner from her parents, her finding Ginger, learning Fred was missing, and offering to help find him, only to have him hit in front of her. Tears streamed down her face as she recalled picking the dog up and carrying him to her car.

Ron moved round the table and slid into the booth next to her. Putting his arms around her, he held her tight.

"Don't cry," he murmured against her hair. "He's going to pull through this. Just watch, he'll be good as new in no time."

Ava looked at him and tried to laugh while she was crying, wiping her wet face with her napkin. She liked how his arms felt around her, and that only served to confuse her, given how she was still feeling about Travis earlier. Although it also pleased her in that it gave her hope there could be life after Mr. Sterling.

Thinking about her conversations with Anne and her best friend's insistence she was going to need a rebound fling to get over Travis made her sad. She knew she could care for Ron if their timing had been different. He was so much better than a rebound fling. Why couldn't the ball have been two months ago, before she ever even met that gorgeous lawyer and daddy-to-be?

One more thing to add to the *not fair* column.

Their dinner was as comfortable as their phone conversations had been throughout the week. He shared he was going overseas again at the end of the month and wouldn't be back until December, but asked if they could Skype while he was away. She frequently talked to her brother Steven over video chat so was comfortable with the idea and easily agreed.

Then she thought about the things she knew Anne did over video chat with men and backtracked.

"You mean actually talking, right?"

He almost seemed insulted at the question, as though she was questioning his honor. "Yes, of course. What else did you think I meant?"

She grinned when she shook her head and replied, "Nothing else. I just wanted to be sure."

\*\*\*\*

*Ron*

When the waitress came to collect their plates, Ava ordered a dinner to-go for Travis. Ron was still uncertain what to think about her and Travis' relationship, and while he loved she was thoughtful by getting Travis food, it didn't do much in convincing him the two really were 'ancient history' as Ava had said they were at the ball.

The general knew there was still a spark between Ava and Travis. Travis had a pulse; Ron couldn't fault the man. He wasn't sure how he felt about the possibility of being Ava's consolation prize though.

They came back to the animal hospital to learn Fred was almost through with surgery. When Ava handed Travis the takeout, he looked at her affectionately and Ron knew he would have hugged her, had the general not been standing right there watching.

"Oh my gosh, I forgot silverware! I'll be right back!" Ava proclaimed and was out the door before Travis could protest he didn't need it.

The two men sat down in uncomfortable quiet until Ron finally broke the silence.

"I'm headed overseas again for a few months," he offered.

Travis nodded his head. Maybe a little too enthusiastically. "Thank you for your service to our country."

"Thank you for all you have done for our returning soldiers who need help. We need more people like you."

Travis shrugged and explained he knew how important it was to take care of our serving men and women, even after they've taken off the uniform.

Ron sat quietly contemplating, then stood up and shook Travis' hand.

"I return in December. If you haven't done something by then, you should know, I'm going to do everything in my power to make her mine." With that, the major general turned on his heel and walked out, meeting Ava at the door to say his goodbye.

Travis watched the man kiss Ava and murmured out loud, "I wish it was that easy."

As Ava was walking back into the veterinarian's clinic, Ron walked out the sliding doors.

"I'm going to be going now," he said with a soft smile.

The look of disappointment on her face made him reconsider what he had told Travis. He might not be able to wait until December after all to woo her.

"Thanks for being so understanding." She paused sheepishly. "About everything. I know canceling dinner to be with the shirtless ex-boyfriend might be asking a little too much of someone on a first date. I can't blame you if you don't want to see me again."

He merely shook his head and gave a smile that said what he was thinking. *You're right, that was a lot to take in, but you haven't scared me off yet.*

She gave an apologetic grin and continued, "I really am sorry about dinner. I was looking forward to it. Can I make it up to you?"

Ron liked her, he had no doubt about that, but after seeing Travis and her together tonight, he knew there was unfinished business between the two, and he wanted her to get that figured out before he started pursuing her. When she was with him, he wanted her with *him*, not thinking about someone else. Then there was the matter of being gone for over two months.

The general looked thoughtfully at her for a second before responding. "Tell you what, if you're available in December when I get back, I'll let you make it up to me then."

When she apologized yet again, he couldn't tell if the look on her face was disappointment or guilt. Touching her cheek with the back of his hand, he leaned over and kissed her gently on the mouth.

"I really do understand," he murmured with his face inches from hers.

She didn't break his stare when she thanked him again. "I really am disappointed we didn't go out on a proper date," she replied softly.

*Dammit, woman, don't tempt me.*

Just then, the automatic door opened to reveal Travis standing in the doorway, and he called, "He's out of surgery," before turning around and causing the doors to close shut again.

Ava hesitated before going inside.

"Will you at least call me before you leave?" she asked hopefully.

He gave her a smile before answering. "Count on it."

# Chapter 19

*Ava*

The vet assured them Fred was going to make a full recovery, and Ava felt an immediate sense of relief, instinctively wrapping both arms around Travis' bicep and squeezing while she leaned her head briefly against his shoulder.

"Thank goodness," she exclaimed.

He leaned over and kissed her head while asking the doctor, "Can we see him?"

"Just for a minute. He's still pretty groggy, and I don't want him to get too excited. Let's see how he does tonight, and maybe he can go home the day after tomorrow."

After seeing Fred and being reassured he was going to be okay, Ava started making her way slowly toward the exit while walking backwards and gesturing to Travis' shirt she still had on.

"Thanks again for this. I'll get it back to you as soon as I can."

He waved his hand dismissively. "No rush. Thank you for getting me dinner. That was so thoughtful of you."

Ava smiled. She didn't know what else to say to him. Now that Fred was in the clear, her mind started to work again. She realized how incredibly hurt she still was by his baby news, and the extremely shitty way he had sprung it on her.

She turned to leave when he blurted out, "Do you want to go grab a drink?"

*Is he fucking for real?*

She looked at him with a bit of disdain now. He was off the market and not by a flavor of the month, by the mother of his child. He shouldn't be asking her to have a drink with him.

Frankly, she was surprised and a little disappointed. That seemed very out of character for the Travis she thought she knew.

****

*Travis*

He immediately realized that was the wrong thing to ask merely by her facial expression. He had allowed himself a glimmer of hope based on how she had touched him and let him hold her earlier. The coldness of her simple one word answer *no* reduced him to feeling like a dirtbag.

He had been thinking all night about everything he had done wrong to not be the one with Ava. Holding her petite body for that brief period of time less than an hour ago felt perfect. She was made to fit in his arms, on his chest and in his bed next to him.

*How could someone as smart as I proclaim to be have fucked this up so badly?* He wanted to tell her about Tara being his sister but couldn't figure out how. How did he say, *Oh hey, I'm a total asshole and made that shit up about me being a daddy. I'm really only going to be an uncle. And by the way, I am in love with you.* You'd think he could find the words, given what he did for a living, but it seemed when it came to her, he had been at a loss lately—at least for the right ones anyway.

Shamefaced, he replied, "Okay, I just thought we could toast Fred's recovery."

She shook her head and once again replied with just, "No."

They stood in silence for a second before she frostily said, "Goodnight, Travis. I'm very glad Fred is going to be okay." And she left.

He needed to talk to her—now. He'd rather she think him a shit for lying than a scumbag cheater. Running after her, he called her name. She turned around with an annoyed look but waited for him to catch up.

"Can I just have five minutes? Please? I need to talk to you."

**** 

Ava

She was taken aback by his pleading tone. She'd only heard that when he was teasing her but never seriously, and the way he said it, it was evident he was serious. Motioning to the bench on the sidewalk, she situated herself so she was angled toward him, legs tucked to the side, and her hands fidgeting in her lap. *What on earth is this about?*

He sat beside her, leaning forward with his elbows on his knees, fingers entwined between his legs. He was obviously trying to figure out what to say to her. Finally, he took a deep breath, sat up straighter, and faced her.

"The night of the ball..." He paused.

Yes, she remembered that awful night but didn't say anything, just waited for him to continue.

He started again. "The night of the ball, I wasn't honest with you."

*What did he mean he wasn't honest with me? We didn't even speak to each other.*

"Tara Whitaker." He paused again.

*What about her? Spit it out, man!*

"Tara is my sister. She is, of course, not pregnant with my child. I made that up to be spiteful."

Suddenly the earth seemed to be spinning too fast for Ava, and she felt nauseous as she tried to process what he had told her. Why would he have done such a cruel thing? He had devastated her with that story, and she felt the tears welling up in her eyes.

"What a horrible thing to do," was all she could manage to whisper.

"Ava, I know, and I'm so sorry." He tried to hold her hands, but she snatched them away. "I don't have a good excuse. I was jealous, and I'm an asshole."

Opening her mouth to speak, then closing it again, not knowing what to say, she looked at him as if she readily agreed with that assessment. He *was* an asshole.

She sat for a moment, staring straight ahead, and finally muttered in a low voice, "I can't believe you did that to me," then looked at him again, anger flashing in her eyes now instead of tears.

"I never meant to hurt y—"

She cut him off right there. "Bullshit. That's exactly what you meant to do. You knew just how to hurt me, and you did it. That practically destroyed me."

"Yeah, you've seemed really destroyed with your marine and all the other men you've been out with," he snarked.

"Screw you, Travis," she said as she got up and started walking toward her car.

Travis followed her this time and grabbed her arm. Ava tried to shrug him off, which only served to make him grab both her arms and shake her a little.

"I'm sorry! Tell me what to do to make it right, and I'll do it!"

"Go to hell," she seethed and tried to break free of his hold.

Rather than let her go, he brought her closer to him. "Baby, I wish I could take it back. I hate that I hurt you."

She was in a state of turmoil, furious at what he had done but oh-so-aware of his body touching hers. Her brain was sending alternating signals to the rest of her. Overwhelmed by the conflicting emotions, she simply started to cry.

Travis enveloped her in his arms, and when she looked up at him, he brought his mouth swiftly down on hers, trying to make up for a lost month as his lips devoured hers. Without hesitation, she returned his kiss and felt a potpourri of emotions wash over her as his tongue sought hers out, as if to offer its own apology. God, she loved how it felt being in his arms. His touch, his smell, his taste, his kiss... it was all intoxicating.

*Ava, he hurt you on purpose, and you're kissing him like he should be rewarded.*

Bells, whistles, and alarms started going off in her head. Suddenly, she broke from the kiss and pushed him away.

"I can't do this Travis," she sobbed as she ran to her car.

He didn't chase after her this time, just stood in the parking lot where she left him and simply called out, "Ava, please don't go."

Managing to unlock her car through her tears, she was still sobbing when she started the engine and hoped not to hit anything as she pulled out of the parking lot.

Instinctively, she started driving towards her parents' house, then realized they were probably already in bed. Anne was on a date and Ava didn't want to interrupt, yet she didn't want to be alone right now. She'd had a few lunch dates with Tracey, the girl from the WWP ball, but decided their friendship was still too new to be confiding something like this, so with a sad sigh, she started driving home.

*I need more friends.* She called her brother Steven, not caring he was three hours ahead of her, but hung up when she got his voicemail. Minutes later, her phone pinged with a text from him inquiring what was up.

*Doesn't anyone talk on the phone anymore*? This was far too complicated to explain via text, so she wrote back, *Can you call me?*

His reply of, *Tomorrow okay*? led her to believe he probably wasn't alone, and the fact of the matter was there was nothing he could do from three thousand miles away anyway except listen, so she responded that was fine.

Throwing her keys on the kitchen counter as she walked in the door, her emotions were all over the place. She was still angry but was also hurt, and even more than that, confused. His revelation he had made up going to be a father and let her languish for almost three weeks infuriated her. Yet, it was also a relief. However, it did not change why they were initially separated—not only his apparent lack of faith in her abilities, but his not coming after her weighed heavily on her mind. He hadn't thought she was important enough to fight for.

That realization had been very humbling and caused her to have a lot of self-doubt over the month following. The night he came home early and took her on his kitchen counter, she had been sure things had changed between them. When he carried her to his room and made love to her repeatedly and passionately, she would have been willing to bet anything he was in love with her. She knew even though she didn't say the words to him, she had left him with no doubt she was madly in love with him.

*That's what scared him, you idiot.*

Over the last month, that reel had been replayed over and over in her head, and she chastised herself each time she got to the part where she had been too forthcoming and open regarding how she felt about him.

Her hands on the back of the counter barstool, she shook her head vehemently. No! She didn't want a relationship like that, one where she couldn't be herself for fear it would scare the man away. What did it say about how Travis felt about her if knowing she was in love with him caused him to make up reasons to flee?

No, she had done some things wrong in their relationship, especially overestimating his feelings about her, but being honest about how she felt towards him was not one of them.

**** 

*Travis*

Travis stood in the parking lot and watched Ava drive off. Pride started to rear its ugly head before he suddenly had the realization it was his pride that had gotten him into this situation to begin with. Pride and fear.

He thought about Ron Thompson's disclosure. Ron was going after her when he returned home in December and Travis almost conceded right there to the man. Yet he couldn't. Maybe Ron Thompson really was the better man, but at that moment he realized he would regret it for the rest of his life if he didn't at least try to get her back. They were made to be together. He might not be a better man than the general, but he was convinced he was the better man for Ava.

Her front door pushed open when he knocked on it. She hadn't made sure it was latched behind her when she came in.

She jumped with a start when she saw him in her doorway, but she didn't say anything as she looked at him.

Her eyes were red from crying, and Travis felt like a shit for being the cause of that. He didn't know how to express with words how sorry he was, so he held her gaze as he slowly walked towards her. She didn't flinch or pull away as he cupped her face in his right hand. Instead, she closed her eyes and rubbed her cheek against his palm while kissing his wrist.

He was still staring at her when she opened her eyes, desire now replacing his previous look of apology. Taking his hand, she led him into her bedroom, where she started unbuttoning the buttons on his shirt, which she was still wearing, her eyes on him the entire time.

"Ava, I—"

She put her fingers to his lips to silence him while she shook her head. "Not tonight. I don't want to think tonight. I just want to feel. Just for tonight."

He groaned as he grabbed her face in both his hands, kissing her passionately, and he felt her completely surrender to his touch. Ridgeport Realty, his sister Tara and the ball, the hurt feelings, none of it mattered tonight. The only thing that mattered was their need for each other.

She closed her eyes as his mouth consumed hers, and let out a little whimper when he broke their kiss to sensually caress her neck with his lips. She arched her back as he made his way to her chest, his fingers entwined and tugging on her hair. She moaned when his tongue flicked over her stiff nipples then drew his head closer when he began to suck on them.

Pulling his head to her face and urgently looking him in the eye, she pleaded, "I need to feel you inside me. Please? Make love to me."

He wanted to make love to her, yet also thought about all the things he still wanted to do to her body. Taking comfort knowing they had all night, he reluctantly pulled away and took off his shirt before unbuttoning his jeans and sliding them off, then watched in amazement at how quickly she removed her clothes and laid on the bed waiting for him, her body beckoning him to hurry.

He crawled up over her until he reached her mouth. The minute his skin touched hers, he felt her get goosebumps from head to toe. He was amazed at how much he had missed her in the month they had been apart. Her body was warm, her familiar apple blossom hair providing a sense of comfort as well as desire, and when she clung to him, willing him to penetrate her, he let out a groan.

He wanted her more than he'd ever wanted a woman in his life, and it took every ounce of his willpower not to slide his cock inside her drenched pussy.

Laying on top of her, his face inches from hers, he whispered, "My test results are still valid. I haven't been with anyone else."

She closed her eyes and nodded. He knew she'd heard him but it was like it wasn't registering as she hungrily thrust her hips against his. She opened her eyes when she finally realized he was waiting for her to validate there wasn't a need on her part for a condom.

"I haven't been with anyone either," she said breathlessly, still straining her mound against his erection.

Satisfied (and secretly delighted), he kissed her mouth while moving his cock against her sex and pushing slightly. She was so tight. If he'd had any doubt about her being intimate with the general, that completely erased it.

The sensation as he filled her made them both moan, and she spread her legs wide to welcome him in. He held her close, kissing her and sucking her lips as she got used to him. Her knees up and on either side of him, they began to move in sync, her back arching as he kissed her neck and massaged her breasts. When he brought his face back to within inches of hers, she closed her eyes while kissing him everywhere her lips could touch, her arms wrapped around him and clinging to his back as he rocked into her. Moaning with every steady thrust, she lowered her hands to his ass, as if trying to push him deeper inside.

Travis loved how she felt underneath him, his arms around her tight body as he kissed and tasted her. He had missed her so much and was somewhat stunned she was actually naked in his arms. Had anyone told him this morning that he would be making love to Ava tonight, he never would have believed it. Watching her react to his touch and feeling her so in the moment with him made his dick hard as a rock. He relished the taste of her skin against his lips, the feel of her touch, and the look on her face as he slowly and sensually slid himself inside her warm, wet pussy.

While looking into her eyes as he moved in and out, twice he almost told her how much he missed her, and once almost told her he loved her. He didn't think either would be well received based on her not wanting to think, just feel. Instead, he told her how good her body felt, and how much he loved making love to her.

He raised up so he was stiff-armed as he started fucking her deeper and faster. Her whimpers encouraged him on as he breathlessly whispered, "Yeah, baby."

Sitting back on his knees, he put her ankles on his shoulders while he picked up the pace even more. Fuck, now he was going to come, and he wasn't ready. He pulled out and kissed her calves and ankles while regaining his composure. He spread her legs wide and began to rub his member in circles around her clit, making her arch her back and silently moan *Oh* with her eyes closed. Sliding his manhood back into her pussy, he used one of her legs for leverage as his fingers took over for his cock on her clit.

Her whimpering and quiet moans were replaced with heavy breathing and cries of, "Oh my God!" as he began to move in and out of her hard and fast. He knew she was close to orgasm when she instructed, "Oh yes, right there. Oh my God, don't stop! Right there!" Expertly polishing her clit while his own impending climax approached, he started moaning when she went still and curved up off the bed with a silent cry, then gasped for breath as her body shuddered. Using both hands now to hold her legs, he plunged with five more deep thrusts before filling her pussy with shot after shot of his thick cream, grunting with each spurt.

Breathing heavy and sweating, he collapsed on top of her, kissing her while hugging her close, as if she might go away if he didn't.

Pressing his forehead against hers and looking into her eyes, he wanted to tell her so many things but was satisfied, for the moment, at the words silently exchanged when she looked back at him.

As he rolled off of her onto his back, she got up to get a towel to clean off and brought him back one, the reversal of their roles in that department striking him as funny for some reason as she crawled back into bed with him. He was anxious for another go but needed to recoup and thought about fingering her to another orgasm in the meantime. Instead she assumed her position on his chest and held him tight while listening to his heartbeat. Fuck, he loved having her there and was about to tell her that, but she raised her head while shaking it no and put her finger to his lips.

"Not tonight."

He knew what she was doing. Tonight she wasn't going to think. Tonight she was going to lie there in his arms like that's where she belonged. Everything else she'd deal with tomorrow. And that's what worried him.

**

Travis woke in the middle of the night, happy to find himself in Ava's bed with her nestled in next to him. *It wasn't a dream.*

The light from the full moon was shining in through her window, and he found himself studying her while she slept. Her features were soft, and her blonde hair almost looked white in the moonlight as it was spread out over his chest. While he watched her breasts rise and fall with each relaxed breath, he couldn't help but look farther down at the rest of her naked body.

Looking at her tiny frame next to him, he had only one thought—she belonged there. Surely she had to know that, or at least feel it too. She had to know in his arms was the safest place she could ever be. He'd always protect her and care for her.

And love her.

Except he hadn't. He'd been a completely jealous asshole, and he couldn't be more sorry.

He'd known since the night in his kitchen he was in love with her, and it had scared the shit out of him at the time. Realizing that losing her scared him a thousand times more, he had to make things right with her. He also knew that night in the kitchen she was in love with him, and that probably scared him even more. She didn't hand that out like it was candy on Halloween. Being loved by her meant something, and right now he was hardly worthy of it, if she even still loved him at all. He had to make her love him again.

Closing his eyes, he breathed in her hair and wrapped his arms around her. He couldn't lose her. It simply wasn't an option.

He hadn't realized it, but he had been kissing her temple repeatedly and hugging her tight as he was lost in his thoughts. When she sleepily looked up at him and smiled her tender smile, he was overwhelmed with his feelings for her.

"Ava," he said as he kissed her hair again. "I lo—"

She raised her head and put her fingertips to his mouth. "Please, Travis."

If she wouldn't let him say the words, he was going to show her. Sliding his arm out from under her, he sat up and leaned over her body, where he kissed her softly on the lips before sucking her neck right below her ear. Groaning, she closed her eyes, and he moved back to her face, where he tenderly kissed her eyelids before moving to the other side of her neck.

When she opened her eyes and looked at him, a thought jolted through him like a lightning bolt. *What if tonight is Ava's way of saying goodbye?* God, he hoped not. If tonight was Ava's farewell to him, he was going to at least know he had treasured every inch and second.

His lips trailed down to her chest above her breasts, where he lightly licked and sucked while his hands moved up and down her sides. He eventually made his way to cup her tits and squeeze them lightly. His mouth found her nipples, and he took his time attending to each one. Over and over he sucked on them and gently bit down, causing her to gasp and hold his head closer to her.

She started pressing her mound against him, and her hands sought out his dick to fondle it. Grabbing both her wrists in one hand and putting them over her head, he murmured in her ear, "This is about you right now, baby. Just relax and let yourself enjoy how good I can make you feel."

Her loud moan of "Ohhh," was immensely satisfying, and he continued where he left off with her tits. Sliding down to her belly, he kissed every inch of her flat stomach and spent an extended amount of time where the waistband of her panties would lay, if she were wearing any, and not going any lower. The tease was driving her crazy, and he could smell how wet she was.

He slid between her legs, bypassing her pussy and stopping at her knee, where he sensually sucked her skin before moving his hands up her thighs and rubbing the inner part of her leg that started forming her body's V.

Arching her back and moaning in approval, she tried moving her sex against his hands as he began working his mouth up her legs to meet where his hands were working. Her juices had trickled down her inner thighs, and he took his time licking her skin clean. She was in torturous, teasing heaven, and Travis could feel the heat generating from between her legs. When he finally moved his hand between her slit to rub her up and down, she moved her head to the side and inhaled sharply, then exhaled in a slow groan, finally achieving some satisfaction from his teasing touch.

He licked her outer lips all over and began sucking on them while running his tongue along her labia taking great care to avoid contact with her clit. When he finally let his tongue flick her, she bucked her hips into his mouth and loudly moaned, "Ohhhh yeessss," sounding like a tire losing air.

Pulling her hood back, he began moving his tongue like a vibrator against it while inserting a finger into her pussy and curving it up, looking for her G-spot. Her shallow breaths and thrusting hips let him know he had found it. She started moaning while his tongue assaulted her erect clit, and his fingers fucked her at a fast pace.

When she grabbed the back of his head and shoved his face into her crotch as she cried out, he felt her wetness all over his fingers as she came. Raising his head, he simply smiled and put a finger to her lips, which she hungrily sucked while looking him in the eye.

Groaning, he closed his eyes, imagining his cock was in place of his finger in her mouth, and moved up to lay beside her and hold her close. He smiled a little smile, loving that he knew how to please her, and was determined to make her come and come again this go-round. If he was going to compete for her, he was going to use the fact he knew what turned her on to his advantage, and at least give Major General Thompson a run for his money.

****

*Ava*

Ava lay in his arms and swore she was in ecstasy as the afterglow of her orgasm washed over her. His scent, his warmth, his touch... what he had just done to her, it was all wonderful. She had been tired of feeling hurt and just wanted to stop the pain. Making love to him wasn't going to solve anything, but it was making her feel better, at least for tonight.

She was straddling his right leg, masturbating her wet pussy against his muscular thigh as she burrowed her face into his neck, when she had an intense need to have his cock in her mouth.

As she began to slide down his leg while kissing his chest, he tried to stop her, whispering, "No Ava. Baby, this is about you."

This time when she said, "Please, Travis," it took on a whole new meaning, and he relented as she insistently worked her way down his body.

She had wanted to tease him as much as he had teased her but didn't have the willpower. She needed him in her mouth and eagerly put his cock between her lips to suck and stroke him with her tongue.

"Oh, Ava!" he groaned while looking down and watching her pleasuring him.

She looked up from between his legs and smiled while she circled her tongue over his balls. Throwing his head back and groaning, he ran his fingers through her soft blonde hair as she sucked each one gently. Her mouth made its way back to his shaft, and she took long strokes up and down it with her tongue before taking him back into her mouth. Sucking his tip like a lollipop and circling her tongue around his hole, she murmured, "Mmm," while squeezing his balls.

She loved how he tasted, and every now and then she could recognize herself from their earlier lovemaking session. She wasn't in a hurry to escalate what she was doing, wanting to savor the experience, unsure what tomorrow was going to bring them.

Every time he tried to touch her, she would move away, concentrating solely on him. Except it seemed all he had in mind was concentrating on her. After only a few minutes of her sucking, licking, and tasting at her leisure, Travis attempted to feast between her legs again. However, when he tried to move her, she wasn't budging from her position. He swiveled her around, laying her across his body, her legs spread, and her pussy in his face while she continued to work on his cock.

He ran his hands over her butt before sliding them to down massage her inner thighs, but returned to her backside. He took his time massaging and squeezing it, while groaning, "Fuck, I've missed this ass!"

He spread her apart and began to lick her with short, shallow strokes up and down, then side-to-side, in between sucking on her clit. When he added darting his finger in and out of her, her rhythm on his cock was disrupted, and she laid still, enjoying letting him lap her up. She felt him smile and knew he was feeling cocky because he still remembered just what to do to turn her on.

Grabbing her ass, he slid her down so her wet slit was right on his mouth and grabbed two handfuls of her cheeks to pull her wide open, murmuring, "Such a wet, pink little pussy," before burying his face between her legs. He was loud with his slurping, sucking, and fingering, and provided a stimulating commentary while doing so.

"You are soaked, baby."

She couldn't deny that. He had a way of doing that to her.

"Do you like it when I fuck you with my tongue?" he asked while darting it in and out of her.

All she could do was mewl. "Oh yes."

He pulled his mouth away and slid one finger in while observing, "Such, a tight, perfect pussy." She was drenched, and he began to assault her clit with his mouth, flicking his tongue fast over her while shaking his head back and forth.

Her gasps of pleasure only spurred him on.

"Mmmmm, you taste so good," he said as he returned to tongue fucking her while maneuvering her lips and clit with his fingers.

Her moans indicated she was close.

"Oh that's it, baby, come for me. Come all over my face," he whispered as she started to grind against him. "Let me taste how good it is."

He increased his speed and pressure in between her legs. Soon she cried out, "Oooohhhhh fuuuuuuuuck!" as she climaxed on his tongue, and he greedily slurped it up.

She moved her body around so she was directly on top of him; her tits mashed against his stomach as her head lay on his chest while she basked in her post-orgasm euphoria. She was cooing with contentment when she slid him inside her puffy, wet pussy.

"Oh baby, I love feeling your cock inside me," she whispered huskily as she began to move up and down on him.

"I love your sweet pussy," he continued. "Can you hear how much you love it when I'm in you?"

The sloshing sounds coming from her were undeniable, and she was still incredibly turned on.

"You make my dick so damn hard," he growled as he started to firmly fuck her from underneath. Ava gasped at how much she loved being taken by him, his strong hands on her hips holding her still while he swiftly penetrated her. When she looked lustfully at him, he groaned and grabbed her face to pull her in and kiss her. Moving one hand in her hair behind her head, he wrapped his other arm around her middle, squeezing her against him before resuming fucking her.

\*\*\*\*

*Travis*

Reaching up to bring her mouth to his again so he could continue kissing her, he wished he could last all night as he watched her face while thrusting deep into her. He loved her and never wanted her to leave his arms. She belonged with him; certainly she had to know that?

Taking over the lead, Ava began to ride him seductively like a sexy cowgirl, rolling her hips as she moved up and down on him, and he reached up to massage her tits while she threw her head back. She was so unbelievably sexy the sight of her alone could have made him come; sliding in and out of her wet, slippery pussy was simply a bonus. But, he had a mission to accomplish—getting her to come again during this session, so coming now for him wasn't an option. Holding her hips again, he brought her all the way down on him and held her there while they both relished the feeling of her being filled with him before moving his thumb back and forth on her clit.

She was staring down at him and he uttered, "Oh, Ava. I—"

She didn't let him finish, instead leaning down to kiss him in an attempt to silence him.

*Why won't she let me say it?* He had a sinking feeling he knew why.

Rolling her over, he once again took pleasure in kissing and touching every part of her body, breathing in her scent and relishing her taste. He wanted tonight to be imprinted in his memory forever. As she responded to his touch, he hoped it was in hers as well. He wanted her to feel his caress every time her new lover put his hands on her, knowing there was no way he could match up to how Travis made her body feel.

He made her climax two more times and was planning on stopping before achieving his own orgasm when she looked at him like she was hurt.

"Don't I turn you on?" she questioned in a small voice as he moved up to hold her after her last orgasm.

"More than any other woman," he replied, his face inches from hers.

"Then why can't I make you come?"

Right then he realized his pleasure was important to her. He thought by only concentrating on her, he was proving how much she meant to him, not understanding she derived almost as much fulfillment from his satisfaction as her own.

"Oh baby, are you sure I haven't worn you out?"

She pulled his mouth to hers where she kissed him gently and long before moving his hand between her legs to show him how wet she was.

"Positive," she whispered with a smile.

He rolled her over onto her stomach where he moved her legs together before entering her from behind. They had both loved that position the last time they did it, and his ego was hopeful to make her come once more with him.

He accomplished his mission just in time before he filled her pussy deep inside with his sperm.

When he slid out of her and came back with a towel, he got a little hard again watching his white cum dripping from her smooth pussy.

It was only a few hours before sunrise, and they fell asleep in their normal position.

*Yes*, he thought as he held her close, *she was made to be in my arms.*

# Chapter 20

*Ava*

Ava woke up the next morning snuggled next to Travis. For the first time since they'd been together, she felt ashamed of herself for having sex with him. She loved how he felt as she lay next to him, and she shuddered at the thought of how he had made her body feel, but now she felt... empty. She had allowed herself to have last night with him and not think about all that had transpired between them, willing their physical intimacy to make up for the hurt, the reality of the situation now hitting her heart as harshly as the morning sunlight did her eyes.

She tried to slip out of his arms, but he tightened them as soon as she did and made no attempt to ease up in order to let her go. Instead, he nuzzled her hair as he whispered, "Good morning, beautiful."

"Hi," she responded softly.

"Are you hungry? Do you want to go get breakfast?"

The idea of food right now made her feel queasy, so she gently shook her head. "No, I think we need to talk."

Other than the deep breath she felt him take in, he didn't move. At first she wondered if he heard her but then realized she hadn't exactly made an attempt to move either. *Maybe they could just lay there forever?* That way she wouldn't have to figure out exactly how she was feeling.

Travis began to stir. She was still unsure how she felt, let alone what she was going to say. Sitting her up, he put his hand under her chin so she would look at him. He had a determined look on his face. It was clear he was going to talk first, before she even had a chance to say anything.

"Ava, I am so sorry I hurt you. I can't tell you how ashamed I am for what I did. This last month without you has been the worst month of my life. Please say you'll let me try and make it up to you, and there's a possibility you can forgive me one day. That you'll give me another chance?" His eyes were pleading with hers.

*Wait. What happened to 'I love you?'* He had been willing to say it last night while they were making love—what changed?

*He hadn't really meant it, and it's morning, that's what changed.* She was suddenly very relieved she hadn't let him tell her last night. She could only imagine how hurt she'd feel now.

Her head was spinning once again. While glad he was remorseful and missed her, as she had missed him terribly, she knew their feelings for each other were lopsided—she cared way more for him than he did her and knew if they continued their relationship, she was only going to fall so deeply in love with him she'd never recover once it truly had run its course. Right now, she still had a shot at healing.

When she didn't say anything, he continued. "We can go as slow as you want. I don't want to pressure you, but baby, I don't want to lose you. I *can't* lose you."

She heard herself suggesting dinner the following night. *What the hell? Where did that come from? What are you doing?!*

He let out a long sigh as if relieved. "Anywhere, you name it. Tell me what time to pick you up."

She hesitated, trying to think of somewhere they would not be recognized. The *Out and About* section of the paper had been having a field day with him being seen with "an unidentified pregnant woman." Ava didn't need to add fuel to that fire.

"Let's go to Sullivan's. You can pick me up at six-thirty," she paused and challenged, "if that works for you." Six-thirty was going to be difficult for him, and she knew it. He normally didn't even leave the office until at least seven.

"I'll make it work." He cocked his head at her. "Sullivan's huh?"

A sandwich and ice cream shop, she knew it was an interesting choice but shot him a look that dared him to criticize it. "Do you have a better idea?"

"No, I love Sullivan's. I used to take my nephews there all the time. When they were five."

She just smiled and he laid back down, motioning for her to nestle in next to him.

"I'm going to check on Fred around lunchtime, if you're interested in meeting me." He hesitated then added with a smile against her hair, "Or I could pick you up, and we could go together?"

She smiled almost apologetically. "I think I will stop by on my way to the office."

"Okay." He sounded disappointed.

Ava was feeling emboldened by the temporary power shift between them, there were things that had been weighing on her mind, and now seemed the perfect time to address them. Rolling onto her stomach so her upper body was on his chest and her head on her fists while looking at him, she asked, "That day at your office... why didn't you come after me?"

She felt him jerk and could almost hear what he was thinking. *Fuck, Ava, are you really going to do this to me now?* But she was going to do it now. If she waited, she might lose her nerve.

"Because I was stupid and arrogant," he said while tucking her hair behind her ear. "Believe me, I regretted it every day," he added before kissing her.

That didn't sound like her Travis. He wasn't one to live with regret. If he truly wanted something, he went after it. She didn't understand how or why she would be an exception, but didn't know what to say to press the matter. She was going to figure it out. That topic wasn't over yet.

"So if Tara wasn't your sister and just a girl you were dating, what would you have done if she showed up on your doorstep pregnant?"

Without hesitation, he stated, "I'd ask her to consider an abortion."

Her body stiffened, and she shifted away from him slightly. Her hopes dashed, she was left to ask him, "What if she wouldn't?"

He shrugged his shoulders. "Then I guess I'd resign myself to writing a check every month."

She felt like she'd been kicked in the guts. There honestly was no possible future with him, even if he did eventually fall in love with her. No kids was a deal breaker, not to mention, was he really that big of an asshole that a baby would simply mean writing a monthly check, nothing more? Had she been so blinded by her feelings for him she failed to see him as he truly was? Was he actually a giant douchebag?

"Oh," was all she could manage to say.

He narrowed his eyes as he looked at her. "Ava, I have always taken great care in that department. I'm not writing anyone a monthly check, and I've never had to ask a woman to make a choice based on my recklessness. There won't be someone showing up at our wedding announcing her child is mine."

*Okay, wait. What the fuck? Did he say their wedding? And something about not having any illegitimate children?*

She was so damn confused. Not to mention mad. Just maybe not so much anymore about his sister and more about this discussion.

And why the hell did he have to be so goddamn gorgeous?

****

*Travis*

Ava sent Travis a text after she stopped by to see Fred, who was doing much better.

She texted him, *Vet says our Freddy should be able to go home tomorrow.*

He replied, *That's great! Dinner at my place tonight to celebrate and welcome him home?*

Travis smiled when he read her next text. *No, tomorrow will be fine.*

He liked that she was playing hard to get. He expected nothing less and was going to enjoy the chase. At least he hoped playing hard to get was all it was. He was astute enough to realize that morning something was wrong when they were talking about pregnant girlfriends. He thought he was proving his commitment to Ava by not choosing his fictitious baby mama over her. (Travis did not take Women 101 in college.)

Yet today his heart was a lot lighter than it had been yesterday at the idea of getting her back. His secretary, Kelli, commented on his better disposition and was floored to learn about Fred. When he explained who had brought his dog to the vet, she smiled as if it all made sense. She had openly wondered about Ava Ericson's significance in Travis' life ever since the day he hurried down to the lobby to meet her for lunch. Kelli had been gracious and tolerant of his horrible mood over the last month, ever since Ava hurried out of his office. He'd never had a woman have any sort of influence over him before, and when he snapped at his secretary a few times recently, he was taken aback at what a dick he was being. After he blew something way out of proportion, Kelli had had enough and told him to quit being stubborn and get the girl back already. It was the best advice she'd ever given him.

Unfortunately, his mood soured again the next day when out of the blue and with no explanation, Ava canceled their dinner plans and would not return his calls or texts.

Travis had his suspicions why, and they had to do with a certain marine.

# Chapter 21

*Ava*

Feeling exhausted, Ava left work early to catch up on the sleep she had missed the night before when she had been with Travis. She had been tired a lot lately. Waking in the middle of the evening, she tried to eat something when she got up but was sick—again.

What the hell is wrong with me? If I didn't know better, I'd think I was pregnant!

The second she thought the words a feeling of panic set in. She was supposed to have had her period a few weeks ago, but it never came. Not having been with anyone that month, she hadn't thought much of it. Now that the idea was in her head, she was rattled and went to the drug store to buy a pregnancy test. When the word pregnant showed up on the little white stick, she began to cry.

Talk about timing. She was a firm believer in things happening for a reason and knew she and Travis having the what if a girl shows up at your door pregnant talk that morning was meant to happen. Realizing she was going to be doing this on her own made any romantic thoughts she'd been secretly harboring about a happily-ever-after with Travis go away. Just like that.

After a brief cry, Ava went into crisis management mode, making a list in her head of everything she needed to do and prioritizing it. First thing that needed to happen was getting a doctor's appointment and finding out how far along she was. That would determine when she would tell Travis—if she told him at all. She wasn't about to tell him while the window for an abortion was still available as an option.

Jumping when her phone rang, she looked down to see it was Steven calling. Knowing she couldn't talk to him right now without spilling everything, she sent it to voicemail. She missed her big brother. Maybe she could look for a job on the East Coast to be near him and away from Travis.

Hiding from Travis was more like it, if she was being honest with herself.

Back in the things happen for a reason mind frame, she wondered if this baby was supposed to motivate her to get back into her beloved profession of organic chemistry. It clearly wasn't meant for her to have a man in her life. Ron Thompson was now, obviously, off the table, and the thought of Travis simply writing a check to her every month was depressing. She was happy she knew she'd be okay financially if she decided not to tell him. The idea of telling her parents made her feel scared to death.

I'm twenty-nine years old, for goodness sake!

It didn't matter. She knew she could be fifty-nine and would still be worried about what her parents thought of her.

\*\*\*\*

*Ron*

Ron called Ava before leaving for overseas. She sounded upset when she asked him to lunch, so there was no way he was going to tell her no.

She suggested they meet at the State Street Outdoor Café, and he was waiting at a table on the sidewalk when she approached. Standing as she came near, he kissed her gently on the cheek and pulled her chair out for her.

Looking at her fondly, Ron sounded concerned when he said, "You seemed pretty serious on the phone. Is everything okay?"

Ava opened her mouth to speak but no words came out, so he sat patiently looking at the menu while letting her collect her thoughts.

Ron thought Travis might have made his move, and she was letting him down in person, so he was not prepared when she finally took a deep breath and quietly said, "I'm pregnant," without looking at him.

He hoped his shocked look was quickly masked with a broad grin before she looked at him again. "Congratulations!"

Giving a weak smile, she offered, "Thank you. I'm obviously surprised," before quickly adding, "pleasantly."

He grabbed her hand and squeezed. "Travis is a lucky man."

His comment seemed to catch her off-guard, and she jerked her head up. "How do you know Travis is the father?"

Smiling, he kept her hand in his and responded, "Isn't he?"

Ava looked down and whispered, "Yes."

Something about the way she answered prompted him to inquire, "Is he excited?"

She wouldn't look at him when she disclosed, "He doesn't know yet."

His sharp intake of breath conveyed he was startled at her answer.

Ron still hadn't let go of her hand when he leaned over and kissed her cheek again. "I think he is going to surprise you," he affectionately told her.

She finally looked at him again with tears streaming down her face as she sobbed, "You are a wonderful man."

He must have looked horrified because she laughed while sniffling. "Hormones."

The marine nodded his head as if he understood. He, of course, had no idea about pregnancy or hormones.

Watching her emotions wreak havoc made him a little glum. Travis better be the stand-up guy Ron thought he was because Ron meant it when he said he thought Sterling was a lucky man. Not only having had this beautiful blonde in his bed but now carrying his child? He allowed himself ten seconds of imagining himself in the lawyer's shoes, at least as far as Ava was concerned. He'd never want to trade his life or career with him, but the idea of having her to come home to was something he realized would make him happy.

Ava received a phone call. She needed to go to her condo immediately—there had been a fire in her building. Ron drove her home and caught her when she fainted at the sight of her unit completely engulfed in flames.

Effortlessly carrying her back to the cab of his truck to lay her down, he found her phone and called Frannie. After Ron explained what had happened, the elder Ericson woman started clucking her concern, and he offered to bring Ava to her mother's home. Ava came to on the drive, disoriented, it took her a moment to realize what was happening, and as they pulled through the guard gates, she implored him not to say anything about her pregnancy to her mother.

"You're the only person I've told," she confided.

He knew that omission wasn't meant to make him feel flattered, but it did.

"My lips are sealed," he said with a sweet smile, noting she was more concerned about her mother finding out she was pregnant than she was about her home that had been destroyed by a fire.

Arriving at the Ericson estate, he went round to the passenger side and carried her in his arms to the front door, where Francine was waiting anxiously. Mrs. Ericson instructed him to deposit her on the living room couch, which he did, then kneeled down to quietly talk to her and stroke her hair while Francine was on the phone to her husband, who promised to leave work as quickly as he could.

"Are you going to be all right here?" Ron quietly asked.

When she nodded her head yes, he continued, "Because you are welcome to come stay with me for a few days."

Ava smiled meagerly. "That's very kind of you to offer but I'll be okay." She grinned a little broader upon hearing her mother's concerned voice. "If not, I'll call you."

Frannie came through the door, still fussing over Ava before turning to Ron. "Thank you so much for bringing her home. I can't imagine what would have happened if you hadn't been there!"

The general stayed a little longer before making his exit. Walking him to the door, Francine told him, "We'd love for you to come to our Halloween party next month."

"I've heard about your famous party, and I wish I was going to be in town to attend. Unfortunately, I leave in a week and will be gone until December."

Mrs. Ericson's disappointment showed on her face. He chuckled, thinking to himself, *That's where Ava gets it.*

"Well, please plan on Christmas Eve then."

Ron leaned over and kissed the woman's cheek without committing to attending. "Take care of your beautiful daughter," he told her before walking out the door.

****

*Ava*

Ava continued to try not to think about Travis over the next month as she took care of her mental to-do list of what she needed to prepare for the baby. Her condominium being destroyed might possibly prove to be a blessing in disguise, as it would allow her to move to the East Coast for a while without having to worry about renting or selling her place.

She got a call from Tracey early one afternoon, upset about her boyfriend, and wondering if Ava had any time to have dinner or drinks later. The two women had met for lunch a few times since the night of the ball, and Ava really liked her. She was spunky.

Ava was supposed to meet Anne for dinner. She was going to tell her friend about her pregnancy tonight. She needed her support more than anything right now. Hearing the desperation in Tracey's voice, however, tugged at Ava's heartstrings—she knew what the girl was feeling all too well.

"My girlfriend Anne and I are having dinner tonight, why don't you join us?"

"I don't want to intrude," Tracey said between sniffles.

"It's no intrusion at all. It will be just what you need—a little girl time to vent." Ava could tell Anne after dinner or tomorrow at lunch. She knew a girl in crisis came first. Being pregnant wasn't going to change, not for several months anyway.

They met at her favorite pizza place, and she was dismayed when the smell made her queasy.

*No! Not this place too!* There wasn't going to be anyplace left she would be able to eat. She took her anti-nausea pill and hoped for the best. Still, she sat on the outside of the booth in case she needed to get to the restroom quickly.

For a girl who was heartbroken, Tracey looked pretty damn good. She had the type of complexion some women paid thousands of dollars to get, and other than the slight bags under her bright blue eyes, you'd never know she had been losing sleep at night. She had her long, dark blonde hair in a braid that seemed to match Anne's. The two girls sitting opposite her almost looked like twins.

They ordered their meal, and her two companions had a beer while she had water. Anne wouldn't be suspicious she wasn't drinking because the only alcohol the restaurant served was beer, and Ava wasn't a big beer drinker.

Ava got down to brass tacks. "So what's going on with Jeff?"

Tracey frowned. "Jeff? Nothing is going on with Jeff, why?"

That surprised Ava. "Aren't you two an item?"

The other girl seemed shocked she knew about them and replied with an apprehensive, "No," obviously trying to see how much Ava knew.

"Oh, I saw you two at the ball and—"

"Oh my god! You saw us!?"

Ava knew she was missing something by the relief on Tracey's face when she said, "I saw him grab your boobs."

"Oh. Well, Jeff and I sometimes mess around if we're both single, but we haven't actually since the ball.

Fortunately, I figured out I needed to let his bullshit roll off my back and not take him too seriously before I took him too seriously, if that makes sense."

It made perfect sense. Ava was sad though; she had liked Jeff the night she met him and thought he and Tracey were cute together. She was sorry to learn they had only been a fling. The thought of being pregnant with her own secret affair's baby almost caused her to warn the girl about flings, although it sounded like Tracey already had that figured out on her own. Maybe Ava should have gotten advice from Tracey about temporary romances.

"So if not Jeff, who?"

Tracey sighed, "Well, I started seeing my ex again right after the ball. Jeff was in one of his moods where he wasn't sure if he wanted to be fuck buddies or just friends. Which is fine, I guess, but when my ex-boyfriend Garrett called, I let him take me out for drinks, against my better judgment, and next thing I know, we're back together. Now I think he's regretting calling me though."

Ava dutifully inquired, "Why? What makes you think that?"

"He knows in his heart we're over but is too big of a chicken shit to just make a clean break, so instead he's being mean hoping I'll do it."

Yeah, that sounded like some of the prick guy moves she had heard about too many times from her sorority sisters in college. Yet, it seemed kind of juvenile. Wasn't Garrett a grown-ass man?

"What is he doing?"

Tracey swallowed a drink of beer then explained. "Just in the last week or so he's made a few snide comments comparing me to his ex-girlfriend—not favorably, by the way. I'm not sure why even. I felt like telling him, if she's so fucking great, then why the hell were you sticking your dick in me the day after you two broke up? But I didn't, I've ignored it. But now, he doesn't even want to sleep with me, and I'm left wondering if maybe he's seeing her again."

Anne and Ava made the obligatory girlfriend comments about what an asshole move that was, why would he do that, and she didn't deserve that.

Tracey nodded appreciatively at the support and continued. "Then last night, I walked out of his bathroom in slutty lingerie I had just bought." Her eyes welled with tears. "He took one look at me," her lip started to quiver as tears began streaming down her face, "and *started laughing*."

*Ooooh. Party foul, dude. Party-fucking-foul.*

Ava thought back to when she had appeared in Travis' home office doorway in only her four-inch heels. She would have died a slow death if he would have laughed at her that night. She couldn't imagine how that must have made Tracey feel. Putting yourself out there to be vulnerable can be pretty nerve-wracking and probably shouldn't be considered when one has a boyfriend who is a fuckhead.

Anne gasped and asked incredulously, "He did *what*?! What. A. Dipshit."

Ava reached over and grabbed Tracey's hand. "Honey, I have no idea why the hell he would laugh at you. You are beautiful, and any other man would kill to have you walk into his bedroom in slutty lingerie. Maybe he's scared?"

The downtrodden girl shook her head. "No, that's not it. I think it's run its course, and this is his way of dealing with it."

Ava shook her head in a sympathetic, understanding fashion. "You don't think it's fixable?"

She had no idea why she asked that. *No, it's not fixable. He's a fucking asshole; why would Tracey even want to repair it?* She felt a little nauseous at the Operation Sex Kitten flashbacks she was having and how her original goal had been to get asshat Brad back in her bed. It was almost laughable how dumb and naïve she had been, and how much bullshit she had been willing to put up with for the sake of 'love.'

*Brad and Garrett, table for two?*

In between tears, Tracey choked out a laugh. "At least it made me get my ass out of bed this morning and to the gym."

They all laughed, each having been there. Anne had lost fifteen pounds after her last breakup.

"Are you interested in maybe seeing Jeff more seriously?" Anne inquired.

Tracey shrugged her shoulders and sighed. "I don't think so. We—" she paused, debating how much to reveal to Ava before just coming out with it. "We had amazing sex, but he can be a man whore and moody as fuck. Besides, it would ruin our friendship if we tried to be anything more than friends with benefits."

As great a couple Ava thought Tracey and Jeff would make, she did have to admit she saw the girl's point.

Tracey took another sip of beer before continuing. "Hopefully Charlie and I are able to keep it platonic when I move in with him, so I can take some time, get my act together, and figure some things out."

"Wait, what? You're moving in with Charlie? Where is Brad going?" Ava asked. She actually couldn't give a shit less where Brad was going but was more curious about why the two men weren't going to be living together.

"I guess he can't find a job here in San Diego. His interview with Carson, Burns, Sterling, and Cooper was a disaster, and Travis Sterling practically threw him out of the building!"

Ava didn't know whether to giggle or feel sorry for Brad. So the stories of Travis being a son-of-a-bitch were actually true.

"Well, I don't have to tell you what a great guy Charlie is. Maybe you two will hit it off?"

"I think I need to be single for a while. It seems like I settle a lot. Why do I do that? Do I think that's all I deserve? The guy will be really good looking but lousy in bed. Or great in bed but a total mind fuck. He's got a great job but can't make time for me. He's a damn slut or he's still in love with his ex-girlfriend. That pretty much sums up my past five relationships, including my secret one."

Ava didn't know much about romances, having only been in two her whole life, but agreed, she shouldn't settle. If Charlie wasn't what she was looking for, she might know a good-looking marine who could be right up her alley.

The women spent the rest of the night laughing and exchanging bad dates and bad boyfriend stories, each trying to outdo the other. Ava felt she had the winner but couldn't share it. Not right now anyway.

The evening didn't do much to restore her faith in men, but it did serve to strengthen her resolve she was going to be okay without one.

**

The day before Halloween and her parents' annual bash finally arrived. The party was quite an affair and getting an invitation was a big deal in the Ericsons' social circle.

Ava had no idea what she was going to do for a costume. She had been doing a pretty good job of hiding her changing body with baggy clothes, but her morning sickness was starting to draw her mother's attention. She knew what she had to do; she just didn't know how to go about telling her parents she was pregnant.

Surprisingly, they took the news better than she expected, her mother shooting her father a knowing look when she told them. Of course they wanted to know who the baby's father was, but Ava wasn't ready to share that yet. Not until she figured out what she was going to do. She also knew her mother's penchant for talking and did not want it getting back to Travis she was almost four months pregnant, lest he do the math and worry he was going to have to pay her a monthly sum every month in child support. So she lied when her mother asked her when she was due.

"Beginning of June." That would put her past any time frame that would possibly make Travis suspect he was the father. When it actually happened in mid-March, she'd blame it on an early arrival.

Mrs. Ericson suggested they keep the news quiet for now, citing it was too early and things could possibly still go wrong. Ava happily agreed, although she had her suspicions her mother suggesting it had more to do with her being an unwed mother than anything. That was not going to go over well at the country club.

Opting for a costume of Greek goddess with flowing robes that would hide her tiny bump, she made her way from the pool house to the main house before guests started to arrive.

"What do you need me to do?" she asked her mother.

"Be your charming self, dear, and circulate! The caterers have everything under control."

Ava did mingle with the guests and was having a nice time as the older judges and lawyers flirted shamelessly with her. Knowing they were harmless, she was enjoying their interesting observations on the world when she caught sight of Travis out of the corner of her eye. She almost didn't recognize him, dressed in dark jeans, brown leather chaps and boots, a red flannel shirt, and grey cowboy hat low on his head. He looked so sexy.

*Now I'm going to have damn cowboy fantasies!* She had been unbelievably horny lately, and how hot her baby daddy looked as a cowboy was not going to help with that.

The sexy cowgirl on his arm in the short shorts, brown cowboy boots, and leather vest that exposed her midriff while accentuating her amazing tits did though.

There was no mistaking her for his sister.

She was beautiful and hanging all over him while having to tilt her brown cowgirl hat up to kiss his face. Her long brown hair was curled but tousled, like maybe she'd had a roll in the hay before getting ready.

Travis had been very active in the *Out and About* section recently, and while she always felt a twinge of jealousy, Ava thought she had gotten over him. Seeing him in person for the first time since the morning after Fred was hit, and with the stunning cowgirl no less, hurt. Not as bad as when he was with Tara at the ball but a close second.

****

*Travis*

For his part, he at least felt uncomfortable when he realized she had seen him. He had been reconsidering his decision to bring a date to the Ericsons' party when he saw Ava alone, although he knew the reason she was alone was probably because her date was overseas.

He had seen her and Ron at a café downtown not long after she canceled their date and wouldn't take his calls. He knew then she was over him and stopped calling, but it didn't stop him from missing her. She looked beautiful tonight, but something about her was different, and he couldn't quite put his finger on what it was.

They did a good job of avoiding each other all night until the costume contest. Mr. Ericson was on the makeshift stage being witty and charming with his audience. Ava was in the middle of a belly laugh when her eyes met Travis', who was also laughing robustly at Robert. The second their eyes met a jolt of electricity went through both of them, and for a moment it was as if they were the only two people in the room. The moment passed, and Ava placed her hands on her stomach and looked away.

Francine Ericson was standing not far from Travis, and when he turned to find a distraction, she was the first person he ran into. She had just witnessed her daughter's exchange with the man and quietly asked him, "So how long did you date Ava?"

He knew there was no use hiding it. "A little over a month."

Fran's eyes filled with tears. "How long ago did you stop?"

"A few months ago."

The disappointment showed on her face. He knew she adored him and thought of all the times Francine Ericson had sat in his office, lecturing him about settling down and dropping not-so-subtle hints about her single daughter being the perfect candidate when he finally decided to.

She sighed wistfully. "That's too bad. You would have been a great father for my grandchild."

He felt the color drain from his face as he attempted to comprehend what Francine was saying. *Was Ava pregnant?!*

His lawyer mode kicked in, and he tried not to appear rattled as he started questioning her.

"Wow, you're going to be a grandma, huh? Congratulations! When is she due?"

"I know, can you believe it? She's not very far along, she just found out recently and told us yesterday."

"So is the general the father? Are they getting married?" He didn't know why he wanted to know if they were getting married, but he did. Not to mention he wanted clarification the general was the father and not him. *Not very far along* was pretty open-ended.

"I'm not sure. I don't even know if he knows. He's overseas, and I don't think she's had an opportunity to talk to him. To be honest, she won't tell us anything about the father yet."

"How far along is she, Francine?" he asked insistently.

Mrs. Ericson finally understood his reason for wanting to know and replied regretfully, "A little over a month, I think."

**\*\***

Travis left the party without seeing Ava again. She seemed to have disappeared, much like his date had. Although he feigned he was looking for the woman he came with, she was secondary to finding Ava. He walked out having found neither. His companion had left without even telling him goodbye. He couldn't really blame her—he'd spent most of his night watching Ava and had barely paid attention to the sexy cowgirl.

Ava was all he could think about the entire weekend, which wasn't new, but the pregnancy presented a whole new facet to his thought process about her, their relationship, and what went wrong. He had accepted his blame in the situation, and there wasn't a day he didn't get up—particularly on Monday mornings—he wasn't filled with regret. She had been the best thing that had ever happened to him. He didn't dare allow himself to fantasize that was his baby, although it was hard not to. But every time his mind started down that path, he made himself stop and think about something else.

By eleven a.m. Monday morning, he couldn't take it anymore and was on the phone to Ridgeport Realty, thinking she'd at least pick up the phone in her office if she wouldn't take his call on her cell. When he was told there was no agent by the name of Ava Ericson there, he grew confused. When he called Oceanside Realty to learn she was still there, he became angry.

Showing up at her office unannounced, he didn't wait for the receptionist to call her up front and meet him in the lobby. Instead he barged his way back to her office amid the poor woman's protests.

****

*Ava*

Ava was startled when she looked up and saw him looming in her office doorway.

*Fuck.*

He closed the door and stood there glaring at her. Even though she'd only seen him angry once, she knew he was mad and was uncomfortable with him towering over her as she sat at her desk, so she motioned for him to sit in one of the empty grey upholstered chairs opposite her.

"You didn't take the Ridgeport job," he stated flatly as he sat down.

"No, I didn't." She provided no further explanation and braced herself.

"That was the whole reason we stopped dating. At least, that's what I thought was the reason. Apparently, there was more to the story I wasn't privy to," he said, his voice dripping with contempt.

She didn't flinch, which seemed to infuriate him more. Her seemingly lack of giving-a-shit was more than he could stand in a civilized frame of mind.

"There was much more to me not telling you, Travis, you're right. Not the least of which was that little stunt you pulled with your sister."

He sneered, "Nice try, Ava. The ball was weeks after you got the job offer. You could have told me you turned it down, and we would have gone to it together."

She looked at him coolly, although she knew she was going to throw up at any time and kept her hands firmly on the desk so he wouldn't see them shaking.

"I guess I'm not a big fan of ultimatums."

He snorted in disdain. "Ultimatums... yeah, okay." The look he gave her was pure anger. "Well, I guess everything worked out for you in the end, didn't it? You got your marine and your baby, and you don't have to give another thought to the lawyer-next-door whose head you thoroughly fucked with. Operation Sex Kitten was definitely a success."

*He knows I'm pregnant! Shit! Wait, how does he know about OSK?!*

Finally, she let him know she was rattled.

"I never fucked with your head, Travis." Her voice was shaking and getting higher as she stood up. "If I recall, *you* were the one playing games, not me. So, if you're done with your accusations, I'm going to have to ask you to leave now."

*Before I puke.*

Seething, he sat in his chair a little longer before looking her up and down. "It's a good thing you had your period when you were with me because if I thought for a second that was my baby..."

He didn't finish his thought until he stood up and walked toward the door, pausing before looking her up and down again as if she disgusted him. "If that was my baby, I'd move heaven and earth to make sure you didn't have custody."

That made her knees buckle a little, but she kept her composure when she opened the door and gestured for him

261

to leave as she hissed, "Well we're both in luck then, because it's not your baby. I don't have to worry about a custody battle, and you don't have to worry yourself with writing a monthly check."

"Goodbye, Ava," he said dismissively as he walked out her door.

She refrained from slamming it behind him as she ran back to her desk, making it to her garbage can just in time.

Ava was a nervous wreck from then on and called her brother in Connecticut. After telling him pretty much everything except Travis' actual name, he urged her to come stay with him between Thanksgiving and Christmas.

"I'll be home at Thanksgiving. You can fly back with me, and then we'll return for Christmas and New Year's."

She knew he was worried about her as he listened to her crying.

"Do Mom and Dad know?"

"They know I'm pregnant, and Mom knows I'm having trouble keeping anything down, even with anti-nausea medicine."

"Little sister, that is not good for your baby. You have to be able to give your child nutrition. What does your OB-GYN have to say about all this?"

"I have an appointment next week, and I'll talk to her more about it then. I'm finding out the sex."

Her big brother took a sharp breath. "I'll be home this weekend to be sure I'm at that appointment with you."

"Steve, I love you, and I love you're concerned, but Mom and Dad don't know how far along I am. You coming here would raise suspicions. My girlfriend, Anne, is going with me.

I promise I will call you the second I know. Hell, I can even Skype with you while it's happening!"

Steven laughed. "I might take you up on that."

They said their goodbyes, and Ava sat on the edge of her bed crying with gratitude she had such an amazing older sibling.

# Chapter 22

*Ava*

The week of Thanksgiving arrived, and all her siblings were back for the holiday. Ava woke earlier than normal and found she was actually hungry enough to join her family for breakfast for once.

She slipped quietly through the French doors and over to the breakfast nook, where her father was already seated in his robe, his silver hair still wet from the shower. He never dressed before breakfast; he didn't want to risk getting anything on his shirt or tie.

"Hey, Ava Bear! Glad you could make it!" He took his feet off the chair next to him and pulled it out, motioning for her to sit in it.

Her mother came over and ran her fingers through her daughter's hair. "How are you feeling this morning, baby? Think you can keep something down?"

Ava nodded cautiously. "I think so. I've been feeling better lately."

"What do you want, Bear Bug? I'll make anything you want," Francine matronly inquired.

"For some strange reason, I've been craving blueberry pancakes. I have no idea why."

Her mother laughed and patted Ava's stomach. "Because that little one wants some, that's why."

"Where is everyone else?" she asked loudly in her mother's direction. Her dad was busy reading something on his tablet.

Her mother hadn't heard her over all the sizzling going on at the stove so her dad answered, not looking up from his digital device. "Well, Steven went for a run, and your sisters are still sleeping." He looked up and smiled at her. "Which I'm sure surprises you."

Ava's younger siblings were notorious for sleeping late. They would probably sleep until noon if their mother allowed them to. Still, when she had asked where *everyone* was, she was trying to be diplomatic and not assume they hadn't changed while in college. But her dad was right; she wasn't surprised. She hoped Steven got back from his run before they finished breakfast. She always enjoyed the banter at the table when her brother was there.

Mrs. Ericson set the butter and syrup down in the middle of the table and gave her husband a scolding look. "Robert, it's only seven in the morning. I'm sure those girls need to catch up on their sleep."

"Oh yeah, because I'm sure they're exhausted from all the studying they've done this semester," her dad muttered sarcastically.

Ava put her hand on her dad's and giggled. "Well, at least your oldest two turned out awesome, Pops."

She had meant regarding her and Steven's education and grades, but then thought about her current condition and was immediately ashamed at what she thought must have sounded incredibly hypocritical.

She looked down, embarrassed, and gestured to her baby bump. "Well, okay, at least you've still got hope with Steve."

Her dad squeezed her hand and gently but sternly said, "I'm still incredibly proud of you, Bear. That hasn't changed for a second."

Tears filled Ava's eyes. Hearing her father say that brought a sense of relief. She had been worried her parents were embarrassed and disappointed with her. Disappointing her mom and dad was something Ava had fretted about ever since she could remember. It's probably why she never got into trouble growing up or ever did anything crazy in college, even though she knew they loved her unconditionally. They had always shown that to all their children. The examples they set while she was growing up were invaluable and were what gave her the confidence and belief she could raise her baby on her own and do a good job. Their love and devotion to not only their family, but to each other was something to be emulated. Sadly, she didn't see herself having that kind of relationship with anyone in the future. It broke her heart she wouldn't be able to give her child that kind of example, but she hoped she would be able to instill a strong sense of belonging. She knew her family would play a huge part in that, and she was going to need her father and brother now more than ever to be the male role models.

Her father's words magically made her feel a sense of peace, like things were going to be okay, at least as far as her baby was concerned. She still had the cloud of dread about Travis discovering the truth hanging over her, but for the sake of her sanity, and her health, she couldn't think about that right now.

Her mother put the pancakes down in front of her and a plate of turkey, bacon and eggs in front of her father, then came back with a small pancake and eggs for herself. Just then, Steven opened up the door, his hair and shirt wet from the sweat of his workout.

"Hey, sis! I didn't think you were going to be here this early! Let me quick shower, and I'll be right down."

The simple fact he was happy to see her delighted her. She had missed her brother; he was her oldest friend and most trusted confidant. Of course he was also the one who glued her bedroom door shut and shaved her Barbie's head, but those memories only endeared him more to her now. She was sure it was her hormones, but as she looked at the plate of pancakes her mother had prepared for her, Ava felt enormously thankful and grateful for her wonderful, supportive family.

Her dad was looking at his calendar on his tablet when he casually said to his wife, "Don't be jealous, honey, but guess who I'll be spending time with today?"

Her mother looked suspiciously at her father, expecting he was teasing her and it was really someone she didn't care for. "Who?"

"Travis Sterling."

Her mother raised her eyebrows, "Why on earth would Travis have a case in Federal Court?"

"It's an eminent domain case against the government." Robert Ericson wiped the corners of his smiling mouth with his napkin and stood up. "I'm going to have to admit to everyone my wife likes the plaintiff's attorney more than she does me." He kissed his wife on the lips. "Thanks for breakfast, my love. I've got to finish getting ready." He looked at Ava. "Bear, try to eat something. I don't want you back in the hospital! My grandbaby needs some food." Then he reached over and pulled his daughter against the side of his hip, hugging her. "Feel better, kiddo," he said before he headed upstairs to get dressed.

Her father must have confused her sudden pale cheeks for morning sickness. The minute the Ericson patriarch said

Travis' name, Ava felt all the color drain from her face. Just hearing his name set off alarm bells, but the fact he was going to be trying a case in front of her father made her dizzy, for so many reasons.

She jumped up from the table, with her hand over her mouth, and ran to the bathroom. Miraculously, she didn't get sick. She sat on the side of the tub for a few minutes, just in case, then got up and splashed cold water on her face. Patting her skin dry, she looked at her image in the mirror. The face staring back looked about how she felt—worn out. Ava took a deep breath and sighed. It was time to face the music.

Knocking on her parents' bedroom, Ava called out, "Daddy?" as she walked in, then shut her eyes tight. *Dammit*, she only called him that when she was in trouble. He was the one who brought that to her attention when she was trying to sweet talk him out of grounding her when she was fifteen.

He came out of his side of the suite as he was looping his tie around itself, his brow furrowed. He knew something was up. "What's wrong?"

She crossed the room and sat down on his bed. He finished his Windsor knot, looking at her through the mirror's reflection as he made the final adjustments.

"I need to tell you something." Ava knew she had no other choice. Her father's career and reputation demanded it. If it ever became known the father of his daughter's baby was an attorney in his court without it being known to all parties, it could wreak havoc. He disclosed the relationship his wife had with Travis, for goodness sake. Granted, he did so not because of the crush her mother had, as he liked to tease her about, but rather because of Travis' generosity with her charities. Judge Ericson never wanted to leave a doubt of impropriety, and he felt it was better to disclose everything. He was the most ethical man she knew.

She lowered her head and whispered, "I need to tell you who the father is."

"Okay." He sat down on the bed and looked at her, waiting for her to continue.

Almost inaudibly, she breathed, "It's Travis Sterling." Ava quickly glanced over and saw a look of shock on her father's face. She implored, "Don't say anything yet to Mom, please!"

Robert shook his head, "How..." He stopped to correct himself. He already knew how. "When... It's not... Does he..." She had never seen her father at a loss for words. He sat for a moment in silence while trying to regain his composure. Swallowing hard, he started again slowly and quietly. "When did this happen?"

"Over five months ago."

He continued, "Are you still involved?"

"No, it only lasted a little more than a month."

Her dad sat thinking for a few seconds. "But, I don't understand. You're only two months pregnant? How...?"

With tears streaming down her face as she shook her head, he gently stated, knowingly, "You're farther along than that." Ava nodded yes.

Her dad sat thinking for a few seconds. "How far along are you?"

"Twenty weeks."

He took a deep breath. "I'm assuming he doesn't know?" Ava again shook her head.

"You're going to have to tell him, Bear."

A strangled, exasperated cry escaped her. "I know I am. I was going to, but I'm too tired to fight with him right now." She needed to make her father understand. "When he found out I was pregnant, he came to my office and threatened to sue me for full custody. He said he'd *move heaven and earth* to make sure I didn't have custody. I lied so he wouldn't know it was his. I don't have the energy right now, Dad." Her shirt was wet from where she kept wiping her tears.

Her dad's expression showed he was still trying to put all the pieces together. "And there's no possible way it could be Ron Thompson's?"

"Not unless I got pregnant through immaculate conception," she sobbed. Her shoulders shook as she cried harder, and her father hugged her tight.

She stopped crying, took a breath, and drew herself up tall. "Steven and I have talked about me going to stay with him for a while." She let out a deep sigh of defeat. "Maybe he'll let me stay forever. Then I'll never have to deal with Travis." She felt so helpless about the situation.

Her father was always the voice of reason. "Honey, ignoring it isn't going to make it go away. Your baby deserves a father, and Travis deserves to know the truth."

"But he doesn't even want to be a father! That's what I'm trying to tell you! He's going to be spiteful and take me to court!" she cried. Her unsettled voice grew louder. "I know how expensive custody cases can be. You and I both know Travis has infinitely more resources to do battle than I do."

She held her hand up to stop him when he started to say, "Your mother and I..."

"No, Dad. I'm not going to allow you and mom to pay hundreds of thousands of dollars to fight this. It's just easier right now if I go to Connecticut with Steve." She continued talking, as if she were trying to convince herself about what a great plan she had. "I can get a job in the private sector anywhere. I'll have the baby, stay there for six months, and when I come back, Travis will have forgotten all about me."

"Ava, that child needs a father too."

She closed her eyes and shook her head and started crying again. She was an emotional roller coaster. Absent mindedly, she rubbed her stomach and said, "I know he does, Dad. I know."

A huge smile spread across her father's face. "He? You're having a boy?" He hugged her again.

Ava laughed and wiped her eyes. "Yes, you're going to have a grandson."

Mr. Ericson let the happiness of learning about the sex of his first grandchild soak in, then gave a sigh of resolution. "Honey, this is your decision and I will respect it, but I have to be on record as saying I think this is wrong. You have to let Travis have an opportunity to know his son."

She shook her head violently. "He was awful, Dad! Awful! He hates me, and he will use the baby to get back at me. You know Travis' reputation. He will not rest until he's won." She started crying again.

"Ava..." Her dad stopped then nodded his head as if in acceptance of her decision and slapped his knees. "Okay, kid. I've got to get to work. I've got a trial I need to recuse myself from!"

"What are you going to say is the reason?" Ava sniffled.

"If I'm asked for a reason, I'll blame it on your mother." He winked and started to put his suit jacket on.

"Please don't tell Mom yet." Ava got a tissue from her mother's nightstand.

"I won't." He took a deep breath. "But don't wait too long. Your mother is going to have a fit when she learns she only has four months to prepare for her grandsss—" He corrected himself and winked at her again. "Grandchild."

She stood up and hugged him. "Thanks, Pops."

He hugged her back. "I love you, Bear." And he headed downstairs.

She knew she was going to have to tell her mother the truth. Nestea-plunging onto her parents' made bed, she thought, *Maybe tomorrow.*

**

Her big brother, Steven, announced he was taking her to the mall that morning. Christmas season was going to officially start on Friday, the day after Thanksgiving, and he posed that it was to get a jump on things, yet the only thing he bought was new clothes for Ava. Not that she was complaining; she needed new clothes. What little she still had that wasn't destroyed in the fire were all too small for her now.

He also treated her to pampering with a haircut and pedicure, since she was starting to have trouble reaching her feet. Every time she would protest at the money he was spending on her, he would grab her by the chin and emphatically say, "You're worth it."

In the middle of getting her toes done she got a call from Ron.

*That is odd.* He hadn't called her once since leaving for overseas.

"Hello, beautiful," he greeted her when she answered.

"Hi!" she replied enthusiastically. "Is everything okay?"

"Well, I take it you haven't told Travis yet he's going to be a father?"

Taken aback at how he could possibly know this from however thousands of miles away he was, she cautiously responded. "No?"

He chuckled and the line began to get staticky. "Didn't think so. He called me today to congratulate me."

It was a good thing she was already sitting because she might have fallen down otherwise.

"Oh, Ron. I am so sorry."

"Ava, I'm actually the one who's sorry and that's why I'm calling. I told him he was barking up the wrong tree when he started accusing me of things against my character."

What a mess this had turned out to be. This was not at all what she envisioned her life was going to be like when she was pregnant with her first child.

"Don't be sorry, Ron. I should have dealt with this, and I didn't. I am the one who is sorry."

The line started cutting in and out. "I've got to go, but I hope everything turns out all right for you."

"You be careful and come home in one piece! I've got a girlfriend I want to fix you up with!"

She was pretty sure she heard him say goodbye before the line went dead. Taking a deep breath, she simply sighed with resignation at what she knew was coming in her near future.

**

Utterly exhausted, Ava put her packages on the couch, sat down, and slumped over sideways onto them. She was just going to lie there for a few minutes...

She woke up, completely disoriented. It was dark outside, and her face was sticking to the shopping bag she had been using as a pillow. She had her jacket draped over her as a blanket and shoes still on her feet.

*This growing a baby inside of you business isn't for wimps, that's for sure.* She stood up and switched on the lamp next to the couch, knowing she needed to eat but had to get into some comfy clothes first. Making her way to the little bedroom, she rummaged through her drawers for anything that could classify as comfortable. She attempted to put on the biggest pair of yoga pants she owned but found even those were too tight.

*Hmph. So much for comfy.*

It seemed everything she owned was suddenly too small. Forget any kind of pants, shorts, jeans... she was now more appreciative of the granny panties she had begrudgingly bought a few weeks ago. Her belly seemed to have popped out overnight. She groaned, glad she'd gotten some cute dresses today she could wear for at least another month or so until she got even bigger. She'd had to have gotten pregnant by someone whose baby was going to be as broad chested as he was. She didn't want to even think about what a natural birth was going to be like with his son.

She caught a glimpse of herself in the bathroom vanity. She still looked tired, but had to admit, she loved her new haircut and was glad Steven pampered her today.

Remembering the cute sleepwear she had splurged on while waiting for her hair appointment, she dug through the bags in the living room until she found the one with the pajamas in it. Looking at the pile of bags, Ava felt a twinge of guilt before shaking her head. *I deserve it!* She smiled, thinking about what Steven had said repeatedly to her earlier that afternoon. She still didn't quite believe it but did know one thing, she was glad she had at least bought the pjs because they had to be more comfortable than what she was currently wearing.

Changing into the silky ensemble, she stood, hands at her side, checking herself over in the full-length mirror. Her boobs were getting huge! She put her hands on her hips and twisted back and forth from the waist. Other than her boobs and protruding belly, she was still too skinny from the morning sickness, but there was no more hiding she was with child, that was for sure. She turned around and looked at her backside. Actually, if you only saw her from behind, you wouldn't be able to tell she was pregnant. Maybe she could just walk backwards for the next four months.

She grabbed her old, ratty robe and put it on while walking towards the kitchenette. She felt guilty when she poured herself a bowl of cereal. The kid wasn't even born, and she was already feeding him cereal for dinner. In order to assuage her guilt, she cut up a banana to put on top of her frosted flakes before pouring milk over it. *And I'll have a piece of cheese with some spinach and peanut butter crackers later, conscience, so shut up!*

Looking at her day's haul still sitting on the couch, she had a dilemma. If she took the time to take everything into her bedroom, her cereal would get soggy. Instead she just pushed it all on to the floor, propped herself against the throw pillows, and put her feet on the couch. Soon she realized she had another dilemma: she couldn't reach the remote control. Straining and stretching, she was finally able to get her fingertips on the end and inch it close enough so she could grasp the whole thing. *Whew, that was a lot of work.*

She was munching her cereal, wiping the occasional milk drip off her chin, and enjoying her favorite gameshow with her feet now propped on a pillow, when there was a knock at her door. With a mouthful of mushy frosted flakes and bananas, she sputtered "Come in!" After no one came in, she switched the TV off, put the bowl on the coffee table and rolled off the couch, yelling, "Good grief, I told you before, just come in!" while walking towards the door.

The door opened before she reached it, and Travis stepped through the pool house threshold. She knew this was coming; she just hadn't expected it tonight.

The room suddenly got smaller, like it had a tendency to do when he was in it. He looked haggard. Finding out you're going to be a father can do that to a perpetual bachelor. They stood there, looking at each other. She wasn't sure what was coming, but she knew she didn't have the energy for it, whatever it was.

"I can't fight with you tonight, Travis. I'm too tired, and I'm too pregnant," she said flatly and turned, defeated, to waddle back to the couch.

The next thing she knew, he had spun her around and seemed surprised at how hard he had turned her as she wobbled back and forth. Putting his hands gently on her arms to steady her, he searched her eyes for the answer he needed to know. The reason he was standing before her.

"I didn't come here to fight. I need to know—is it true?"

She had no idea why, but she decided to play dumb. Maybe to buy some time until she could think straight. "Is what true?"

He shook his head vehemently back and forth. "Don't, Ava. Don't do that."

She looked down but stayed silent. She wasn't going to give him any ammunition to use against her later. He let go of her arms and rubbed the back of his neck hard, obviously frustrated.

"I talked to Ron today," he said matter-of-factly.

Ava needed a barrier between them, so she picked up the cereal bowl still full with milk and the last remnants of her dinner flakes and carried it to the sink.

"I know. He called me." She didn't offer anything else.

"I thought it was odd your father recused himself from presiding over my case when suddenly, the pieces fell together."

She didn't say anything, instead, rinsed her bowl and ran the garbage disposal. After she shut it off, she looked over at him, waiting for him to continue before starting to wipe the counter.

He came around to where she was standing in the kitchenette, took the dishrag from her hand and tossed it on the counter, then guided her to a bar stool. She looked at the stool, then at her belly, then at him, and started laughing. If he thought she was going to be able to get onto that, he obviously hadn't seen her try to get off the couch.

Putting his hands around her waist, he boosted her up, then grabbed her hands and scanned her face. He looked almost... desperate.

"Why Ava? Why didn't you tell me that's my baby? I have a right to know."

She thought of the conversation she'd had that morning with her father. Of course he did, but she had her reasons and they were perfectly acceptable ones as far as she was concerned.

Out of nowhere, tears started streaming down her face. *These goddamn hormones.* "You said you didn't want children, remember? That you'd ask someone to get an abortion if they were pregnant with your child. I didn't want to go through that with you, and then in my office you said you didn't want anything to do with me, remember? That if this baby was yours, you'd get full custody and never let me see my child. I couldn't risk that, Travis. Not with how much hate you have towards me right now. I thought maybe in a year, maybe you'd be more reasonable, and I would tell you then."

He took his hands away from hers and paced the floor in front of her. He was now visibly angry, like he'd been in her office that dreadful day. "And let me miss out on the first year of my child's life? How do you think I'd react then? You think I'd be okay with that?" He hissed at her, "How pregnant are you exactly? I thought you were supposed to be on birth control? Was that a lie too? Was that what Operation Sex Kitten was? A ruse so I'd be your little sperm donor, and you could go off and have a baby by yourself?"

*Goddammit, how did he know about OSK?* Shaking her head, she decided it didn't matter, then allowed herself to feel a flash of anger. "Sperm donor? *Sperm donor?!* Do you have any idea how much I loved you? You think I *want* to be a single mother? You think I didn't want to share this with you?" She slid off the bar stool and started poking him in the chest. "Let me tell you something, buddy, if things had been right between us, and if you wouldn't have said you didn't want children, I would have told you the minute I found out."

She started to walk toward the other side of the counter, then reeled around and came back at him, her robe flapping open as she strode toward him. She saw his eyes drop to her chest and paused to tie it closed.

"That night we—" She stopped. She wasn't going to talk about that magical night when she had been so sure he had fallen for her. "That morning when we got food poisoning, I vomited my birth control. Unfortunately, I hadn't realized I could get pregnant after the fact. That bleeding you mentioned in my office was actually our son—" She poked him again in the chest with each word she uttered next, "Attaching. Himself. To. Me."

He put his hand on her belly, his eyes wide, and asked in happy wonderment, "We're having a boy?"

Dammit, she had to remember to keep her words gender neutral!

She was caught off guard at his sudden change and couldn't help but smile tenderly at his excitement before nodding. "Yes, we're having a boy." She hoped she at least sounded stern.

Travis dropped to his knees and began rubbing and kissing her belly. "Hi, baby. It's your dad." He kept talking into her stomach while kissing and caressing it, over and over, smiling broadly.

She looked down at him. He was so happy and excited, and she was so confused. Wasn't this the guy who didn't want children? They were nothing but a monthly check he'd have to write. Instinctively, she ran her fingers through his hair. When she realized what she was doing, she stopped. Man, she had missed doing that.

*What the hell is going on? I know I have pregnancy brain, but weren't we just arguing?*

He stood back up, but kept his hand on her stomach, looking at her like he was in awe and amazement of her.

His face suddenly got dark, and he quietly said, "Ava, I know I scared you when I was in your office and told you if that was my baby, I'd get custody."

The painful memory was seared into her brain, and she wouldn't look at him. He tilted her chin towards him. "You have to know, I said that out of hurt and anger." She tried to look away, but he wouldn't let her, keeping hold of her chin as his eyes locked on hers. "I could never hurt you like that. Ever."

The weight of the last few months was suddenly lifted from her shoulders, and she could feel the sense of relief on her face. Tears streamed down her cheeks once again.

"I am so sorry," Travis whispered while her body shook as she muffled a sob. "I should have been here."

He pulled her close and stroked her hair while she continued to cry. After several minutes when she had finally stopped, he stepped back and held her around the shoulders while looking pleadingly into her glistening, wet eyes. She had never seen him defenseless like this before. "Can you ever forgive me?"

She noticed he still hadn't told her he loved her.

She wiped her eyes with the back of her hand and gave a weak smile before lightly touching his shoulder. "Of course I can forgive you, Travis. I'm not completely innocent in this. I know I should have told you, no matter the consequences. My only defense is I was afraid." She walked over and started to wipe the coffee table where her cereal bowl had sat before continuing. "Thank you for coming to talk to me and being able to get past your anger. Thank you for being so kind. That gives me hope that we can figure out how we're going to do this."

He looked confused.

"I want to be there when our child is born. I want to try to make this work between us."

Tears started to stream down Ava's face once again. He wanted to make things work so he could be there when the baby was born. What happened after that? He would grow tired of her once again, and she would be destroyed when he left her. Only this time she'd have to grieve in the presence of their boy.

Maybe he wouldn't leave?

That wouldn't work. She knew they couldn't be together simply because of their child. She'd seen that end in disaster.

She was unable to speak, so she stood there silently and looked at the colorful shopping bags on the floor, so many thoughts still going through her mind.

Finally, she was able to muster up the word, "No," and gently shake her head.

He rubbed the back of his neck furiously again, then ran his fingers through his hair. Letting out a whoosh of air, he asked, "What do you mean, *no*?"

All of it was happening too fast. He had just been mad at her, then he was apologizing for hurting her, next rubbing her belly, then he was asking her if they could make it work. Did he actually love her? Or was he doing this simply to be with his baby?

This was exhausting her. She needed to lie down and told him so. He was cute as he walked her into the bedroom, like she was going to break, and moved things out of her way so she wouldn't trip before turning on the lamp on her nightstand. He removed her robe, then rotated her around to face him. As she did so, she saw his face suddenly change as he muttered, "Oh my God."

"What's wrong?" she asked, then noticed he was staring at her boobs. It was her old Travis, openly leering at her.

She looked down. "Yeah, the gods needed to make up for the baby belly somehow."

He started untying the front of her pajama top.

"Travis, I really am tired."

He shushed her and removed her shirt, leaving her bottoms untouched. He stared at her body carrying his son then walked over and shut off the overhead light before stripping down to his boxers. She noticed he wasn't aroused. He climbed into bed and threw the sheet back, motioning for her to lie down next to him. When she did, he burrowed in next to her, pulling her tightly against him. The feeling when his bare skin met hers was electric. She sighed at the familiar scent of him and nuzzled into his neck.

"I just want to hold you and our baby in my arms all night, if that's okay. Nothing else, I promise." Then as if he couldn't resist, he added, "Even if you begged me."

She leaned back on her elbows and shot him a challenging look with her eyebrows raised.

"Darling, don't make a liar out of me." This time she refused to avert her gaze. He tenderly started caressing her body, murmuring, "Or do, that's okay too."

She closed her eyes and let herself enjoy the feeling for a moment before stopping him and whispering, "We can have this baby together, but we can't be a couple again. And you don't need to be with me to be in the delivery room. You're welcome to be there." Her pride had taken over. She wasn't going to give him another chance to hurt her.

He nodded and gave a half-smile. "I had to give it a shot."

She honestly hadn't expected him to give up so easily. That wasn't the Travis she knew. The Travis she knew never took no for an answer. He almost seemed thankful when she told him she wasn't interested. He was very noble, wanting to do the right thing, but it must have been a huge relief she let him off the hook.

Yet, he still held her in his arms with no indication of leaving. She pecked him on the cheek before switching the lamp off, then turned over and nestled her butt against him in a spooning manner. She really was tired and frankly, she was glad she was, otherwise she'd lay awake all night trying to figure out what was going on.

But then she wished that wasn't the case when she felt his cock move against her when she wiggled her butt while trying to get even closer to him. Fuck, she was horny! But exhaustion trumped horniness, and she was asleep in no time with Travis keeping his arms around her, one hand on her belly. Besides, they weren't going to be together as a couple— having sex would only complicate things.

# Chapter 23

*Ava*

Ava woke to the dawn coming in her room. She had been enjoying having breakfast with her parents and was happy she hadn't overslept and missed it today. It took her a moment to remember she had fallen asleep snuggled against Travis, but now he was gone, and she felt sad for a moment.

Maybe it had been a dream?

She got up and made herself presentable before throwing her fuzzy slippers and old robe on and heading to the main house for her mother's breakfast.

On the short walk over, she conceded today was the day she was going to have to tell her mother about Travis. She wasn't looking forward to it but knew it had to be done. She was fairly certain her father would keep his word about not telling her, knowing he didn't want to be the one to break it to his wife her grandchild's baby daddy was none other than Travis Sterling.

Ava opened the door and instantly smelled the delicious aroma of Francine's breakfast.

"I'm so glad that smell doesn't make me puke anymore!" she announced as she closed the door. Looking over at the breakfast table, she first saw her mother's smiling face, her father taking a sip of coffee, and then her eyes focused on... Travis. Judging by how little food was left on their plates, he'd been there a while. Why did she suddenly feel like she was about to enter the principal's office?

Mrs. Ericson jumped up and immediately hugged her daughter around the shoulders as she guided her to the table.

"Me too, dear! Now what can I fix you? Pancakes seemed not to agree with you yesterday."

Ava had forgotten she had almost gotten sick yesterday when she learned her father was going to be presiding over Travis' case.

"I think I want to try them again anyway."

Her father pulled out a chair next to him, across the table from Travis, gesturing her to sit down. She walked over and slumped into it without saying anything while trying to figure out what Travis was doing there. She thought maybe he hadn't said anything yet, so she kept her mouth shut until she understood exactly what was going on.

Her mother brought over a glass of juice and set Ava's prenatal vitamins on the table next to it. "We need to keep that baby healthy!" She smiled, then looked at Travis and smiled broader. Okay, so her mother obviously knew. Now what?

Francine asked, "More coffee, Travis?" then gestured to her husband. "Dear?"

Both men indicated they would like a refill, so she brought a carafe of coffee when she brought Ava's pancakes. Sitting down between Ava and Travis, she slid her chair up to the table and looked back and forth between them before simply saying, "So."

Ava looked over at Travis as she began to butter her pancakes. So. She opened her mouth to speak but heard Travis' voice before she could utter any words.

"So, your daughter and I are having a baby together."

"Yes, I know, but what does that mean, exactly? Are you two going to get married? Live together so your child grows up with both parents under one roof?"

Again she was about to speak when Travis beat her to it. "We haven't quite got all of that figured out yet, Frannie."

Her mother started to tsk and cluck when her father finally spoke up. "My dear, go easy on the man. He just found out yesterday he was going to be a father."

Ava was mid-bite of her breakfast when her mother shot her a disapproving look. "Yes, I know."

Might as well get it all out in the open. Taking a deep breath, she blurted out, "You need to know something else, Mom. I'm actually twenty weeks along, not eight." Mrs. Ericson gasped. Ava tried to soften the blow with, "And we're having a boy."

Tears immediately filled the older woman's eyes, and she grabbed her daughter's hand with one hand and Travis' with the other. "A boy! I'm so happy for you two. You're going to be wonderful parents to my grandson." Then she looked over at her husband, who didn't seem as surprised as she was. Reading his wife's mind, he said, "I found out yesterday but was sworn to secrecy." When Francine's mouth gaped open he continued defensively, "I told her she better tell you soon or I would have to."

Frannie squeezed both of their hands tight, maybe a little too tight, before releasing them and exclaiming, "We've got a lot of work to do and not a lot of time to do it! We're going to have to wait until the first of the year for your shower, but I need to get invitations out as soon as I can! I'm going to ask your aunt to host it, of course, but we can still have it here." Her mother was very traditional and was going to hold on to as much etiquette as she could, even if her daughter was going to be an unwed mother, and that included immediate family not hosting a shower.

"Mom, I don't need a shower."

"Nonsense."

Ava looked over at Travis. She hated having to say this in front of him. "Hardly anyone even knows I'm pregnant, and even fewer know Travis is the father. I think it would be too awkward to have to explain everything."

Before Francine could disagree, Travis chimed in, but not like Ava was hoping. "Let's have a New Year's Eve party, and we can announce it then. We can co-host it so you can have your friends and family, and I can invite who I'd like. We'll get it all out in the open at once, so we don't have to repeat our story over and over."

Ava was starting to shake her head no when her mother clapped her hands in excitement. "Yes! That's a wonderful idea! Are you two free to look at some venues this afternoon? If we could get the location booked, I can get the invitations to the printer's today. I've given them enough business over the years. They will do a quick turnaround for me, and we could have them in the mail no later than Monday!"

Travis shot Ava a smirk and without taking his eyes off her said, "Frannie, do you think you can arrange for us to look at The Plaza at noon?" Her mother nodded enthusiastically. Ava could see the woman's planning wheels turning in overdrive. Travis knew dangling a party to plan in front of her mother would get the woman on his side about it. Ava shot him a glaring look that didn't seem to faze him in the least because he continued, "Judge Ericson, would you care to join us?"

At least she could still count on her father not to fall for his charms.

Her father patted Travis on the back. "Son, I think given our circumstances, you need to start calling me Robert." He then smiled and surprised Ava by saying he'd love to come along.

What the hell?

Travis wiped his mouth with his napkin, stood up, and pushed in his chair. "Terrific. Robert, I'll pick you up at eleven forty-five. Ladies, shall I pick you up as well or do you want to meet us there?"

Before anyone could say anything else, Ava firmly said, "We'll meet you there."

Travis kissed Francine on the cheek and thanked her for breakfast, shook Robert's hand, and, knowing she wouldn't turn away in front of her parents, leaned over and kissed Ava softly on the lips. He looked into her eyes with amusement and said, "I'll see you later."

Ava felt her cheeks flush. She wasn't sure how, but she was going to make him pay for this.

Just then Steven came through the back door covered in sweat from his run.

He stood at the center island, with an eyebrow raised, and looked at Ava, then at Travis in the doorway on the opposite side of the room as him.

Travis crossed the kitchen and held out his hand. "Travis Sterling."

Steven stayed on the other side of island counter and eyed the man with a frown. He slowly wiped his sweaty hand on his shorts and cautiously held it out. "I'm Ava's brother, Steven."

Travis said, "Nice to meet you, Steven. I was on my way out, but maybe you can join us this afternoon."

Steven continued scowling. At least her big brother had her back. He shot Ava a look. "What's this afternoon?"

She jumped to her feet before her mother could start explaining their afternoon plans and went over to stand next to Steven.

"Nothing. It's not a big deal. Travis wants to have a New Year's party where we'll announce the obvious news I'm pregnant." She gulped. "With his baby."

"*This is the father?*" Steven looked at Travis like he was going to throttle him.

Travis took a step back. God bless her brother. He always did watch out for her.

Steven looked over at their parents. "How can you even let this guy in your house? Do you have any idea what he has put Ava through?" He directed his anger back at Travis. "My father should have thrown you out instead of feeding you breakfast. My sister was so distraught over you we thought she was going to lose the baby. She couldn't keep anything down. Look at her, she looks like hell."

She knew he was being melodramatic on her behalf, but still, *I look like hell? Thanks for that, big brother.*

Their mother scurried over next to Travis and gazed at Ava, saying, "I think she looks beautiful," before focusing on her eldest child. "Steven, she couldn't keep anything down because of morning sickness. Travis was not the reason she ended up in the hospital. You can't blame him."

"The hell I can't, Mother. She told everyone it was morning sickness, but it was her nerves, her doctor even told me so. She has been a wreck over this whole situation with him. She'd almost gotten it under control when he paid her a visit and made it worse."

Mrs. Ericson shushed her son. "Stop it! That's in the past, and we're going to put it behind us. He's here now, and he's that baby's father, so you're going to have to deal with it!"

Her brother started to continue berating Travis when their father spoke from the breakfast table. "Steven, that's enough."

That was all that was needed to shut her brother up. Robert Ericson's children knew when he spoke, that was it, there was no arguing. Even as adults they held their father in the utmost regard.

Ava had watched the scene unfold in front of her and was surprised Travis didn't give it back to Steven. She knew he was more than capable. He was famous for it and she'd seen it firsthand. Instead, he stood there as though he was taking his punishment, not offering an excuse or better yet, putting the blame where it belonged—on Ava for lying to him. He just let her brother lambast him without saying a word.

Right then, Hope and Grace appeared in the doorway in their pajamas with mussed hair, rubbing their eyes. "What's all the yelling about, Steve?" Hope asked as she shuffled toward the refrigerator.

Their brother looked away without saying anything. Francine interjected, "Girls, this is Travis Sterling. He's the father of Ava's baby."

Just like that, her mother dropped the bomb and threw him under the bus. Maybe there was hope for the woman after all.

The younger girls looked him over, sizing him up.

Grace cocked her head and said, "You look familiar." She squinted and stared at him, her eyes getting wide when she realized where she had seen him. The night after the party her parents still knew nothing about, when Ava introduced him as Patrick's uncle. The man who sent the cleaning crew.

"Really nice meeting you, Travis," Grace cooed.

Ava knew her sister recognized him and wasn't going to draw any attention to the fact she had already met him, lest she have to explain the circumstances. Hope took the youngest girl's lead and also gushed over the handsome man that had knocked their older sister up.

With that, Travis looked at everyone and said he had to get to work if he wanted to take the afternoon off. His eyes were no longer smug when they met Ava's with an almost business-like expression before nodding at her brother. He kissed and thanked Fran again for breakfast, told the girls it was nice to meet them, nodded appreciatively at her father, then turned and saw himself out.

The girls scurried over to where Ava was standing, "He's gorgeous! Nice job, Ava!" Hope said in a congratulatory tone.

Grace simply said, "I like him. He seems nice."

*Yeah, you like him because he didn't rat you out to your mom and bailed your sorry hung-over self out from hard work.*

Their brother stood there, glowering, but not daring to say anything while their father was still in the room. As if on cue, Robert Ericson made his way to exit the kitchen. Before leaving, he turned to his son and said, "Let's talk later." Steven knew better than to talk about it further in front of their mother.

\*\*

Ava and her mother pulled up to the valet at The Plaza precisely at eleven fifty-five. The elder Ericson woman had phoned three venues and because of all the business she had sent their way, was given a same day appointment at all three.

Francine made her way to the concierge desk and asked for Kimberly. Within two minutes, the woman appeared. "Mrs. Ericson! So lovely to see you again! Thank you so much for thinking of us." Just then, Travis and Robert walked through the lobby doors. Frannie offered them both a warm greeting before turning to Kimberly. "Everyone's here. Let's get started, shall we?"

They walked into the elegant ballroom with crystal chandeliers hanging above each table. It was currently set up for an event, so they could picture what the room would look like for the party.

After a brief rundown of the amenities the hotel could offer for a party, her mother asked Kimberly, "What are our menu options?"

Kimberly must have misunderstood the purpose of Mrs. Ericson's question.

"We can go as inexpensive as you'd like." Obviously the woman did not know who she was in the presence of.

Travis had been looking through the window to the outdoor patio, hands in his pockets. He turned around and drawled, "And what if I'd like it to be expensive?" He was clearly offended at the mere suggestion he would host a cheap party.

This flustered the woman, and she tried to recover. Francine Ericson, ever the gracious socialite, attempted to put Kimberly back at ease by picking up a printed menu off a table and asking clarifying questions about the entrées listed. Her father chuckled as he walked around the space.

*What am I doing here? This is silliness. We should just send out announcements like normal people.*

Except their situation was far from normal, and a far cry from what she was sure her mother had envisioned for announcing her first grandchild to society. The guilt of that kept Ava from walking out the door.

"What day are we looking at?" Kimberly loudly inquired, directing her question to Travis.

Francine ran interference and answered with a smile. "New Year's Eve."

"Oh," the woman said morosely. "That's just a little over a month away; the ballroom is already booked that evening for an event The Plaza is hosting. If you had given me more notice..." She wrung her hands. "There's a side ballroom we could look at. That one may still be available."

Travis looked at Francine and the woman then flatly and coolly said, "Unfortunately, we hadn't the luxury of being able to plan far enough in advance to meet your schedule. I understand that puts us at a disadvantage, and I understand there are consequences by not booking in advance, so whatever you need to charge for us to have the room for New Year's Eve, I don't care. I am prepared and more than capable of paying it. Please tell me the price to make this happen, so we can let you get back to your day."

The woman looked anxiously at Travis, then back at Francine. She was clearly in a quandary.

Ava smiled when she remembered wondering what it would be like for someone to tell Travis no. Apparently this was it.

Francine again ran interference. "Travis, I arranged for us to also look at The Lodge and Las Montanas Verde this afternoon. Why don't we wait and—"

But he cut her off, trying to be gentler this time. Smiling patiently, he said, "Francine, I know the two other locations. We've hosted the Warrior Project ball at both of them at one time or another. I've been to several events at all three locations and The Plaza has always outclassed the other two by far. This party is a big deal." He looked over at Ava. "Your daughter and I are going to announce we're having a child without the benefit of being married. I want this to be such an elegant affair that people will barely flinch at that detail."

Ava knew the people who would flinch. The people he was talking about were in the Ericsons' social circle, particularly Francine's. While having a baby out of wedlock was no longer considered scandalous in today's society, it was still frowned upon in the circles her parents ran in. Ava's sphere not so much, but she was still willing to do whatever would help lessen the blow to her parents' reputation. Travis might also have been concerned about his partners, and how their older clients might feel about such news, although she highly doubted it. Travis could have fifty children out of wedlock with fifty different women, and people would still hire him. She wasn't sure if she gave a damn or not about how this was going to reflect on Travis in 'society', but she did relish the blow his unobtainable bachelor status was going to take, if at least temporarily. He'd probably become more eligible as the doting, single father who needed a woman to mother his child.

If she didn't recognize his name, Kimberly at least understood Travis was someone she wanted to make happy.

Not to mention being able to name the fee would be quite a coup.

"Maybe we could move our event to the other hall." She excused herself to go talk to her superiors.

Ava was going to say something to Travis about how it wasn't a big deal—they should look at the other locations, but thought better of it. Instead, she tried to make chitchat to break up the uncomfortable silence. Her mother took over instead with talk of decorations and centerpieces. Ava could tell Travis wasn't paying attention. He was lost in thought elsewhere, knowing he could entrust Frannie to make this the party of the decade.

"Ava, what colors are you thinking?" her mother asked her.

She hadn't given a single thought to a color scheme. Off-the-cuff, she suggested pink and black. Francine shrieked. It was a fabulous idea. "Actually, Mom, what if we did a black and white ball?"

"Oh, I like that idea even better!" Frannie scurried around the room, notepad in hand, jotting ideas and drawing schematics. Ava was surprised her mother hadn't brought a tape measure with her.

Travis appeared at her side, hands back in his pockets, and nudged her with his arm as he said, "I like that idea too."

She felt obligated to be nice to him. He was going to an awful lot of trouble for this party. "Hey, I'm sorry about this morning, with Steven. He is the quintessential older brother. He'll come around."

Travis shrugged. "I had it coming" was all he said about it.

"Still, I know I share more than half the blame. I should never have lied to you, no matter how scared I was. You had a right to know."

"I can't argue with that, but if I hadn't been such a prick to you, it probably would have been a helluva lot easier for you to."

She smiled. "That's true."

Just then Kimberly appeared, paperwork in hand. The hotel was requiring one hundred percent of the ballroom rental up front as a deposit. Ava choked at the amount but Travis didn't even flinch. They would meet again within a week to finalize the menu and the open bar options. Guests would be given a preferred rate if they chose to stay in one of the hotel's rooms, and there would be a large dance floor and a stage with a microphone. The only sticking point, that Travis of course won by putting up more money, was what time they would have access to the room. Francine insisted it had to be the evening before in order to decorate it properly.

With the stroke of a pen, they had their location. Her mother looked at them, practically beaming. "Don't worry about a thing. I will handle every detail."

Ava was relieved. She was tired just looking at one ballroom. Travis hugged Frannie at the shoulders and said, "I'm counting on it."

Mr. Ericson knew what a tizzy his wife was going to be in over the next month, especially having the holidays thrown in the mix. "Dear, you need to be sure to delegate." His wife hushed him, grinning ear to ear at the idea of how amazing this party was going to be.

They walked out to the lobby, and Travis asked her parents if they wouldn't mind riding together, so he could take Ava to lunch alone. She was a little irritated he didn't even ask her, just assumed she would be willing. As if he could read her mind, he turned to her. "If that's okay with you?"

Dammit, now she couldn't be annoyed about that.

"Depends on where you're taking me," she teased.

He replied, "We can go anywhere you want, but I was thinking Barrio. You seemed to enjoy it the last time we were there and—" He paused, recognizing how surreal what he was about to say was, "I need to make sure you're eating so my son isn't going hungry."

"Barrio sounds lovely—" She thrust her index finger at him, "—as long as you don't molest me this time." Last time they were there he had seductively kissed and licked her wrist and hand causing the whole restaurant to stare, not to mention what he secretly did to her thighs under the table.

He threw his head back and laughed. She hadn't seen him do that in so long. She had missed it.

"I promise I will behave myself. This time."

The whole inappropriate behavior talk got her parents' attention, as they both snapped their heads to look at them. Ava answered their inquisitive looks with a laugh and, "It's a long story."

"No wonder you want to go alone." Her father chuckled as he escorted his wife to the valet station.

**

The ride to the restaurant was a bit somber. Travis wanted the details of her hospital stay Steven had brought up that morning. She tried to be as nonchalant about it as she could, but his brows were furrowed the entire time she was talking about it.

"How long were you in the hospital?" he queried.

"Just overnight." She continued to try to downplay it. "They wanted to keep me for observation while they decided if I needed a feeding tube." She laughed and tried to make it sound like a joke.

"Steven said you weren't eating because of nerves."

"I didn't have much of an appetite," she conceded.

"Because of me?"

"Well…" She paused, debating if she should bring up the next point, but then decided it was what it was, and there was no sense avoiding it. "I was worried how I was going to keep him from you." She thought she saw him wince ever-so-slightly. "Then I was scared because every time I ate, I vomited."

She continued, chuckling, "I was so nervous about having to eat it made me sick to my stomach. Talk about irony."

"Did you really almost lose our baby?" He sounded sad.

"There was a concern about his development if I didn't start to keep food down. Anti-nausea medicine wasn't working very well."

"Are you still taking that?"

Ava smiled brightly. "I am, but not as often, and I've gained five pounds in one week!"

With a half-smile, he said, "You're the first woman I've ever known who was happy to put on weight."

His face became somber again as he put his hand on top of hers and gave it a little squeeze. "I wish I had been there for you. I'm sorry I wasn't."

She smiled and shrugged, not able to think of a good way to respond. He didn't talk any more about it, but he didn't take his hand away until they reached the restaurant.

Not surprisingly, he was recognized the minute they walked through the doors. There was the same amount of fuss over him as last time, only now she was far more self-conscious about people staring, given her obvious pregnant belly and page six unknown status. Travis whispered something to the maître d', and Ava saw him slip the man some money, then they were immediately shown to a corner booth out of the way.

Their conversation started out awkwardly, but it didn't take long for them to be laughing and enjoying each other's company. She realized that, other than the mind-blowing movie sex, simply talking to him was what she had missed most. He was brilliant about so many topics, but humble enough to know she could teach him things too.

Somehow the topic turned to baby development. She explained she was currently in the second trimester, and she then would enter the last phase of her pregnancy.

She touched his arm when she told him, "You were smart to start talking to him last night. Soon he will begin to respond to familiar voices."

"You shouldn't have told me that. Now you're never going to get rid of me. I'm going to be talking to your belly every night. Maybe I'll even sing."

She giggled at the thought, and he continued in a quieter, questioning tone. "I want you to think about staying with me, so I can talk to him in the mornings too."

He had said it with trepidation, like he already knew the answer, but couldn't resist asking.

She put her hand over his and smiled. "Let's stick with you visiting me."

He responded in a teasing tone, "You could have your own room and everything." As if that was the one thing she couldn't resist that would tip the scale in his favor.

"I've got my own condo. Well, at least I hope to again. If they ever start rebuilding." She shook her head when she realized she was not making a very good case for not staying with him. "For now, I've got my very own pool house. I can swim any time I want, and my mother takes excellent care of me."

"I had your mother's breakfast this morning. You're right, I can't compete with that."

Once again, he gave up way easier than she had expected, reinforcing what she already knew. His offer was given out of a sense of duty. She didn't want him to feel obligated to her. The small fortune he was dropping on this party to try and salvage the Ericson reputation should be more than enough to ease any form of guilt or obligation he might have.

"You do realize you created a monster, don't you? My mother is going to be relentless about making this party perfect."

He smiled. "I know."

She teasingly frowned at him. "Yeah, well you're not the one who has to live with her!"

He grabbed her hand and started kissing her wrist. "My offer still stands," his lips murmured against her skin.

She snatched her hand back and pouted. "You promised!"

He flashed that familiar wicked grin and put his hand on her thigh. "I couldn't resist."

They finished their meal, and she slipped off to the restroom while he waited in the lobby for her. They were standing in line at the valet when Ava commented about what a beautiful, sunny California day it was.

"Want to walk around for a bit?" he asked.

She thought about it for only a second before nodding. "Yes, that sounds great."

He put his valet ticket in his pocket, offered her his arm, and they started up the sidewalk toward the center square.

"Thanks for lunch. You're right, I do enjoy their food."

"I noticed," he teased.

Playfully slugging him on the arm, she feigned offense. "Hey! I'm eating for two!"

"Oh, it was a compliment! Like I told you earlier, I want to make sure our baby is getting fed too!"

Holding onto his upper arm with both hands, she leaned her head against his shoulder and laughed as they continued to walk along, talking about nothing in particular while enjoying the conversation and the company.

She hadn't realized how far they'd walked until they were standing in front of his building.

"Do you have a few minutes to come up? I want to talk to you about some things."

Sounded serious. She looked at her watch, wondering if she should get back to help her mother with the plans, although she knew her mother didn't need her for a single thing. "Sure."

He opened the door to the lobby and immediately took her arm again as they walked toward the elevator. The girl in the headset behind the huge desk smiled and offered, "Good afternoon," as they made their way through the reception area.

His secretary, Kelli Adamson, smiled at her as they walked into his office suite, then looked startled when she noticed her baby bump. Ava giggled inside at the quick recovery the woman made.

"Ms. Ericson! So lovely to see you again!"

"For the last time, please call me Ava!" she pleasantly replied, then hugged her soundly.

The secretary glanced down again at Ava's protruding stomach. "How long has it been? Three months?"

The woman was not at all subtle.

"Three or four, something like that." She smirked.

Travis had grown impatient with the pleasantries and guided Ava towards his office. He turned to shut the door and said to his secretary, "I'm not to be disturbed," before closing it all the way.

They were seated in his sitting area. She looked down and wondered if he was having the same flashbacks she was of the last time they were on that couch. His evil smirk answered her question, and she felt her cheeks go red. This time, thank God, he sat in the chair opposite her.

"So what do you want to talk about?"

"A couple of things. First, do you have health insurance? I'd like to get you on our company plan. It's first rate."

*Of course it is.*

"I have a policy. I think it's okay. Except for my brief hospital stay, I haven't had a lot of out-of-pocket expenses, and I checked into when he comes. As long as he's healthy with no complications, it should be affordable."

He frowned. "What if there are complications?"

She shrugged and said sheepishly, "I haven't allowed myself to even think about that."

He was all business. "Well, I'm going to put him on my plan. I think that takes effect the second he's born. I would like you to consider going on my plan too. Until then, I'm going to cover any of your out-of-pocket costs, including your hospital stay."

"Travis, I'm pregnant, not destitute."

"I realize that, but this is the least I can do. Please humor my male ego and allow me to do this. Please."

She appreciated the gesture and knew arguing with him would be of no use. "That's very gracious of you," was all she said. She was not, however, going to be turning any bills in to him for payment. "What else did you want to discuss?"

"I'm going to set up a trust for him, and one for you as well. I don't want you to ever have to worry if something were to happen to me."

He had known for one day he was going to have a son, and he was already putting a trust in place for him. She assumed the trust for her was so he would be assured his child was adequately taken care of in the event for some reason he was not around. That sounded par for the course. He never left any detail undone.

She wasn't sure how she should respond. Thank you? Out of politeness and habit, she almost said it wasn't necessary, but then stopped. Of course he felt a trust for his child was necessary. It was most certainly necessary.

"Is there anything special you need from me in order to do that?" was all she could think to say.

"Just your social security number. You can give it to Kelli on the way out."

"Anything else?"

He moved over and sat down next to her. His proximity both excited and scared her. At first, he draped his arm along the back of the couch cushions, but soon he was leaning forward, taking her hand in his and absent-mindedly stroking it before he actually started talking. "Have you given any thought to a baby name?"

"Not really. I mean, I've tucked a few away in the back of mind when I've come across one I liked, but I haven't given it a lot of consideration. Why?"

He paused and took a breath. She could tell this was weighing on him heavily. "It would mean a lot to me if we could name him after my dad."

Ava didn't respond, thinking there was more to the story and not wanting to interrupt him as he explained. Instead, he merely added, "Would you at least think about it?" His eyes were kind and tender, and she suddenly wanted to make him happy. Actually, she wanted to kiss him, but that was not a good idea.

But then she did kiss him, only it was gently on the cheek, and not at all how what she had in mind. "I don't even have to think about. Of course we'll name him after your dad."

His face lit up with a smile so big she thought his cheeks must hurt. It was contagious, and she found herself smiling with him. He leaned over as though he was going to kiss her but then hugged her instead, holding her tight, kissing her hair, and stroking her back. "Thank you," he whispered. He sounded like he might be tearing up. Good grief, that only made her want to kiss him more.

As an afterthought and to lighten the mood, she pulled back and asked suspiciously, "What is his name?"

He laughed at her question. "Alexander."

"Alexander Steven Ericson," she teased. "I like the sound of that."

"Steven? Ericson?" he growled.

"Okay, I'm open to negotiation on the Ericson but Steven is non-negotiable. He and I made a pact when we were kids."

"Alexander Steven Sterling has a much better ring to it," he declared.

"Like I said, I'm open to negotiation."

He winked at her and said, "So am I."

*Oh dear. There was that wink.* The one that had made her knees go weak and her legs fly open. The effect had not diminished in her current condition. If anything, it amplified it. She was still indescribably horny. She knew it was normal, having read all about what the hormones were doing to her, but the tingling in her pelvis indicated it was time to make a retreat, lest she attempt to repeat their couch performance from her last (and only other) visit here. She didn't trust herself at the moment not to jump him right there so she hastily scrambled to her feet.

"Okay, I need to get home. I'm sure my mother is climbing the walls waiting for me."

She didn't wait for his response and headed toward the door. Her hand was on the knob when he called after her.

"Ava?"

She spun around and avoided looking at him, certain he would be able to read her mind. Her dirty, naughty mind. "Yes?"

"I'm your ride home."

*Shit.*

"Oh my goodness!" she laughed almost hysterically and slapped herself against her forehead. "Pregnancy brain!"

Without letting him reply, she prattled on, "You're busy. I can call a cab or Uber."

Travis looked at her like she'd lost her mind and seemed to speak slower as if she might be having trouble understanding him.

"No, I'm not too busy to take you home. I was planning on it. Things always start to slow down during the holidays. Actually, the entire office will be closed the last two weeks in December. We mandate no one is allowed to come in during that time, even partners. We're wrapping up loose ends now."

She had a hard time imagining him not working for two whole weeks. He probably just took everything home and worked on it in his office there. The one with the desk. The magic desk. Dammit! She needed a new dildo. Maybe that would calm her down. Losing her old one in the condo fire made masturbating a harder option now for relieving her pent-up frustrations. She giggled when she thought of the fire inspector going through the charred remains of her bedroom, holding it up and wondering aloud what it was.

She needed to think of something, anything else that didn't involve her pussy being fondled and probed.

Ava wanted to ask him how the Ridgeport Realty case had turned out but her pride prevented her from doing so. *Maybe another time.*

"How is Fred doing?" was all she could think to say.

\*\*\*\*

*Travis*

She actually dozed off on the couch of his office while they waited for someone from the mailroom to run and pick up his car from the restaurant. It was barely past three o'clock and the events of the day appeared to have worn her out. She continued her nap in the car on the way to her parents'. He had never seen anyone get so tired so quickly.

Travis carefully walked her to the pool house, where he sat her on the bed and took off her shoes. She tugged on her new blouse and gave up, exasperated, when she couldn't get it off. "Lift your arms up," he commanded, and she willingly complied in her sleepy state. He couldn't help but notice her heavy-duty bra supporting her amazing boobs and had a brief flashback of things he had done to those tits in the past, causing him to get a little rise in his pants.

*Down, boy; now is not the time.*

He went to unbutton her pants, only to find she had none on her elastic waistband. Instead, he just slid them down as she lifted her bottom to help him take them off. Pulling her socks off, he laid her down on the bed and stared in wonderment at her pregnant belly as the realization came over him that was his son growing inside this beautiful woman. This amazing, adorable, smart, stubborn, perfect woman. He stood watching her for a minute before tucking in the covers around her and kissing her hair repeatedly.

As he turned to leave, she mumbled, "Will you hold me for a little while?"

If her father walked in and found him in bed with her in her state of undress, he was fairly certain he'd leave with a black eye. If her brother walked in, he had no doubt he'd leave on a stretcher. Still, he wasn't going to pass up the opportunity. Last night had been heavenly, and something he could get used to on a regular basis.

"Sure. Let's put your nightie on first, okay?"

"Okay." She pleasantly sighed with her eyes still closed. She was drunk with exhaustion. He couldn't imagine how hard her body had to be working to keep their little one growing.

He found what she had been wearing last night and went to slip her arms through it. She stopped him and without opening her eyes, unhooked her bra and slid it off before raising her hands for him to put the sleepwear on her. He was proud of himself for only hesitating a second to get a good look at her naked breasts. He was even more proud he had managed to keep his hands to himself. While he had been able to keep his physical attraction for her at bay last night— at least somewhat—after waking up to her in his arms this morning and spending a wonderful afternoon with her, all bets were once again off.

She scooched to the middle of the bed and turned over so he could spoon her. He lovingly remembered she often ended up that way in the middle of the night when they slept together. Travis dutifully laid down next to her, putting his left arm around her, breathing in her apple blossom hair and sighing. Laying there next to her without taking both their clothes off and making love to her seemed like the hardest thing he had done in a while. Second only to not dialing her number every time he had picked up his phone to call her over the last few months.

When she couldn't seem to get comfortable, he gestured towards his chest. She wrapped her arms around him and assumed her usual place, albeit a modified one, while sighing and grinning contently once she'd been able to find a comfy position. He smiled and stroked her hair as he ran the back of his other hand along her cheek. He loved watching her sleep.

He woke to her gently shaking him and it took him a second to register where he was. He knew it was dark and his arm was around Ava. Anything other than that, he didn't really care about.

"Hey," she said softly. "You fell asleep with me."

"Well I certainly like waking up with you." He smiled and stretched. "What time is it?"

"Believe it or not, it's only six-thirty. I hate that it gets dark so early this time of year."

"Are you hungry?" he asked her.

She shook her head. "No, but I know I need to eat something."

"You stay here. I'll find us something."

He went into the kitchenette and opened all the cupboards and small refrigerator, only to find nothing he would deem as a suitable dinner. Calling out "I'll be right back," he headed to the main house.

In a few minutes he was back with Francine in tow.

"Nonsense," Frannie was saying as they walked through the pool house door, "I'm happy she's eating so well today."

Mrs. Ericson walked into the bedroom carrying a tray with two bowls filled with spinach salad and two plates of lasagna with garlic bread. There were also two large glasses of milk.

"I'm so glad Travis came and got something for you to eat," Francine said to Ava while smiling at Travis appreciatively. "I always worry if I bring you dinner you'll be sleeping, and I'll wake you up, especially when I can't tell if the lights are on."

"Oh, Mom, thank you so much for this. Just set it on the table. I can get up."

Frannie retreated back to the kitchenette area, along with Travis. Ava followed and sat down at the table in her ratty robe. She began to tear up, then hugged her mother around the waist.

"Thank you so much for taking such great care of me."

Francine looked at her daughter's eyes brimming over with tears and burst out laughing. "Oh honey, I remember those hormones and mood swings! Your poor father does too!"

Travis sat watching. He was still coming to grips with all that had happened in the last twenty-four hours and could not wrap his head around why Frannie was laughing about the fact her daughter was crying, nor could he understand why Ava was crying in the first place.

Mrs. Ericson leaned over and patted him on the cheek. "Remember to be patient and even though it's probably not your fault, hug her and tell her you're sorry anyway."

"Huh?"

"You'll see." She smiled knowingly, then stood up. "Enjoy your dinner."

She turned around before she reached the door. With a hopeful voice, she asked, "Will we be seeing you at breakfast, Travis?"

Travis looked over at Ava, who was pushing her spinach around and deliberately not making eye contact with him after her mother posed the question. "We'll see, Frannie. I've got to play a little bit of catch up with work after playing hooky this afternoon."

"Speaking of playing hooky, we have an appointment next Monday at two-thirty to sample dinners for the party."

He smiled and said, "I look forward to it."

Francine's eyes got wide. "Oh my goodness, I have to stop talking or your food is going to get cold! Good night!"

Travis thought their food was delicious, and their conversation was even better. After dinner, he insisted she lie on the couch with her feet on some pillows while he cleaned up. When he was through with the dishes, he came over and sat on the floor next to the couch and proceeded to talk in a low voice into Ava's stomach, all the while stroking and kissing it like he had last night.

She didn't say anything as she laid back with her eyes closed and a smile on her face while listening to him tell their baby about how they were going to play baseball together.

Travis gently covered Ava with a throw so not to wake her but couldn't resist kissing her. He had intended for it to be on the cheek but somehow found his lips softly on hers.

He stood up and was surprised to hear her say, "That was nice. Do that again."

Sitting down on the edge of the couch, he willing obliged her, only putting his lips more firmly on hers this time. Almost instinctively, her arms came around his neck, pulling him to her. His tongue sought out hers, teasing and demanding she respond, which she did. Their breathing got more ragged, and soon he was nuzzling her neck, heading to her delightful breasts. She was holding the back of his head against her body, arching her back with anticipation. He was so damn aroused.

All of sudden, Ava let out a cry of "No!" and pulled away from him.

He slid off the couch and kneeled onto the ground, looking into her eyes, bewildered, his breathing still unsteady.

She started to cry. "I just—we just—can't."

He was confused but remembered what Frannie had just told him not more than an hour ago, so he hugged her tight and told her how sorry he was, careful not to tell her it wouldn't happen again. He might be an attorney, but in spite of their reputations, he wasn't (usually) a liar, and he wasn't about to start being one now.

"Come on baby, let's put you to bed."

He had tucked her in when she looked at him as though she were upset.

"Aren't you going to stay?"

*Jesus Christ, woman, you're killing me!*

Sitting on the edge of the bed, he brushed her hair away from her face.

"Tell you what, I'll lay with you until you fall asleep, and then I'll go and get some work done and hopefully be back before you even know I'm gone."

She smiled and sighed.

He was determined not to give up. "Or you could just come home with me now."

Had she not looked so warm and cozy in her bed, he probably would have pushed harder. Especially when she seemed as though she was actually considering it and didn't flat out tell him *no*.

He considered that progress.

# Chapter 24

*Ava*

They appeared together the next morning at breakfast with her parents, to the delight of her mother. Thanksgiving was the following day, and Fran made it a point to invite Travis for dinner when she set his breakfast in front of him.

He looked at Ava while replying to Mrs. Ericson. "Thank you. I'd love to come, but I'm hoping Ava and I will go to dinner at my family's. I want to introduce her and share the news with them before the New Year's Eve party."

Ava sat there for a second. That sounded an awful lot like something a couple would do. Was she setting herself up for heartbreak if she said yes?

Travis stroked her arm, not having taken his eyes off her. "I would consider it a huge favor."

Her mother shot her a look that suggested she had better agree or else. When she didn't say anything, Fran took the lead.

"What time is your family's dinner, Travis? I'll be sure to plan ours so you two can make both."

*I guess I'm going to the Sterlings' Thanksgiving dinner.*

Without actually saying the words she was going, she inquired in between bites of her breakfast, "What should I wear? Is it more formal, like ours, or is it like my friends who watch football and wear jeans and sweatshirts?"

He thought carefully for a second. "I think it's something in between. Slacks and a sweater will be fine."

Ava scowled. "My wardrobe is in short supply of slacks and sweaters these days."

He smiled. "Babe, wear whatever you're comfortable in. It's not a big deal."

For whatever reason, she felt like being surly. "Fine," was all she replied before taking a drink of juice.

*And stop fucking calling me babe.*

\*\*\*\*

*Travis*

Ava looked nervous as they pulled up to his older brother Tim's brick two-story with the immaculate green lawn. Tim was the father of Patrick, the boy who'd started all of this by calling Travis to rescue him from being held hostage at Grace's party.

His little sister Tara was also going to be there with her husband, Jim, and their new baby.

Travis winked and held her hand as they walked in the front door. He took a deep breath, not knowing exactly what to expect next. He had told his family he was bringing a date, which was a big enough deal in and of itself since he had never once brought a woman to any family gathering, but hadn't mentioned she was with child. As his siblings warmly greeted their brother, they were also very welcoming to Ava as Travis introduced her, all the while trying not to stare or act surprised by her pregnant belly.

Tara's newborn was sleeping, but Travis couldn't help but stare at the little girl in wonderment. They were going to have that in four short months. He smiled widely when the baby grasped his finger. Ava grinned when she watched him quickly step away when the little one started to fuss.

Kissing his sister on her temple while hugging her, he beamed. "You done good, kid."

Tara blushed before disappearing to breastfeed.

Everyone was milling around the gourmet kitchen that rivaled Travis', nibbling on appetizers and enjoying a glass of wine, or its non-alcoholic equivalent, when Tara returned. Travis decided it was time to make his announcement and made sure everyone's glass was full before clanking a spoon on his glass to get their attention.

"If you don't mind, I'm going to start the toasts this time," he said making sure they were all listening before continuing. "Tara and Jim, congratulations. I love that you've made me an uncle once again. Little sister, I've never seen you more beautiful than when you hold your baby girl in your arms." He beamed at her before continuing. "Tim and Sandy, you continue to be the example for the rest of us. The love and care you show each other and your family is amazing and enviable." He paused and took a deep breath. "This is a particularly special Thanksgiving for me, and I love that I'm able to share it with all of you. As I'm sure you've probably figured out, my friend Ava—" He pulled her next to him. "—is pregnant—" He paused for dramatic effect. "—with my baby." The men smiled, Tim's wife and kids murmured their surprise, and Tara clapped her hands in excitement, waiting for him to continue. "Our son, Alexander, is due in mid-March."

The family swarmed them with hugs, tears, and not too intrusive touching of Ava's belly before continuing their tradition of toasts.

His big brother went next. "Ava, I can honestly say I never thought I'd see the day Travis would be a father. You are obviously very special, and we want to welcome you to our family." He smiled kindly at her then continued. "Travis, I've always been proud of everything you've done, but I think this is the best news you've ever given me. You're going to be a great father, and I'm so happy you are naming your son after our dad." He got a little misty eyed. "I know Mom and Dad are looking down and smiling right now." He directed his attention to his little sister. "Thank you for finally making me an uncle, and to a little princess no less. I love you all." Then he raised his glass and offered, "Cheers."

After *cheers* in unison from everyone in the room, it was his sister's turn. Remembering what Travis did at the ball, she took a little different tone.

"Tim and Sandy, Travis is right, thank you for continuing to be the example. I hope to be half the parent you two are." She faced Travis and Ava. "It doesn't happen very often, but when my big brother screws up, he does it in grand fashion." She shot Travis a look, then looked at Ava with a smile. "But Ava, you are proof he eventually figures it out and finds his way. We are so happy for you both and are here for whatever you need." She took a breath and then closed her eyes tight, balled her free hand into a fist, stamped her feet, and squealed, "I can't believe Travis is going to be a father!"

Glasses clanked and the siblings' spouses gave speeches about what a wonderful family Ava was joining and made mock warnings about the Sterling stubbornness. He couldn't help but smile when he looked at the woman growing his baby inside her.

Ava was talking with Tim's wife, Sandy, when Travis went in the other room with his sister.

Grabbing him by the arm, Tara whispered, "Oh my goodness, Travis! Congratulations! I thought for sure you had blown it with her at the ball!"

He grimaced. "Tara, I still have blown it. We are not together—yet." Then he offered his sibling some assurance. "I'm trying like hell though."

She squeezed his hand and said, "Be patient. There is no doubt in anyone's mind she loves you; that much is obvious every time she looks at you." She punched his arm. "You are just as obvious, by the way."

He smiled a knowing smile. "I don't know what to do to get her back," he lamented.

"Be attentive, be caring," she laughed, "and be available when she gets super horny."

"She's going to get horny?" he asked as his eyes widened.

"Big brother, she probably already is."

That definitely held some possibilities.

While they were all seated at the dinner table, Travis made a point of making sure everyone knew to look for their New Year's Eve party invitations in the mail by next week.

"Oh no!" Sandy exclaimed, "We have already made plans."

Travis gave his brother a look. "Cancel them. You need to be there." He never asked anything of his family, so he hoped Tim understood this was important.

Sandy started to protest when Tim cut her off. "Of course, we'll be there."

****

*Ava*

Tim had three boys and one girl, the exact opposite of Ava's family makeup. Watching the brothers together, she almost felt sad for Steve not having a brother to wrestle and horseplay with when he grew up.

*What am I talking about? He horseplayed with me.*

She also watched them wistfully when she realized Alexander wasn't going to have a full biological sibling. She was going to have two different fathers for her children. Ugh. Holidays were going to suck as they tried to juggle family schedules.

Her rational side took over. *Let's wait and worry about that when we have to, okay?*

The afternoon had been wonderful. They made her feel so comfortable and she loved the toasts welcoming her into the family.

Except she wasn't joining their family. Her baby was, not her. Still, she allowed herself to admit it would be a wonderful family to join. She decided she'd let Travis deal with the detail that they weren't a couple when he needed to and instead just enjoyed the rest of the time with his warm and loving relatives.

After their meal was finished and things were cleaned up, they made their way to the living room, Sandy in the oversize chair with Tim on the floor leaning back between her legs, Tara and Jim on the sofa with their baby in the car seat on the floor next to the couch, and Travis and Ava on the loveseat. Travis' arm casually draped around Ava's shoulders. They started reminiscing about past Thanksgivings when their parents were alive and teasing each other about bad hair and wardrobe choices, among other missteps from their youth. By their stories of their parents when they were kids, it was obvious they were very loved children. That made Ava happy. Travis also had a great example of parenting that seemed to match her own experience. She gave an internal sigh of relief. Their kid might be okay after all.

Checking the time, Travis announced they needed to be back at the Ericsons' for Round Two of their Thanksgiving dinner. With a warm sendoff, they were on their way.

"Your family is wonderful." She smiled with her head against the headrest as they drove off in his BMW.

"Thanks. I think so too." He grinned. "Except my sister's baby is ugly. I hope our son is cuter than she is!"

That made Ava laugh out loud. "You are going to think Alexander is the most beautiful baby you've ever seen. Even if no one else thinks so. I promise!"

He grabbed her hand and squeezed it.

"Thanks for coming. That meant a lot to me."

She kept hold of his hand and smiled again. "I'm glad I got to meet them."

She really was glad. It helped her know what kind of family her son was going to be with when he spent his holidays with his dad.

All of a sudden, she started to cry.

"What's wrong?!" he asked. "Did someone say something to upset you?" Poor guy. She knew he needed a roadmap to deal with her feelings. Her fragile, extra-sensitive, hormone-fueled feelings.

She sobbed, "I just realized I'm not going to be with him at every holiday!"

Travis frowned and slowed the car down so he could pull over. Putting it in park, he undid his seatbelt, then turned to face her. She thought he was going to yell at her by the somber look on his face. Instead he undid her seatbelt, cupped her face in his hands, and looked into her tear-filled eyes.

"Ava Faith, I love you, and you are going to be at every holiday with our son because you are stuck with me whether you like it or not. I know you loved me once, and I'm hopeful you'll be able to love me again someday. You are the best thing to ever happen in my life, and I'm never letting you go again. Never. Not without a helluva fight."

She stared at him, not sure she was believing what she was hearing. *He loves me?*

He then kissed her on the mouth firmly and ardently, and she let out a small groan as she wrapped her arms around his neck. He loved her! His mouth felt so amazing on hers. His tongue sought hers out and she gladly welcomed it. Breathing harder, he started sucking on her lips while exploring her body with his hands. Finally, he pulled away and asked her to put her seat belt on as he buckled back up.

She groaned internally, *noooooo!* Dinner was going to be torture. She knew all she would be able to think about was making love to him. Maybe they could play footsie under the table.

When he missed the turn to the Ericsons', she made no objections as he pulled onto his street instead. They were in the house immediately, their lips locked as they stripped on their hurried way to the bedroom.

She heard the barking of Fred and Ginger, incensed they were not being let out of their room to say hello. That sound made her happy. She was so glad Fred was okay.

Her mind quickly went back to the hands roaming all over her body, and he gently laid her down on the bed. Although he had been kissing and fondling her with a fervor that left them both panting, he was very careful as he helped her remove the last of her clothes before pausing to admire her for a few minutes.

Completely naked with her swollen belly, she looked directly at him and simply said, "I love you."

She had missed his touch so much. The last few days with him back in her life had been wonderful. She truly did enjoy his company when he was clothed, but the things he made her feel when he was naked were almost indescribable.

\*\*\*\*

*Travis*

What the fuck did I do to deserve her?

He smiled as he finished removing his clothes. He wasn't sure what he'd done but he was going to do his damnedest to be worthy of her from now on. Crawling up her soft body, he paused to kiss her stomach and of course, her breasts, before reaching her face, where he looked at her tenderly.

"I love you too," he whispered before placing his mouth on hers and kissing her with passion.

He wanted to explore every inch of her changed body, kiss each part until neither of them could stand it. She clung to him like she was never going to let go. Holding her in his arms the last few nights without actually touching and caressing her beautiful body had been torture. A wonderful, awful torture.

As he was tasting her skin, he had an ugly thought: it was going to kill him when he had to take out a condom to use. He knew it was going to hurt her too and prayed it didn't bring things to a halt. He'd have to make sure she was too turned on to want to stop.

Wait. That's kind of shitty. Definitely not behavior worthy of her.

He needed to stop and be upfront with her now, before they were past the point of no return, while she still had some of her faculties.

He moved back up to her face and kissed her softly on the mouth.

"Baby, we're going to have to use a condom tonight," he shamefacedly told her. He didn't offer to stop. He was trying to be a good guy, but even he had his limits. He'd let her make that call.

It was obvious by the look on her face she was hurt by what that meant.

"Okay," she said in a low voice.

"I'm sorry."

"It's okay, Travis. I understand. Do you want to put one on now?"

"Are you kidding me? We're not even close to that yet, baby."

He then proceeded to make his apologies to her body by touching and kissing every part covered in skin. Finally, he slid between her legs and breathed in her scent before plunging his tongue inside of her, not bothering to make acquaintances with the other parts of her pussy. She gasped and bucked her hips a little until he withdrew his tongue and replaced it with his finger so he could tend to her lips and clit with his mouth.

He attacked her pussy with a fervor, and because he knew her body so well and it had been so long since the last time he'd touched her down there, it didn't take long until she was moaning and gasping her appreciation as an amazing orgasm wracked her body. He didn't stop as it did and was surprised she let him continue; normally she was pushing his head away by now. He proceeded to lick her to a second climax not long after her first and was feeling pretty proud of himself when the thought of what he had to do next surfaced.

He was glad he had made her come first. Now, if she wanted to quit, she could without her hormones being in complete control. When she drew his head to her and kissed him thoroughly while moving her hand down to stroke his cock, he was even more glad because he knew she was doing it because she wanted to, not because her desires were making her.

She swung her legs round to straddle his muscular thighs and began to rub his cock while watching his face. He didn't take his eyes off hers as she moved her hand in a steady pace up and down his shaft. Lowering her head, she peeked up at him with a small smile through the hair covering her face, then bent down to moisten him with her tongue. Taking long, wide licks as she cupped his balls, he heard her murmur, "Mmm," then he threw his head back with a gasp when she completely engulfed him between her lips. Deliberately dipping him deep in her mouth and sensuously pulling him out slowly, she was obviously enjoying teasing him as she started to roll her hips in rhythm with her mouth and hands.

Travis was somewhat timid about fucking her. Were there rules when making love to a pregnant woman? Was he going to hurt their baby?

He didn't have to worry as Ava took the lead. Getting the dreaded purple package from his nightstand, she rolled the condom on him before sliding her body up to his groin and putting his cock at her entrance. He pushed forward slightly as she rocked down with little thrusts, letting her body get used to him gradually. When he finally was completely inside her, he could have sworn he heard the hallelujah chorus, that's how good it felt, and how much he had missed her.

Closing her eyes, she moved up and down on his cock slowly and steadily and let out a little moan. Watching her, he wondered how it was possible to feel such lust and love at the same time because he was over-the-moon in love with her but still wanted to fuck the shit out of her.

She began to thrust her hips urgently and laid forward onto his chest, riding him even faster. When he held her waist and took over, he was so turned on that it didn't take long before he came hard. He heard her sigh and felt her smile against his chest when he was finally still.

They laid there quietly for a few minutes relishing the moment until he lifted her up off of him and made his trek to the bathroom to clean up.

"Do you think we should get ready and go to your parents' now?" he asked as he tossed her a towel.

****

*Ava*

*Oh shit!* She had completely forgotten it was Thanksgiving. Actually, she had forgotten almost everything except her name when he licked her to multiple orgasms. That was a first, and she wondered if the pregnancy hormones had something to do with it. Happiness exuded from her when she realized she'd have the opportunity to find out after the baby was born.

"Oh my goodness! Yes!"

She brushed her hair and tried to get the *Just Been Fucked* look off her face, but it wasn't happening. She was positively beaming, and every single member of her family noticed it when they arrived late. Her mother had been annoyed at first that they had been kept waiting, but then noticed Travis and Ava's change in displays of affection toward each other. Travis protectively having his arm around her chair during dinner, and Ava leaning into him when she spoke, her happy smile as she touched him lovingly... and their goddamn googly eyes for each other.

Ava excused herself not long after dinner to go and lie down. Travis walked her to the pool house, where he asked her what she thought about him going back to talk with her family and hopefully win Steven over, or at least make the man dislike him less. He made headway when he mentioned he had attended Stanford Law; Steven had studied at Stanford for his undergraduate degree. Her brother also had noticed how much Travis doted on Ava at dinner, and that once he realized it was dark out, went to check on her, causing Steven to relent his previous position and admit Sterling was going to take good care of his sister.

She heard Travis bump into a barstool before she felt him sit on the edge of the bed. When he reached down to stroke her hair, he seemed surprised when she rolled over and smiled at him.

"Hi."

"Hi yourself. How are you feeling?"

"I'm okay. I was just tired."

Continuing to run his fingers through her hair, he asked, "Do you feel like getting up and coming out? Your family is about to start some game I'd never heard of."

Oh yes, her family and games. She had to admit, she did enjoy them, particularly when Steve was home because the two of them were ultra-competitive with each other. When they were younger, their father actually forbade them from playing Monopoly because it was ending in fights between them.

She smirked. "Are *you* up for some Ericson family game time?"

Leaning over, he kissed her on the mouth. "I'd rather have naked Ava Ericson time, but that can wait a while longer."

Kissing her again, he then added with his mythical powered wink, "I guess."

She hoped he enjoyed spending time with her family as much as she had with his. He and Steven were like long-lost brothers when they partnered to gang up on her. Travis didn't seem like he was worried when she threated he was 'going to pay for that.' On the contrary, he acted like he was looking forward to it.

The evening ended, and Ava started making her way to the door towards the pool house, looking at him as if to ask if he was coming. His expression when he looked back at her and shook his head indicated she should know better. When she pretended she didn't understand what he meant, he strode over and scooped her up in his arms, then marched out the front door with her. The pool house was now no longer an option; she was going home to his bed, for good.

**\*\***

From Thanksgiving until Christmas Eve, the two behaved like newlyweds, spending more time in bed than out. They decided to host a party the night before Christmas for both their families to meet and get to know each other.

This was Ava's first time hosting what she referred to as 'a grown up' party. She was impressed with how much knowledge her mother had imparted to her over the years and was pleased with how things had come together. She was hoping they could blend both their family's traditions and maybe make a few of their own.

After everyone had arrived, but before dinner was served, Travis was standing with his arm around her waist when his family started their custom of making toasts at family gatherings. When it got to Travis, he smiled and stepped forward as if to take the floor.

"I want to thank all of you for coming and spending your Christmas Eve with us." He reached for Ava's hand and pulled her toward him. "We are so blessed to have such a caring family and hope you'll all be there when we welcome our son into the world. If you are, then the only thing that could make that day more perfect is if Ava was my wife when he arrived."

Ava felt her stomach drop. *Did he just—?*

She looked to find him in the traditional proposal pose—on one knee while he held out a ring.

"Baby, will you marry me?"

Tears streamed down her face, and she could barely talk. He looked at her, worried when she didn't answer him. Laughing and crying, she nodded yes.

Finally being able to find the words, she cooed, "Of course I'll marry you."

After slipping the ring on her finger, he stood and picked her up to swing her around while kissing her, her arms wrapped tightly around his neck. There wasn't a dry eye in the room.

**\*\***

She later learned that her parents were surprised at their tears, thinking they were prepared. Travis had taken them to lunch to ask their permission to marry their daughter. They all understood it was simply symbolic since he hadn't asked their permission to screw her ninety minutes after meeting her, but she knew her mom and dad appreciated the gesture anyway.

Frannie volunteered to go ring shopping with Travis, but he had already gone to see a friend who was a jeweler and had her ring custom made. He designed the dainty channel band to completely surround her flawless three-carat pear-shaped diamond. He confided to Ava that his mother had a pear-shaped stone and he felt he was somehow paying tribute to her by giving his future wife something similar. She cried when he told her how he wished Ava had gotten to meet her—

meet both his parents, actually. He knew they would approve of his union with her.

When they laid in bed that night, Ava sat admiring her ring and said, "I just had an idea! The New Year's party can also be our engagement party!" She thought she was brilliant for thinking of it.

He didn't say much, just sighed and responded with, "Mm hmm."

She sat up suddenly and turned to face him. With an accusatory tone, she asked, "Did you plan that? Is that why you wanted it to be such a big deal?"

He laid there quietly for a second before sitting up to look at her.

"No, I want that to be our wedding reception."

She was taken aback. This was too sudden; they didn't have time to prepare.

"But we haven't booked a church or anything! There's no way we could find something with this short notice."

Sliding his hands around her back and nibbling her neck, he said, "Let's have it here. In our backyard. We'll be surrounded by our closest family and friends. Nothing too big. Your dad can marry us." Pulling away from her neck, he looked at her with an eager expression. "Whaddya say?"

Ava sat dutifully still, as if she were pondering the idea, which she wasn't doing at all because the second he suggested it, she loved it.

"I think that sounds perfect," she said as she kissed his lips and brought her forehead to his.

Lowering her body back down onto the bed so he could make love to her, he couldn't have agreed more.

# Epilogue

*Ava*

Their New Year's Eve party/wedding reception was just about perfect, except for the photo from it that somehow managed to end up a quarter-page size in the *Out and About* section the next day. It was a wonderful picture of the two of them during their first dance, Travis gazing lovingly at her while she smiled up at him in her beautiful pink gown with the headline, *Off the Market*!

The ball's theme was black and white, but her mother insisted she stand out, and they found a pink dress that in no way hid her pregnant belly. When Ava was lamenting that fact, Travis smiled and emphatically told her he thought that made her look even more beautiful.

My, how she loved that man.

Ava introduced Ron to Tracey but could tell right away there wasn't a connection between the two. "I gave it a shot," she mused. "They're on their own."

\*\*\*\*

*Ron*

As Ron watched Travis and Ava together, he couldn't help but feel a bit envious. This was the second time he had not gotten the girl and decided the next time an opportunity came along, he wasn't going to play nice and let it pass by. He wondered if it was serendipity that the moment he thought that, the most beautiful blonde he had ever seen smiled as she took her seat at his table and introduced herself as

Brenna Roberts. She charmingly looked down shyly when he caught her eye.

The older woman sitting next to Brenna put her hand sympathetically over hers and said, "I'm so sorry about Danny." The gorgeous woman just gave a meager smile and offered her thanks and said she was doing all right.

*Danny Roberts? As in,* the *Danny Roberts, baseball player for the San Diego Padres?*

He knew Danny had been killed in a car crash a few years ago and sizing his widow up, had no trouble believing she had been a professional ball player's wife. She was damn-near flawless, even if some of her parts were probably not authentic. No woman in her forties had real boobs that perky, but he was perfectly fine with how high hers sat. Perfectly fine. Genuine was overrated. He was applauding his decision to attend Ava and Travis' party after all when he asked if he could get her something from the bar, and she flirtatiously offered to go with him.

*Thank you, whoever made the seating chart, for putting her at my table.*

\*\*\*\*

*Travis*

Travis took Ava's hand not long after their first dance and unapologetically exited his expensive party with his bride. He was going to make love to his wife before the day's events caught up with her and she was too exhausted. After they finished their first love-making session as man and wife in the penthouse suite of The Plaza, Ava turned to Travis and asked out of the blue, "How did you know about Operation Sex Kitten?"

He grinned at her wickedly. "I honestly have no idea what it was. I just saw it flash on a text Anne sent you one time when your phone was sitting on the counter."

She smiled and shook her head at him. "That explains it."

\*\*\*\*

*Ava*

Travis brought it up years later when their oldest daughter was about to go on her first date.

"He better not have any sex kitten operations in mind," he growled in Ava's ear as they watched their girl's date follow her out the front door.

"I have some in mind, Mr. Sterling," she purred while tracing his cock over his pants with her finger.

"You do? Didn't you learn your lesson the last time, Mrs. Sterling?" he teased as he pulled her hard and tight against him.

She just grinned and continued stroking him. "Not in the slightest, baby."

Kissing her neck, he threatened, "Good thing you finished your research project yesterday because I don't think I'm going to let you out of bed this weekend."

Pulling away from him, Ava asked in mock concern, "Who will feed our three children?"

"We'll have pizza delivered," he replied with a wink.

She was still a sucker for that wink, even after all these years.

<h1 style="text-align:center">The End</h1>

# A Note From Tess

Thank you for reading my debut novel. I loved writing it and fell in love with Travis AND Ron, so it was hard to decide who Ava should end up with. I think Travis was the right choice, but I wanted Ron to have his happily-ever-after too. Please read Ron's story in *The General's Desire*, Book 2 of the San Diego Scene.

I hope you will leave me a review wherever you purchased *Operation Sex Kitten*. Reviews are so important for authors – especially new ones like me.

Join my newsletter (BookHip.com/SNGBXD) to be the first to know about upcoming releases and for exclusive content.

# *The General's Desire*
## San Diego Social Scene, Book 2

*Falling in lust is easy but falling in love is more than they ever imagined.*

Brenna Roberts hasn't had the best luck with men—from her deceased philandering husband to most recently being stood up for a date and having it announced in the gossip section of the newspaper. She's beginning to doubt that good guys still exist. Then she meets decorated Marine General Ron Thompson. Stoic, handsome, and all alpha... he's literally her hero when he saves her from a bad situation.

Decorated Marine General Ron Thompson isn't looking for love. Lust maybe, but not love. As a military star on the rise, he'd rather keep his head down and his focus on the prize—promotion. But when the widow of professional baseball player Danny Roberts sits down at his table at the Sterling wedding reception, everything changes. Lucky for him, he's always been the type to go big or go home, and he's going big when it comes to her.

But she's not sure she's cut out to be with a military man for anything more than just a fling. The sex may be amazing, but the long periods apart and his inability to discuss his work might be too much for her to handle. Except he keeps saving the day, making it impossible for her to stay away.

This is Book 2 in the San Diego Social Scene series. Each book is a stand-alone with an HEA and no cheating.

https://bit.ly/TheGeneralsDesireTess

# *Playing Dirty*
## San Diego Social Scene, Book 3

Cassie

I'm a career woman. I wear success like a second skin, and I'm rarely satisfied with anything less than the best. This includes my love life. If you want to date me, you better bring your A game because I don't play with the B team.

The only type of commitment I'm interested in is the one I have with my career. There is no man strong enough to tame me. Bold enough to rattle me. Or confident enough to win my heart. But then again, I have never met a man like Luke Rivas.

Luke

Cassie is one feisty, fiery, demanding woman who has enough confidence to intimidate even the bravest of men. She's driven, ambitious, and clearly has no interest in anything more than a casual fling.

But here's the thing. I want her, and once I have her, there will be nothing casual about it.

I will crack through that tough exterior she wears so well and bend her into submission. I'll make her break every one of her own damn rules just for me. And in order to accomplish just that...

I'm willing to play dirty.

Get your copy here: https://bit.ly/PlayingDirtyTess

# *Cinderella and the Marine*
## San Diego Social Scene, Book Four
*One night. No strings attached. What could go wrong?*

Cooper Johnson was happy living the carefree life of a successful bachelor. Money to spend, a revolving door of women, no commitment, no relationship troubles—it was perfect. At least that's what he thought until he held his friends' newborn baby in his arms, and she smiled at him.

That was the moment he realized what life was all about. That was also the moment it occurred to him that he needed a baby mama—stat.

So...the hunt is on for the perfect candidate. But first, he might have to have one last fling—go out with a bang. Literally.

Kate Connelly made a few wrong decisions along the way and is now busting her ass waiting tables while putting herself through college. It's not ideal, but she's determined to stand on her own two feet and take care of her responsibilities the best she can.

But she's still a woman with needs. She just don't have the time for any kind of commitment. Naturally when a smoldering hot Marine offers her a no-strings attached one night stand, she's on board.

Turns out...he wants more than she's willing to give.

https://bit.ly/CinderellaandtheMarine

# San Diego Social Scene

*Operation Sex Kitten*: (Ava and Travis)
   https://bit.ly/SDSSOperationSexKitten
*The General's Desire*: (Brenna and Ron)
   https://bit.ly/TheGeneralsDesireTess
*Playing Dirty*: (Cassie and Luke)
   https://bit.ly/PlayingDirtyTess
*Cinderella and the Marine*: (Cooper and Katie)
   https://bit.ly/CinderellaandtheMarine
*The Playboy and the SWAT Princess*: (Craig and Maddie)
   https://bit.ly/ThePlayboyandtheSWATPrincess
*The Heiress and the Mechanic*: (Harper and Ben)
   https://bit.ly/TheHeiressandtheMechanic
*Burning Her Resolve*: (Grace and Ryan)
   https://bit.ly/BurningHerResolve
*This Is It:* (Paige and Grant)
   https://bit.ly/SDSSThisIsIt
*Sloane:* (Ashley and Sloane)
   https://bit.ly/TessSloane
*San Diego Social Scene Boxset 1*
   http://www.bit.ly/SDSSBoxset1
*San Diego Social Scene Boxset 2*
   https://bit.ly/SDSSBoxset2

# Agents of Ensenada

https://tesssummersauthor.com/agents-of-ensenada-1

*Ignition*: (Kennedy and Dante prequel)
https://bit.ly/TSIgnition
*Inferno*: (Kennedy and Dante)
https://bit.ly/TSInferno
*Combustion*: (Reagan and Mason)
https://bit.ly/TSCombustion
*Reignited*: (Taren and Jacob)

https://bit.ly/TSReignited
*Flashpoint*: (Sophia and Ramon)
https://bit.ly/TSFlashpoint

# Boston's Elite series

https://tesssummersauthor.com/bostons-elite-2

*Wicked Hot Silver Fox:* (Preston and Xandra)

    http://www.bit.ly/WickedHotSilverFox

*Wicked Hot Doctor*: (Steven and Whitney)

    https://bit.ly/WickedHotDoctor

*Wicked Hot Medicine*: (Evan and Hope)

    https://bit.ly/WickedHotMedicine

*Wicked Hot Baby Daddy*: (James and Yvette)

    https://bit.ly/WickedHotBabyDaddy

*Wicked Bad Decisions*: (Zach and Zoe)

    https://bit.ly/WickedBadDecisions

*Wicked Little Secret*: (Maverick and Olivia)

    https://bit.ly/WickedLittleSecret

*Wicked Grumpy Heart Doc*: (Aiden and Dakota)

    https://bit.ly/WickedGrumpyHeartDoc

*Wicked Little Thief*: (Liam and Utah)

    https://bit.ly/WickedLittleThief

*Wicked Boxset 1*

    https://bit.ly/WickedBoxset1

*Wicked Boxset 2*

    https://bit.ly/WickedBoxset2

# Wounded Heroes

https://tesssummersauthor.com/wounded-heroes

*Callahan*: (Adam and Lainey)
https://bit.ly/TSCallahan

*Sergeant O'*:(Brian and Jade)
https://bit.ly/SergeantO

*Alleged Husband*: (Alan and Jessica)
https://bit.ly/CaptainAllegedly

*Dr. Weaver*: (Justin and Kristy)
https://bit.ly/TessSummersDrWeaver

# San Diego After Dark

https://tesssummersauthor.com/san-diego-after-dark

*Highest Bidder*: (Jeff and Vivian)
https://bit.ly/TSHighestBidder

# The Mister Series

https://tesssummersauthor.com/the-mister-series

*Mr. Infuriating*: (Gabe and Gretchen)
https://bit.ly/MrInfuriating

*Mr. Inappropriate*: (Beau and Angela)

# About the Author

Tess Summers is a former businesswoman and teacher who always loved writing but never seemed to have time to sit down and write a short story, let alone a novel. Now battling MS, her life changed dramatically, and she has finally slowed down enough to start writing all the stories she's been wanting to tell, including the fun and sexy ones!

Married over thirty years with three grown children, Tess is a former dog foster mom who ended up failing and adopting them instead. She and her husband (and their dogs) split their time between the desert of Arizona and the lakes of Michigan, so she's always in a climate that's not too hot and not too cold, but just right!

# Contact Me!

Sign up for my newsletter: BookHip.com/SNGBXD
Email: TessSummersAuthor@yahoo.com
Visit my website: www.TessSummersAuthor.com
Facebook: http://facebook.com/TessSummersAuthor
My FB Group: Tess Summers Sizzling Playhouse
TikTok: https://www.tiktok.com/@tesssummersauthor
Instagram: https://www.instagram.com/tesssummers/
BookBub https://www.bookbub.com/profile/tess-summers
Goodreads - https://www.goodreads.com/TessSummers
Twitter: http://twitter.com/@mmmTess